Why Not Both?
Sarah Neeson

Happy Reading :)

SPN

18 Street Press

Why Not Both?

The Blue Vista Crew Book 1

Copyright © 2024 by Sarah Neeson

www.18streetpress.com

All rights reserved. No portion of this book may be reproduced, distributed, or transmitted in any form or by any means without prior written permission of the publisher, except in the case of brief quotations for review purposes.

This book is a work of fiction. Names, characters, businesses, organizations, places, events, and incidents are either the product of the author's imagination or used fictitiously. Any resemblance to actual persons, living or dead, events, or locales is entirely coincidental.

This work is intended for adults, aged 18+ and contains adult language, adult themes, and explicit sexual content.

Cover Designed by Sarah Neeson
Character Art by TheCaprica (Gonda)
IG: @thecaprica

Developmental Edit by Melanie Yu, Made Me Blush Books
IG: @mademeblushbooks

ebook ISBN: 978-1-7383602-0-8

Version: September 2024

For Jenn – because there would be no book without you.
And for Ryan – always

Author's Note

Welcome to the world of Blue Vista Events. This book was written by a Canadian and takes place in Vancouver, BC. As such, you will find Canadian spelling within these pages. Some of it will look weird, but I promise, it's on purpose.

Chapter 1

Lis

"So I was just wondering. What's your blood type?"

I pause with the fork halfway to my mouth and look across the table at my date. Grant had seemed like an interesting person online. We had a few things in common, including both having pet corgis. Our coffee date a few days ago had also gone okay. But this dinner is crashing and burning. After the conversation at the cafe, it turns out we have nothing left to talk about.

"Excuse me?" I ask, not sure if I heard him right.

"Your blood type. Do you know what it is?"

"Yes." I donate blood regularly, so I know I'm B positive. Not that I have any intention of telling this man who I've known for only a week. "Why do you want to know?"

"Well," he says, stalling by taking a drink of water. "I actually had hoped to discuss this once we knew each other better, but I need a kidney transplant."

I'm glad I hadn't taken that bite of food because I certainly would have choked on it. I'd held my fork suspended, so now I set it down on my plate. "You need a kidney," I say, slowly.

"Yes. I'm on a list, but if I find someone willing to donate their kidney, I won't have to wait anymore." He takes a bite of food as though he asks people for their kidneys every day.

"Right." I look at my plate, then at my glass of wine. "I, uh. I need to go to the bathroom. Excuse me."

I get up, bringing my purse with me, and escape to the ladies' room. I stand at the sink, staring at myself in the mirror. Why does this always happen to me? Weird guys, creepy guys, assholes. I can't find one regular, cool guy. Someone I can laugh with and feel at ease with. I have to find the guys who need kidneys.

I went all out getting ready for this date. My blonde hair is scooped up into a stylish ponytail with the rainbow dye exposed. My favorite red top matches my bright red nails. My cute skinny jeans show off my ass. Even my winged eyeliner is symmetrical and on point. I look hot. All that preparation, wasted.

I'm second guessing everything. Had he simply asked me out to ask for my kidney? He said he'd hoped to bring it up when we knew one another better. Had he brought it up now because, like me, he knew there wasn't going to be another date? Did he even have a corgi?

I sigh and take my phone from my pocket, sending a quick SOS text to my sister before I go back to the table.

"What's *your* blood type?" I ask Grant as I sit down.

"A positive."

"Oh. That's too bad. I'm not a match." At least I won't feel guilty later when I never speak to him again. I mean, really. Who asks someone for a kidney on their second date?

My phone rings.

I lift it, seeing my face staring back, with shorter hair and no dye.

"My sister is calling. Excuse me." I answer, "Hey, Daze. What's up?"

"You told me to call. Is it really going that bad?" my sister asks.

I let my face fall from the polite smile I'd been wearing to a concerned expression.

"Oh no. Is she okay?" I ask, adding some anxiety to my voice.

"That bad then. Well, it's Saturday night, and you spent all that time getting ready. Sophie and I are taking you out."

"Do you want me to come?"

"Obviously I want you to come. We'll go out dancing. Soph was already trying to convince me."

"Okay. I'll be right over. See you soon." I hang up the phone and turn to Grant. "I'm so sorry. I have to go. My sister's girlfriend was in an accident."

"Nothing too serious, I hope."

"No, no." I pull out my wallet. "They think it's just a broken leg, but Daze needs me, so I have to go."

"I can get the bill," he says.

"I insist." I set a few bills on the table. No way am I letting him pay. "That should be enough for my meal. I had a great time."

I grab my jacket and leave the restaurant, calling Daze back as soon as I'm outside.

"I just want to go home and sit in a hot bubble bath and feel sorry for myself."

"Amaryllis Stone. Did you or did you not shave your legs for this date?"

I wince. I hate it when she full-names me. "I shaved everything."

"Exactly. You primped and prepped for tonight. Just because the date wasn't worth it doesn't mean the night won't be. Sophie and I are already heading out the door. You're coming with us even if we have to drag you kicking and screaming."

I know they'll do it, too. "Where are we going?" I ask, resigned. "Should I call an Uber or can I walk? Reminder: I'm wearing three-inch heels."

My twin laughs. "Where are you?"

We settle on our favourite place, which is conveniently close to home, but far enough from me that I decide to take an Uber. On the drive, I delete the dating app off my phone. I'd gone onto the app about ten months ago after a three-year hiatus from dating. My last relationship had exploded in a raging inferno, almost taking my career with it. I'd finally decided to try again, but this online stuff just wasn't worth it.

By the time I arrive at the bar, Sophie and Daze are already there. It's still somewhat early, so we get inside and find a booth. After our drinks arrive, I tell them about what Grant said. Sophie howls with laughter, tears streaming down her cheeks, drawing looks from the other tables.

"Fuck, Lis! I did my mascara and now it's ruined."

Daze looks at her with such fondness that my heart aches. "You still look beautiful, hon."

Sophie smiles and asks, "So, back to the drawing board? Or message board?"

"Nope. That's it for me. I already deleted the app. I need a break from the online dating game. In fact, I think I need a break from the whole fucking thing. I'm starting my dream job on Monday and I'm just going to focus on that."

"Okay," Daze says. "I get it. But. What if. We're sitting here, minding our own business, and the man of your dreams walks up to you and is smoking hot and asks you to dance. Are you going to say no?"

I roll my eyes. "*If* some smoking hot guy comes up to me and asks me to dance, I will say yes. Happy?"

Daze grins. She lifts her glass and I clink my strawberry daiquiri against it. "Ecstatic." Then she sobers. "Seriously, Lis. I know you want to find someone to love. But you don't *need* someone."

"I know. I just want what you guys have."

Sophie nudges me with her shoulder. "Your problem is you're batting for the wrong team," she says, waggling her eyebrows.

I flutter my eyelashes at her and she laughs. Then I heave an exaggerated sigh. "I wish. But I'd miss the D too much."

Chapter 2

Spencer

"Here's to best friends, and another year in the black," Adalie says next, raising her beer. Derek and I clink with her.

"Here's to the last free Saturday before wedding season," Derek says, and we toast again.

"And here's to ex-girlfriends who absolutely did us a favour," I say, for our final toast.

Sitting at a table with two of my three best friends, I feel more relaxed than I have in a long time. The only thing that would make it better is if Vic, the last member of our fantastic foursome, had come out as well. She'd wanted to be her usual workaholic self instead and stayed at Blue Vista, the event venue we all run together, going over schedules and finances. Granted, it's the beginning of our busiest season, and our cook just left us for greener pastures, but it's all under control.

"So, Spencer, who are you going to take home tonight?" Derek asks, scanning the crowded bar.

Adalie and I groan at his question. Derek is always such a man whore.

"Don't be a dick," I say. "I never said I was taking anyone home." But I scan the bar as well. I won't say no to finding a beautiful woman to dance with, should one be interested.

"We're here in part because of you," Derek says. "You need to shake off the break-up."

"The break-up doesn't bother me. I meant it when I said she did me a favour. I should have broken up with Lucy a long time ago. I didn't realize how tense I was with her until it was over."

"Here, here," Adalie says, raising her glass. We clink again and I smile at my best friends.

I'm about to say something else when my gaze snags on a blonde and rainbow ponytail, long and silky, hanging down a red-clad back.

"That one," I say, indicating in her direction.

Derek grins and Adalie rolls her eyes. I flash her a smile.

"I don't mean I'm planning to take her home. I mean, I'm going to ask her to dance."

"As long as you're not turning into this one," she says, hooking a thumb at Derek.

"Dancing is the first step in taking a girl home," Derek says.

"That, my friend, is no girl," I say. "That is a woman."

"Well, what are you waiting for?" He takes a drink of his beer while looking at me expectantly.

"She's hanging out with her friends, and we just got here. I'm in no rush. Besides, I want to text Vic. Make sure she's okay. See if she's changed her mind."

I send a quick message to my boss and friend of twenty-five years.

Me:
> How are the numbers coming? Having fun yet?

We drink and talk while I wait for her answer. Adalie tells us about the new painting she started working on while Derek and I listen with bemused smiles, understanding about half of what she's saying, but enjoying her enthusiasm, anyway. My phone buzzes. I pick it up as I drain my glass, my eyes sliding to the rainbow hair for what feels like the hundredth time. The woman still hasn't turned this way. I adjust my focus to read Vic's response.

Vic:
> You know how much I love numbers. Especially ones that look like these.

Me:
> We're doing well this year then?

"Spencer," Derek says, pulling my attention away from my phone. "There's something you should see."

My phone buzzes again.

> **Vic:**
> It's shaping up to be almost twice as good as last year's numbers. I'm thinking we might be looking at expanding sooner than I thought.

> **Me:**
> You should be here celebrating then, not in your office.

"What is it, Derek?" I ask, waiting for the little dots to change to Vic's response.

> **Vic:**
> I'm in my happy place. Leave me alone. Get laid tonight. I probably won't be home until late.

> **Me:**
> :sunglasses emoji:

"What did she say?" Adalie asks.

"She's not coming out. She's having too much fun."

"Spence," Derek says sharply. I hate the shortened form of my name and he knows it. So now he has my undivided attention. "Incoming."

I look up just in time to see Lucy striding toward me, her short brown hair framing a face lit up with excitement.

"Spencer, honey," she says, her voice sugary sweet. "I'm so happy to see you."

I raise an eyebrow and cast a look at my friends, who both shrug.

"I don't know why."

"I've just been doing so much thinking, and I may have acted a little rash."

I lift my glass to take a sip of beer, only to frown when I remember it's gone. "I'm going to get a refill. Anyone else?"

"Ooh, me please," Adalie says.

Derek nods and I get up and walk to the bar, Lucy trailing behind me.

"I mean it, Spencer. I shouldn't have listened to Megan. She said you were wrong for me, and I believed her. It's not like you made it difficult. I'd been dropping hints about us moving in together and you weren't picking any up."

I'd actually picked up every hint. And ignored them.

Lucy continues. "I've had some time to think about it, and she was wrong. We should be together. I should have been more direct."

I walk past the booth where the rainbow haired goddess sits. Her face is as exquisite as her back—lush red lips, wide blue eyes. Or are they green? They lock with mine for just a moment. Something electric sparks between us making me want to stop right where I am, but Lucy huffs behind me and the woman's eyes drop from mine to her drink, breaking the spell.

WHY NOT BOTH?

"Spencer, please," Lucy begs. "I'm sorry I was so quick to break up. I shouldn't have."

I make it to the bar, waiting for a bit until the bartender comes around. Lucy lingers impatiently next to me, not taking the hint. I place the order for the table, then turn to her.

"Lucy. You broke up with me. You wanted me out of your life, and you were right to want it. So why are you really talking to me now? Is it just because you saw me out having a good time? Maybe you're upset that I'm not upset?"

Her eyes drop to the side, and I know I'm on the right track. I've always had a knack for reading people quickly. Almost like a sixth sense. I tilt my head as her gaze comes back to me, guilt flashing in her eyes for about half a second.

"No," I say. "That's part of it, sure. But the real reason is more than that, isn't it?" I pause, searching her face. "You found out who my father is, didn't you?"

The guilt flashes again before it's replaced by a cool look of haughtiness.

"I don't know what you're talking about," she says, turning her nose up.

I smile. "You cute little mercenary. Can't say you're the first. Would it change your mind at all to know I'm completely cut off? My father and I are basically estranged. I don't have access to any of his money."

"I can't believe you'd think that low of me, Spencer."

She keeps her head held high, as though the very idea that she could be a gold digger hadn't crossed her mind, but I know I've just called her out on the truth. She confirms it when she says nothing more to defend herself—because what can she say?—and turns with a huff, stalking away as the bartender returns with my drinks. I slide him my credit card and he swipes it before handing it back. I walk past the rainbow-haired woman again, hoping to snag another glance at her face, but she doesn't look up. She is, however, watching me from the corner of her eye.

I suppress a grin and return to my friends, handing out the drinks.

"Lucy's gone?" Derek asks.

"For now."

"You going to talk to the blonde?" he asks.

I sip my beer, watching as that silky hair sways when she talks animatedly to the other people at her table. Why am I not there right now? I take one more drink of my beer and stand.

Then I start toward the siren who has caught my attention. She looks up again when I reach her table. Her eyes are definitely blue. I cast a quick glance at her tablemates. "Ladies," I say with a polite nod, before turning back to The One. "Hello."

"Hi," she says, her voice quiet enough that I barely hear it over the noise in the bar.

"I've been wondering all night what I might say to convince you to dance with me. Then I figured I'd just come over and ask. So. Do you want to dance?"

She looks at her friends. "Did one of you put him up to this?" she asks.

My lips lift in a smile, even though I'm confused.

"I've never seen this man before in my life," one of the other women says. "But you said…"

"I know what I said," she snaps before turning to give me a look of consideration. I just wait while she glances back at her friends, one perfect golden eyebrow arched at them.

Then she turns back to me, her eyes alight with mischief and interest despite her odd conversation. "More than you can imagine."

She holds out a hand and I take it in mine, noting the bright red nails before I help her to her feet. She's about six inches shorter than me in those fuck-me heels she's wearing. I can't help it as my eyes rake down her body, so close to mine, and I lead her to the dance floor where the DJ is playing something with a heavy beat.

I lift my arm and spin her under it and away from me, noticing a pretty flower tattoo on her arm—a daisy and something that looks like a vibrant red lily—before tugging her back. She laughs up at me as her body meets mine.

"Who taught you how to dance?" she asks.

I give her my most mysterious smile. "You can't open the book of my life and jump in the middle. Like Woman, I am a mystery," I quote from one of my favourite shows.

She squints her eyes at me. "You just quoted something," she says.

"I did. You know it?" I ask, surprised. It's not one of the more popular quotes from the sci-fi show. And *Firefly* itself isn't as well-known as it should be.

She thinks for a moment. "I can't remember."

I think I've just found my soulmate. Even if she can't remember what it's from, she has to have seen it enough times to recognize it.

I spin her out and back a few times, delighting in her laughter every time and the way her hair flies with the movement. As the song comes to an end, I pull her against me.

"What's your name?" I ask.

"Lis," she says.

"Liz? Like Elizabeth?"

She shakes her head. "Lis, with an S."

I smile and lean closer. "I'm Spencer. Also with an S."

She tilts her head back and laughs again and it takes every ounce of willpower not to capture that sound with my lips. She's a perfect firecracker.

WHY NOT BOTH?

"You want to take a break?" I ask.

Her eyes search mine. In the darkness of the bar, I'm no longer certain they're blue. They're more green now, or maybe some colour in between. Either way, right now, they're shining for me.

"I'm right where I want to be."

The next song is slower than the first and I hold her against me, swaying to the beat, our eyes locked together. My head dips toward her until our foreheads touch. I want to press my lips to hers so much, but I also don't want to move too fast.

"Spencer," a shrill voice says from right next to me. I lift my head to find Lucy standing there, a calculating smile on her lips, and I can see in her eyes she's come back to fuck with me for blowing her off. As Lis turns in my arms, Lucy alters her expression into a look of outrage.

I sigh, leaning down to say to Lis, "This is Lucy. My *ex*-girlfriend. She broke up with me about a week ago and, for some reason, is having trouble remembering that tonight." I don't want Lis to have any doubt that I'm free to dance with her however I want.

"How could you, Spencer? After all we've been through."

"You broke up with me, Lucy," I remind her again.

"I made a mistake," she whines.

I roll my eyes and am about to respond when Lis does instead.

"Sweetie, it's over. Sometimes people make mistakes. But you need to stop stalking him." Then she turns in my arms and tugs my lips down to hers.

Just like everything else about her, it's perfect. Her lips are soft and when I dip my tongue into her mouth, she tastes like strawberries. I lose all concept of time and space as our kiss deepens, and she moves against me. Lucy disappears, the bar and the dance floor disappear. My whole world narrows to the feeling of Lis' body pressed into mine. I need her more than I need to breathe.

I break the kiss, keeping her close.

"What do you want to do now?" I ask.

She swallows hard, her gaze dropping to my lips.

"Do you want to get out of here?" she asks.

My arms tighten around her, and I can't help but kiss her again.

"More than you can imagine," I tell her.

"I have to tell my friends I'm going," she says.

I nod and we separate. I can't tear my eyes away from her ass as she walks back to her table. It's rude to stare, but fuck if she's not the most beautiful woman I've ever seen. And I'm going to take her home.

Chapter 3

Lis

When I get back to the table, Daze and Sophie are watching me with sly grins.

"He's staring at you," Daze says.

"He is smoking hot," Sophie says. "Even I can appreciate it."

"I'm going with him." I drain my daiquiri and meet my sister's gaze.

"Text me the address where you end up," she says, one hundred per cent on board with my absolutely crazy plan. "If you take him back to our place, let me know and we'll be quiet when we come in. What's his name?"

"Spencer." I hesitate. "I trust him."

"Can't be too careful." Then she winks. "Have fun."

I blow her a kiss and turn to find him still staring at me. He hasn't moved from his place on the dance floor. He is as smoking hot as Sophie said. His dark blond hair is cut long on top and shorter on the sides, so it falls in front of his clear blue eyes. The blue shirt he wears shows off his broad shoulders, flat stomach, and the orange, red, and black tattoo sliding down from inside the short sleeve. It looks like the tail feathers of a bird. He is so tall he makes me feel tiny, even in the three-inch heels.

People move around him, but he doesn't seem bothered. He's just watching me as I make my way back to him. As soon as I'm there, he pulls me against him and dips toward me, capturing my lips in a kiss that curls my toes.

"I missed you," he says.

"I was only gone a minute."

"Too long. Let's go."

I follow him outside and he takes his phone out. "Your place or mine?" he asks as he loads his Uber app.

"Which is closer?" I ask.

He shoots me a look that steals my breath, the desire flashing in his eyes stoking mine. "Where do you live?"

I tell him my cross-streets and he nods. "You're closer, but not by a lot. My roommate promised she won't be home until late."

"Your place it is."

He taps the screen, then finds a group chat. He doesn't try to hide it from me, so I watch as he types a message saying *heading home* and hits send.

"I thought you said your roommate won't be there."

"She won't. But that group includes the two inside."

I laugh at him and he tugs me closer again, like he can't stand us being apart. I understand the feeling. "You could have told them in person."

"Then I would have had to take my eyes off your perfect ass."

His hands slide down my back to grab said feature. I gasp as he pulls my pelvis into his and I feel the erection I hadn't known was already there.

"Spencer," I say on a sigh as my eyes drift closed and his lips find mine again.

A car arrives and we separate. It feels like tearing off my skin to let him go. He confirms the ride is here for us, holding the door open for me before getting in the other side. He takes his phone out as the car starts toward our destination and I do the same.

"What's your address?" I ask.

He rattles it off and I send the message to Daze, like she asked me to.

We put our phones away at the same time, turning toward each other. "Sorry," he says. "I just wanted to make sure Vic knew I was bringing someone home. Just in case she comes home earlier than I thought."

"No problem," I say with a laugh. "I just had to text my friends your address so they know where to send the police if you try to murder me."

He shakes his head, his eyes alight with laughter. "Murdering you is not on my agenda tonight. I have some other things in mind I want to do to you."

He's sitting right against me, my body hot where our legs and arms are touching. He takes my hand in his, twining our fingers together.

I lean toward him, needing his lips on mine again. Those beautiful, full lips with a hint of my lipstick on them. He lets go of my hand to cup the back of my neck, drawing me closer. Our lips brush once, twice, before he crushes me to him, and we're lost in each other again. He trails kisses along the edge of my jaw, then someone clears their throat.

Our driver.

"We're here, man," he says.

The car has stopped in front of a building looking out over English Bay and Vanier Park on the other side of the water.

"This is where you live?" I exclaim as we get out of the car.

The moonlight shines off the ocean, and I could stare at the picturesque scene all night. Spencer comes up behind me, wrapping his arms around me, looking at the view as well.

"This is where I live. Vic owns the place. I rent a room from her."

I turn in his arms, suddenly so curious about the man who has demanded my attention from the first second I saw him. Now is not the time.

"Take me to it," I whisper, pressing a kiss in the soft spot below his ear.

"As you wish," he whispers back and I giggle, placing the famous line from *The Princess Bride* easily.

We don't say anything more as he links our fingers together and tugs me with him, getting us in the building and into the elevator quickly. Then he pulls me against him, leaning on the wall as he kisses and nips along my neck, making me moan. The ride up is too short. He leads me to a door and unlocks it, tugging me inside and pressing me against the cool wood, leaning in to capture my lips again.

"Fuck, Lis, you are so gorgeous," he says against my skin, sending shivers through my body.

"You're not so bad yourself."

He wraps his arms around me and takes us through another door on our left. Inside he separates for a moment to turn on the light and there's the bed, massive in the small space. Just like that, a wash of anxiety floods me.

"I've never done this before," I blurt.

He looks at me, blue eyes wide. "Had sex?"

"With a practical stranger."

He lets out a breath, moving forward to hold me gently.

"I don't usually either. I want you, Lis. A lot. But if you're not comfortable with this, we can just chill. Watch a show or something. Or I can get you a car to take you home. It's your choice."

I search his eyes and see nothing but sincerity in them. That makes up my mind. I haven't ever had sex outside of relationships before. But I want him. And I don't want to consider why it might be wrong or why it might not work out. I just want to take this one thing he's offering without worrying about the consequences.

So I kiss him. Hard. Biting his lip before I move to kiss along his jaw this time. While I do, my fingers find the top button on his shirt and undo it. Then I work on the next and the next until it's open and I reach my hands inside, dragging my nails along his skin.

"You're driving me crazy, firecracker," Spencer says while his hands rove over my back and ass until his fingers find the hem of my shirt and pull it over my head.

"Firecracker?" I ask, my mouth watering as he shrugs off his shirt letting me see the toned muscles and that tattoo, a bird starting at the top of his shoulder and stretching to his elbow wrapping around his chest and back.

He tilts my chin up and I realize I've been ogling him. The look on his face tells me he doesn't mind.

"Yes. Firecracker." His hands skim over my shoulders, slipping my bra straps free, sending shivers along my skin.

WHY NOT BOTH?

"Exciting, vibrant." His fingers find the clasp on the bra, undoing it. "Dazzling, explosive."

The garment falls to the floor, leaving me bare to his gaze and his mouth. His hands splay against my back, bending me backward as he dips further to tease one hard nipple with his tongue and teeth. I moan as heat floods my core, a wave of pleasure shivering through me. I make more sounds I've never heard from myself before as he switches to the other breast.

"Fucking perfect," he says, before closing his lips over the other nipple.

He turns us, his lips never leaving my body, and leads me toward his king-sized bed. I barely notice he's undoing the button at the top of my jeans until he slides them and my underwear down my legs, releasing me to take them off, my skin chilled in the night air.

I sit on the bed as he pulls them off my feet and tosses them aside. His gaze drags up my body and I can't find it in me to be self-conscious when he's looking at me like that.

"You're overdressed," I say, pointing to the pants he's still wearing.

He grins, locking his eyes with mine. He unhooks the button on his black slacks and they fall to the floor with his underwear. His erection points toward me, hard and thick and long. My eyes grow wide, but I'm more intrigued than nervous. I reach out and gently touch him, my fingers brushing his head before I lower myself to my knees in front of him. Almost in a trance, I kiss the velvety tip. Then I wet my lips and take him into my mouth.

He groans, and when I look up at him, his head is tilted back. "Fuck, Lis."

I set to work and suck him in deeply before withdrawing. I wrap my hand around his shaft because I can't comfortably fit him all the way in. He removes my hair tie, then plunges his fingers into the strands, pulling tight enough to bring tears to my eyes, but not so tight that I want him to stop. I move faster, my tongue swirling over him as I bob my head back and forth. My other hand cups his balls and he groans again, shifting so he's in control, holding my head still as he pumps into me, deeper than I thought I could take him. My hand that had been holding him moves to his tight ass, and I relax my throat, loving the feeling of his dick sliding along my tongue as he fucks my mouth. His balls tighten and he tries to pull out, but I grip his ass, digging my nails in, keeping him in place as he comes, swallowing it all down. He shudders and goes still. I take a moment to lick all the evidence away, then I look up at him, still licking my lips.

He shakes his head in awe, then hauls me to my feet, practically throwing me onto his bed. I land with my legs wide and he's there in an instant, mouth over my clit, tongue moving relentlessly against me. His hands hold my thighs open with an almost bruising force, but

WHY NOT BOTH?

I don't care as long as he's sucking on me with that single-minded intent. One of his hands slides toward my core, dipping a finger into me while his tongue continues to ravish my clit. I let out a long moan when a second finger enters me, sliding in and out in a slow, lazy rhythm that's at odds with his mouth.

I don't know if my eyes are open or closed as the world narrows to the pleasure arcing through me. It's my turn to thread my fingers into his hair, pulling his face closer, though I don't really need to. He sucks on my clit and I scream, the pleasure ratcheting higher and higher. I'm so tense, on the brink of breaking. It takes one last flick of his tongue, one last pulse of his fingers, and I shatter into a million pieces, screaming again as the orgasm shakes my whole body. He slowly eases the pressure of his tongue, drawing the orgasm out for as long as possible until I lay completely boneless against his mattress.

My eyes are closed, bliss sweeping through me, when he says, "Fuck." Not in a good way.

I blink one eye open. He's standing next to the bed, fully naked, fully hard again, searching in the drawer of the bedside table.

"What's wrong?" I ask.

"There are no condoms in here."

I whimper and he turns to me with a smile, leaning over my spent body to kiss me. I taste myself and lick his lips, wondering when I decided I love the taste. He chuckles and pulls back.

"There's more in the bathroom. I'll be back in thirty seconds. I promise."

"What do I do while you're gone?"

He kisses me again. "Get comfortable. Because you're not going anywhere for a while, sweetheart." Then he kisses me again. And again. Finally, I laugh and push him away.

"If you don't get going, we're going to forget all about it."

Lust flashes in his eyes, but he stands and walks backward out of the room, staring at me until he's gone. I start counting and move further onto the bed, spreading my hair out on the pillow and watching for his return.

When he comes back, I grin. "Seventeen seconds. Not bad."

"I had an excellent incentive to hurry."

He sets the whole box on his bedside table before climbing onto the bed with me.

"I missed you," I say as I wrap my arms around his broad shoulders.

"I was only gone seventeen seconds."

"Too long."

He kisses me deeply, and my body throbs with anticipation. He pulls away only long enough to grab a condom out of the box and roll it on. Then he settles between my legs, sliding them up so my knees are bent on either side of him. He leans down, kissing me, beginning his first slow thrust.

"Fuck. You're so tight."

I gasp as my body stretches to accommodate him. He continues to move slowly, letting me adjust. I wiggle my hips, finding just the right angle for him to slide all the way in.

He rests there for a moment.

"What do you need?" he asks.

I search his eyes, consumed with lust and something more.

"Hard. Fast. Give me everything."

He flashes me a grin before kissing me, biting my lower lip, and drawing it into his mouth as he starts to move. Slow at first, then faster and faster, harder and deeper with each thrust. I moan and grip his shoulders, meeting his hips with mine. In love with the sound of our bodies coming together and the headboard rattling against the wall. I try to keep up with the rhythm he sets, but after a while, it's too much and I wrap one leg around his waist to anchor myself to him and ride the wave. He buries his face in the crook of my neck and drives into me, the pleasure building and building.

"Spencer," I say, barely recognizing my own voice. "Fuck. I—"

I lose the ability to formulate words. I grip his shoulders tighter and he moves faster, harder. I can't take anymore. My body breaks for the second time. I scream as my release floods me, rushing through my body. He continues to move, sending my orgasm higher until he groans against me, my name on his lips, his body shuddering as his own orgasm takes him as well.

We both breathe heavily, a tangle of bodies on the bed. He stirs first, kissing my shoulder and neck where his head still rests.

"You are a goddess," he says, his lips sliding along my skin.

"Does that make you a god?" I ask, laughter in my voice.

He lifts a shoulder in a shrug and moves to hover over me. "It's up to you, firecracker. Was I a god?"

I hold up my hand, squeezing my thumb and finger together. "Almost."

"You deserve a spanking for that," he says, rising off of me. "Turn over."

I laugh again and reach up to pull his face back to mine, kissing him dreamily. He strokes his thumb over my cheekbone, lifting his lips, but not going too far. "Let me get cleaned up, then we'll start on round two."

"Round two?" I ask, anticipation already swirling in my core.

WHY NOT BOTH?

"I need a chance to change that almost into an absolutely." He kisses me and winks. Then he's up, getting rid of the condom and cleaning up. I watch from my place in his bed. He is so hot, just looking at him is making me want him again. I smile as I realize, the night is young.

Chapter 4

Spencer

In the morning, I wake to sunlight streaming in through the window and a soft, warm weight on my chest. I look down at the tangled rainbow and blonde hair spread around slim, satin shoulders.

I close my eyes with a smile, enjoying the simple pleasure of waking up with a firecracker goddess in my arms. It doesn't take long for her to stir against me, lifting her head to smile at me.

"Good morning, gorgeous," I say. "You didn't leave."

She rolls her stunning eyes, more blue than green this morning. "How could I? Every time I woke up and thought about it, you woke up as well and we ended up having sex again."

I grin. "Yeah, we did. Do you want to get some breakfast?"

She hesitates, a worried look in her eyes.

"No pressure, Lis. I just figure we're both probably hungry."

"I thought this might be…"

"A one-night stand? Not if I can help it." I slide my hands down her back and grip her hips, pulling her over me, letting her feel the erection that has grown since we woke.

She gasps and laughs, settling down on my chest, her hands folded under her chin as she looks at me through golden lashes. At some point last night, she'd gone to the bathroom and washed off all her makeup, just as fucking gorgeous without it as she had been with it.

"A couple problems with going for breakfast," she says. "My shirt is all wrinkled. I left my jacket at the bar and it's going to be pretty cold out there this morning. And I don't exactly have the right shoes for anything other than clubbing."

"I can easily fix the first two for you. The shoes… you may have to suffer."

I give her a lingering kiss before shifting her off me and grabbing some clothes from my closet and dresser. I hand her a plain white t-shirt and my black *Evil Dead* hoodie.

"I don't care much about the t-shirt, but that's my favourite hoodie," I say. "I expect it back."

"Maybe."

She sends me a mischievous smile and pulls them on, not bothering with her bra. Now I want the t-shirt back as well, just to have something she's worn against her bare skin. After we're dressed, I gather the things she isn't wearing, putting them in a backpack, then we head out and I lead her away from the beach, promising the restaurant I'm thinking of isn't far.

I lace our fingers together and it's the most natural thing in the world. She looks amazing in my hoodie, her hair twisted up on her head, a riot of colours, her feet still in those fuck-me shoes.

"So have you figured out that quote yet?" I ask.

She looks at me out of the corner of her eye. "Not yet."

"No Googling. That's cheating."

She places a hand over her heart. "I would never!" she says, in an intensely offended way that sounds familiar.

"Now you're quoting."

She grins at me, and I realize I'm already gone for this woman.

We reach the restaurant and get seats within a few minutes. Lis' phone rings and she answers, sending me an apologetic smile.

"Hey," she says. "No, I'm fine. We're just out for breakfast."

Her face turns bright red, and she slides her gaze away from me, but the smile remains on her lips.

"I'm going to go now. I'll talk to you later. Goodbye. I love you."

She says the last as though she's talking over the other person, then hangs up.

"Sorry. My sister."

"You have a sister?"

"My identical twin," she says, like I should already know. "She was at the bar last night."

"There were two of you?" I should have noticed there was a second perfect looking woman at the table. How had I noticed Lis and not her sister? "What's her name?"

"Daze."

I blink a few times. "Lis and Daze? You must have pretty cool parents."

She laughs. "They are, but not in the way you're thinking. Lis and Daze are shortened."

"Shortened from what?"

She holds my gaze with a grin. "You can't open the book of my life and jump in the middle. Like Woman, I am a mystery."

I erupt into laughter and she laughs with me.

"It's been driving me crazy," she says. "What is that line from?"

I lean toward her. Why did I sit all the way on the other side of this table? I should be sitting next to her. I want to be touching her. "Guess."

Her eyes sparkle and she leans forward as well. "Let's play a game. Twenty questions."

I narrow my eyes. "Twenty is too many. If you're who I think you are, you'll guess long before twenty."

"Five then. But they don't have to be yes/no."

"Fine. One-word answers only."

She nods. "You can't ask about actors. That would make it too easy."

"Agreed. You *can* ask the gender of the speaker." I drum my fingers on the table. "To win the game, you have to guess right within… twenty-four hours."

"What does the winner get?"

"One favour of any kind."

Her smile grows and I can see her thinking of all the favours she's going to ask me for. Instead of feeling nervous, I'm excited.

"Movies and shows only? Or books as well?"

I consider the question for a moment. "We can do books, but they won't count toward winning or losing."

"Okay. Your quote. First question. Movie or show?"

"Show."

She regards me for a long moment. "Fantasy or Sci-fi?"

I grin. "Sci-fi."

She holds my gaze as she thinks. Then she smiles. Then it gets wider. "Malcolm Reynolds. *Firefly*."

She has never been hotter than she is at this moment.

"Will you marry me?"

She throws her head back and laughs. She knows I'm joking. I know I'm joking.

But if she says yes, I will be an engaged man.

Our food arrives and we eat, a breakfast sandwich for her and a chili and cheese omelette for me.

"Your quote," I say after the first few bites. "Movie or show?"

"Movie."

"Genre?"

She taps her lips, thinking. "Action/adventure. Maybe a little bit horror?"

"That was more than one word."

She smiles sweetly. "Freebie."

"Is the speaker a man or woman?"

"Woman."

I eat some more of my breakfast while I consider my options and what next question I want to ask. She's watching me with that sparkle in her eye, like she's considering what favour she's going to ask for when I get this wrong.

"Older or newer?"

"Older. Definitely. Like late nineties, I think."

I grin. "You're really no good at the one-word answers, are you?"

"I'm just answering the questions, Spencer. You shouldn't be complaining. I'm making it easier on you."

I have one more question. And I need to get this right. She guessed my quote after only two questions. I'm watching her closely.

"Is this your favourite movie?"

She props her chin on her hand. "How is that going to help you figure out what it's from?"

"It isn't. I just want to know."

She takes a breath, considering. "It's not necessarily my favourite. But it *is* my comfort movie. I watch it whenever I'm sad or sick or just feeling blah."

"Oh yeah. Like *The Dark Crystal*."

"What?"

"My comfort movie. It's *The Dark Crystal*."

"I don't think I've seen that one."

I slump back in my seat. "You haven't? How can you not have seen *The Dark Crystal*?"

"I don't know. I'll have to fix that."

"We'll watch it together," I say. "Give me your phone."

She hands it to me, and I save my number in her contacts. Then send myself a text with one word. *Firecracker*. I hand back her phone.

"There."

She reads what I've done before bursting into laughter. "God?"

"I think it was well established by the end of last night."

She shakes her head as she changes the contact to my name instead.

"You prefer Spencer and not Spence, right?"

My good mood freezes for a second at the shortened form of my name, sending a flash of ice through me. I really hate being called Spence.

Lis looks up, waiting for my answer.

"Yeah. I prefer Spencer."

Her smile eases the tension and we fall back into the easy teasing we've been enjoying. We finish eating and I get out my wallet.

"How much do I owe?" she asks.

"I'm not letting you pay," I say.

She arches an eyebrow. "Was this a date?"

"Abso-fucking-lutely."

Her cheeks flush and she gives me another smile. I could live on her smiles alone.

"Fine. I'll let you pay. This time."

The waitress brings the card reader, asking what the day holds for us. I want to spend all of it with Lis, but she says she has to get home and get ready to start a new job tomorrow. I don't let my disappointment show. We've already had an incredible morning. And night. I'll be thinking about last night until the next time I can get her into my bed. Or until I can get into hers. Or until I'm dead. Probably all three.

I grab her hand as we leave the restaurant and start down the road to the bus stop. Her place is far enough away that she doesn't want to walk. I insist on coming onto the bus with her, even though she says it isn't necessary.

It's only three stops and we decide to stand instead of getting a seat. I hold her against me with one arm while I hold on to a bar with the other. The ride is too short before we're standing in front of her building. I hand her the backpack with her shirt and bra inside.

"Give it back later. When you return my hoodie."

She grins up at me, wrapping her arms around my waist. "I'm not giving this hoodie back. You shouldn't have given it to me if it's your favourite."

I sigh and capture her lips in a swift kiss. "You can keep it for now. But I want to see it next time we go out. I need to see you're taking care of it. Maybe I can take it off you."

She laughs and kisses me again. "I have to go. I have to wash my hair and remove my nail polish."

"Your rainbow isn't going to wash out, is it?" I ask, alarmed.

"No. It's permanent. It's pretty new, though, so the colours will fade over the next few months. Some more than others. But I need a shower before I start a new job. If you remember, I got a little sweaty last night."

"I don't want to let you go. Not until I know when I'm going to see you next."

She searches my eyes and I notice they're more green now than they were earlier. What made them change? Was it her emotions? Or just the light?

"I'm going to be pretty busy for the next little while. And I'm not sure what my schedule is going to be until I start. I'll let you know?"

"That's as good as I can get, I suppose. You want me to walk you up?"

"No. I'll save you from Sophie and Daze giving you the third degree. For now."

She lifts onto her tiptoes to touch her lips to mine. I hold her against me for as long as she allows. When she slips away, I force myself to let her go, watching through the glass doors as she crosses the lobby. I'm rewarded for my patience when she turns and waves before getting into the elevator. When she's out of my sight, I start toward the beach a few blocks down, intending to walk along the Seawall back to my place, feeling like everything is absolutely perfect.

Chapter 5

Lis

I wake early Monday morning to a text from Spencer and a heavy weight on my feet.

Spencer:
> Evelyn. The Mummy.

Me:
> You Googled it, didn't you?

He sends me a picture of a movie collection spread out on the floor around his crossed legs. A DVD copy of *The Mummy* starring Brendan Fraser sitting right in front of him.

Me:
> Did that take you all night?

I sit up while I wait for his response and scratch Cerberus between the ears. He gives me his most forlorn expression. He's a tri-coloured Pembroke corgi with a brown face, black body, and ears far too big for his head, which are currently tipped back in concern.

"I know lazybones, but if we get up, I'll take you for a run." His tail flops on the bed a few times and my phone buzzes.

Spencer:

> Not all night. I had the idea at 2am. Figured it out around 4 but didn't want to wake you. I didn't wake you did I?

Me:

> You didn't. I was just getting up. What were you doing up at 2am?

Spencer:

> Thinking about you and what you might be wearing.

I laugh out loud, hesitating for only a second before turning on the camera and taking a picture of my pyjamas: cozy pants and his hoodie.

Spencer:

> You look hot in my clothes.

A shiver tingles through me, settling between my thighs, making me want to skip taking my dog out and just run to Spencer's apartment instead. Then Cerberus moves up the bed to get more head scratches, and I know I can't give in to my desires. As much as I want to.

Me:

> Leave me alone. I have to get ready for my new job.

I give my dog his required scritches and wait for the message Spencer is typing.

Spencer:

> You're gonna kill it firecracker. Call me when you're done and tell me how it went.

I set my phone down to find my running gear. Since I don't start for a few hours, I have time for a short run, the most Cerberus can do anyway with his stubby legs. My phone buzzes again.

Spencer:

> And what it is. We never talked about what we do.

Me:

> I'll tell you all about it later. I'm heading out for a run along the seawall. Watch for me?

Spencer:

> Are you asking me to stalk you? Because yes please. I'd offer to join you but gross.

Someone knocks on my door and I tell them to come in while I get my sports bra on.

"Is that Spencer you're texting?" Daze says when she enters.

"Maybe."

"Did you sleep in his hoodie?"

I pull on my pants, then turn to her. "Why do you ask questions you already know the answer to?"

She just grins at me. "I'm heading to work. Have an awesome day. Sophie and I want to take you out to celebrate tonight. Unless you have other plans?"

I glance at my phone. He hasn't asked me out tonight. I want to see him again. Soon. But I also don't want this to move too fast. Whatever *this* is. Especially since I *just* said I was giving up on dating.

"No plans," I say.

"Great. See you later, then." She kisses my cheek, gives Cerberus a pat, and leaves.

I finish getting ready and Cerberus finally gets up, doing his funny little hops down the stairs I'd bought for him to be able to get onto my bed. They take up more space in my tiny room than I like, but when I read about what can happen if he jumped down from too high a height, I bought them the next day.

When we get outside, I connect my headphones and turn on my favourite running playlist. Then my little buddy and I begin our run.

I pass Spencer's apartment in only a few minutes and a text buzzes my phone, interrupting the music. The text has no words. Just the eyes emoji followed by the kiss emoji. I find his window and blow a kiss toward it. Then I get another text from him.

Spencer:

> I didn't know you had a dog. You are so full of mystery firecracker. Looking forward to talking to you later.

I don't bother to fight the stupid grin. Cerberus and I run all the way to my new place of employment before turning and running back to my apartment for a quick shower and to change. I get my dog settled with Sophie—who works from home—then walk the same route back to Blue Vista Events.

I enter the building and am immediately greeted by the owner, Victoria Sterling. She'd done my two interviews, saying someone else usually conducts them, but she'd been called away that week.

Victoria is stunning with long black hair, crystal blue eyes, and a statuesque figure that makes me jealous. I left my heels at home in favour of shoes I would normally work in, black Doc Martens. Though they're fancier than the ones I usually wear with embroidered flowers on the sides. My clothes are also ones I would never consider working in, a bright red blouse and black slacks, dressing professionally to meet the full team for the first time. My rainbow hair is scooped back and twisted up, kept in place with a large claw clip, but still showing off the color I'd paid a lot of money for.

"Victoria," I say as I hold my hand out to shake hers. "It's good to see you again. Thank you so much for this opportunity."

"The pleasure is all mine, Amaryllis. I'm glad it worked out. Yours was by far the best application we received." She leads me to a conference room just off the lobby.

"Please. Just call me Lis."

Her smile slips for half a second and I wonder what I've said wrong.

"Did you say Lis?" she asks.

"Yes, I—"

"Lis? What are you doing here?"

I turn away from Victoria and my heart stops beating. Spencer is there on the other side of the conference room with two other people. I can't see them as my vision narrows to the man I spent all night with on Saturday. My face grows hot as we stare at each other.

"Lis is our new head chef," Victoria says into the growing silence.

I can't tear my gaze away from Spencer. The dots start connecting in my fried brain. I was scheduled to meet with the top staff at Blue Vista today. The owner, the event coordinator, the acquisitions coordinator, and the staff coordinator. Victoria and three other people.

I wrench my gaze away from him to look at my new boss. Then back at him. I swallow, terrified of what she knows. He said his best friend's name is Vic. That she's his roommate as well. That he was going to text her to make sure she wasn't coming home early.

"Give us a few minutes?" Spencer says, and everyone leaves the room until it's just me and him.

"Do they know?" I whisper.

He grimaces as he stands and comes around the table to me, leaning against the edge of it.

"They do. Derek and Adalie were at the bar with me. They saw us together. And Vic is my roommate." He scratches the back of his neck. "I may have mentioned you once or twice. I swear it was because I thought I was going to call you and take you out again. Not because I was bragging or anything. I really like you, Lis."

My heart is breaking. Because he really likes me, and I really like him. We had so much fun together. And he's a nerd, just like me. And he thinks I'm beautiful. And—

"We can't see each other again," I say. The words feel like claws on my soul. "Not romantically, I mean."

"Lis," he says. I can hear the protest, so I stop him before he can say more.

"No, Spencer. I can't." I bite my lip, searching for a way to explain. "I'm head chef here. Do you know how many female head chefs and executive chefs there are in Vancouver?"

"I'm going to guess by your question the answer is not many."

"No. This is an unbelievable opportunity for me. Something I've been dreaming about for years. I can't do anything to mess it up."

"Being with me won't mess it up."

"Maybe that's true. But what if we get together and it doesn't work out? What if we break up and it's weird and we can't stand each other anymore? Victoria is your best friend. You think she'll choose me over you?"

"Vic. Her friends call her Vic."

I smile sadly. "I'm not her friend, Spencer. I'm her employee."

He straightens, catching my hand in his. "But what if it does work out? What if it doesn't end? What if we have the greatest love story ever told?"

My heart is pounding in my chest because I want to. God knows I want to try. I want to see where this could go. But after last time, I just can't risk it.

I shake my head. "I'm sorry, Spencer. We had one night together and one date. They were amazing. But I can't."

He stares down at me for a long time. Then he lets go of my hand to cup the back of my neck. My eyes close at his touch and he leans down, pressing a gentle kiss to my lips. A kiss that says goodbye. My heart shatters into a million pieces at the thought that I'll never get to kiss him again.

He pulls away.

"Okay. We'll do it your way. For the record, I think you're wrong."

He lets me go and my whole body feels frozen. He leaves the conference room to call the others back and as the space between us grows, the colder I get.

Chapter 6

Spencer

I listen with half an ear as Vic goes over the broad outline of the next few months. Wedding season has started and Blue Vista is booked solid. Every Saturday—starting the one coming up until the middle of September—is booked for a wedding. I know all this. I booked the fucking things.

Still. I need to be here with the team. If Vic needs me to step in to explain some detail, I need to be ready. But my focus is split between what she's saying and the rainbow-haired beauty sitting across from me. I keep myself from looking at her, mostly staring at the folder in front of me as Vic goes over things. I don't really see what I'm looking at, every cell in my body pulled in Lis' direction.

"That's it," Vic says. "Any questions?"

"When can I meet the kitchen staff?" Lis asks.

"I've asked them to come in for a couple hours this afternoon," Adalie says. "They'll be here around one."

Lis turns toward me and I hold my breath.

"Can we set up a meeting to discuss the events in more detail?" she asks.

"Whatever you need."

She turns away again, and it hurts. I thought we could have had something. But she wants the job more than me.

Don't be a dick, Spencer. You've known the woman for less than forty-eight hours. You can't expect her to choose you over a job she's been dreaming about for who knows how long.

"I guess that's it then. Come on. I'll take you for a tour." Vic stands to lead Lis out of the conference room, but I stand as well.

"I'll do it," I say. "You've probably got a lot to do. After I show Lis around, we can have that meeting about the schedule."

I'm being an idiot. I should let Vic take Lis on the tour. I should give her some space, like she asked. But we're colleagues now. There's no reason I can't give her the tour. I know the building better than Vic does, anyway.

Vic lifts one black eyebrow at me, but nods. "Fine. Start with Adalie's office. She has your contract for you. Read it over and hand it in before you leave today."

"Absolutely," Lis responds before I lead her out of the conference room and we're alone in the halls for just a few minutes.

I want to say a million things. I want to beg for a chance. Instead, I take her to the storage room first, which is right next to Adalie's office. I shove my hands in my pockets as we walk around the space.

"We'll give Adalie a minute to get everything sorted," I say. "This is our storage room. Elevator to the upper floor is there." I point it out. "It's staff only, unless there's a special request and the person is accompanied by staff."

"Is there anything I need in here?"

I consider her question for a moment. "I think a few of those warming tray things are in here somewhere. Our last chef, Mark, had things where he liked them. You can move them if you find a spot that suits you better."

"You can make decisions like that?"

"Vic won't mind. If it worries you, just let her know what you're doing."

"You know Vic really well, then?" she asks.

I turn to her, the exaggerated nonchalance in her tone making me wonder if there's something more behind that question.

"We've been friends since we were five."

"That's a really long time to be friends with someone."

"Yep. Twenty-five years."

Lis doesn't look at me when she says, "You live with her. Work with her. Known her for twenty-five years. That's quite a relationship."

I watch her carefully in the room's dimness. I hadn't bothered to turn on the lights, figuring the sun from outside would be enough. Is she jealous? Or is she worried about something? Though why would she be worried if we're not going to be anything more than colleagues?

"I'm not with Vic. Our parents always hoped we'd get together, but by the time either of us were interested in dating people, we already felt more like siblings."

She finally looks at me. "But you're not."

"People don't always get me and Vic right away. They assume because we have all this history and she's a woman and I'm a man, there must be something between us. But there has never been anything. Not even in high school when our hormones were going crazy. She's always felt like my sister."

"How did you two get to be so close?"

It's my turn to look away. I don't want to talk about my past. "That is a long story, and not all of it's mine. Come on. Let's go see Adalie."

We stop in and Adalie hands her the paperwork that will make her a full employee for the next five months—a sort of probationary period to make sure she meshes well with the team and gives us the guarantee of a head chef for the duration of wedding season. We stop by Derek's office then Vic's. Last is mine, which I just gesture to since it's empty right now. I show her the staff lounge on the far side of the conference room and the bathrooms on this level, usually only used by staff, but guests can use them if they come for meetings. There are a couple of rooms where the wedding party can get ready if they need the space, usually only if the ceremony is happening here as well as the reception.

Finally, I take her to the kitchen and watch as she lights up. It's spectacular. She wanders through the space, touching a counter, the stove, the sink. She opens the fridge and peers inside. I have no idea what she's looking for, but when she turns to me, pure excitement on her face, I am officially jealous of a kitchen. I'm insane.

We spend a long time wandering around her domain, which takes up a large portion of the ground floor of the building.

"Most event venues don't have their own chef," Lis remarks as we make it to her office. "Unless it's a hotel."

"When we came up with the business plan for this place, we wanted to have exclusive contracts with high-end companies as a sort of draw for the clients. Mark was a big name in the cooking world."

"But I'm not."

"You will be."

As we leave the kitchen, Lis asks, "You and Vic came up with the business plan for Blue Vista together?"

I nod. "Along with Derek and Adalie."

I take her upstairs to the venue space and show her where the elevator lets out. She can bring food up that way and we usually set up buffet tables close to the elevator to limit the distance she'll need to bring the food.

We end the tour on the roof—the whole reason the business is called Blue Vista.

"This is gorgeous," Lis breathes as she stares out at English Bay.

But the sight holding my attention is the rainbow-haired firecracker who watches the waves.

"You removed your nail polish," I blurt, wondering why it seems so important to bring it up. My eyes had strayed to her fingers all day and I miss the bright flash of red I remember.

She looks down at her hands as though she'd forgotten about them. "I said I was going to. Besides, I can't wear nail polish in the kitchen. If it chips while I'm working, it would get in the food."

"But you're not cooking today."

She searches my eyes and I know she's confused. Shit, so am I. Why does it matter if she's wearing nail polish or not?

She shrugs. "I figured it wouldn't make a good impression coming in with chipped nail polish on my first day. And I wasn't going to reapply it since I'd have to take it off for tomorrow."

"Yeah. That makes sense," I say, feeling a little off-kilter, like my whole world has been thrown off its axis and I'm trying to remember how to navigate. I need some time to think. "Hey, the tour took a bit longer than I thought. You want to take a break before we get to the meeting?"

"Sure. How long?"

"We usually take an hour for lunch."

"Okay. I'm going to head out. I'll meet you in your office in an hour, then?"

"Great," I say. Then watch her leave, taking a piece of me with her.

Chapter 7

Lis

Spencer and I spend an hour going through the menu before my team comes in and I get to meet my staff. Which is the most fun thing I've ever gotten to say: my staff. I introduce myself and we discuss everyone's roles, making plans for the coming week, then I send everyone home. I duck into Vic's office with a quick knock on her open door. As Spencer had mentioned, she'd told me to call her Vic during the morning meeting.

I step inside her office, a completely monochrome space except for one splash of colour in the form of a bi-flag coloured mug and a small pride flag sitting in it.

"I'm heading home. I'll see you tomorrow."

"I'll walk you out."

We have to pass Spencer's office to get to the doors, and I catch his eye without meaning to. He's on the phone, so he doesn't stop me. I tell myself I'm glad. It felt awful to be near him all day and not be able to touch him. Not be able to laugh with him the way we had on Saturday night and Sunday morning.

WHY NOT BOTH?

I don't know if she catches me staring or if she'd meant to say something all day, but when we're alone in the lobby, Vic stops me before I can leave.

"You know, there's no policy against dating at Blue Vista. Within reason. Obviously, you shouldn't date your kitchen staff."

"I appreciate that. But it's my own policy. I don't date people I work with." *Anymore.*

"All right." She pauses, but I can tell there's more she wants to say. It only takes her a second to continue. "I've known Spencer a really long time. He's a good guy. If you decide to change your policy for him, I won't hold it against you."

"Why are you saying this? Wouldn't a relationship between your employees be messy?"

"Undoubtedly." She sighs and stares out at the water across the street. "But when he came home Sunday morning, he was happy. Happier than I've seen him in a long time. I can take on a bit of messy if it makes my best friend that happy." She shrugs and turns back to me. "The choice is yours. I just wanted to make sure you knew it was your choice and not mine."

I smile ruefully at her. "Thanks for making it harder."

She laughs and claps a hand on my shoulder. "No problem. See you tomorrow."

I walk home along the Seawall. When I get there, Sophie is sitting at her desk in her bedroom, working with headphones on. Cerberus gets up from his bed and wanders over to me on his stubby legs, tail wagging. Not disturbing Sophie, I lead my dog to my room, closing the door and taking the hoodie out from my blankets. I should wash it and give it back to him tomorrow. I sit on my bed, holding it to my face, breathing in the scent of him on the fabric, something spicy and citrusy.

Cerberus whines and climbs his stairs to sit next to me, laying his head on my knee.

"I know, baby. I need to get over this. We were only together one night. It's stupid to be this hung up on him."

I gather up some of my clothes, the hoodie, and the t-shirt and throw them all in the washer, refusing to mourn the loss of his scent. Then I let Sophie know I'm going to take Cerberus for a walk. We go to the dog park a block away from the building and I let him off leash, throwing the ball until he's panting, his tongue lolling out of a doggy grin.

"Doesn't take much to make you happy, does it, buddy?" I say, patting his sides and hooking up his leash again. After we return home and I'm filling up his water dish, Daze comes in.

"How was it?" she exclaims, and Sophie emerges from their bedroom.

I manage a smile at her enthusiasm. Cerberus ignores us all and goes to his water bowl.

"It was terrific," I say. "I love my kitchen. The staff were really excited to meet me. My boss is friendly. And everyone keeps their office doors open, so it's literally an open-door policy."

Daze scans my face. "So what's wrong, then?"

My smile falls apart. For about half a second, I debate saying nothing is wrong, but Daze will see through that in less time than it takes me to say it.

"Spencer works there." I swallow hard past the lump forming in my throat, meeting my sister's eyes as mine fill with tears. "I'm not going to be… seeing him… romantically… again."

Daze doesn't say anything, just wraps her arms around me. Sophie wraps her arms around me from the back, and I'm sandwiched between them. They'd been there before, when my whole world exploded because I dated someone I worked with. They'd helped put the pieces of my life back together.

"Do you want to cancel going out?" Daze asks. "We could order in instead."

"That would be great. Maybe we can put on a movie?"

"Sure. *The Mummy*?"

My heart cracks a little more. How can I watch that movie again now that all I can think about is Spencer spending two hours going through his movies to find the one with my quote? My eyes prick with tears, but I won't let them fall.

"It was only one night. Why does it hurt so much?"

"Everyone could see you had a real connection with him," Sophie says. "I know what happened before, but Blue Vista is a different place. Are you sure you can't make it work?"

I shake my head.

The dryer buzzes, and I look at Sophie. "I switched it over while you were walking Cerberus."

I pull out the hoodie and hug it against me. His scent is still there, barely. It must really be his favourite. I bring it with me to the couch. Sophie and Daze kindly don't mention it.

Daze orders sushi. Sophie gets *The Mummy* started. It turns out I can still watch it. Even though I think of Spencer the whole time, it's still my comfort movie. The sushi arrives and we eat. Daze pours white wine and we drink. Brendan Fraser saves the day and kisses Rachel Weisz and they live happily ever after.

"Why can't I find my Rick O'Connell?" I ask. "Someone who will come rescue me when I'm kidnapped by a mummy."

"Well, Rick lived in the 1920s in Egypt," Daze says.

"And Vancouver has a limited quantity of mummies," Sophie adds.

"Details. I want a man who looks at me the way Rick looks at Evie." Spencer's face flashes through my mind. "Ugh. I'm going to bed. Thanks, you guys."

Daze kisses my cheek. "Love you, Lis."

"Love you, too." I bring the hoodie with me, slipping into it when I get to my room. Cerberus gives me a look. "I know, I know. I'll give it back tomorrow. I just want one more night." I settle into bed and pull the covers around me. Cerberus climbs up as well, and I snuggle against him. At least I have a warm body to snuggle up with. Too bad it's the wrong one.

Chapter 8

Spencer

I'm on my third beer before anyone broaches the subject. I've known it was coming since I got here tonight. The four of us are at Derek's house for game night, the last Monday of every month. Tonight we've decided on a game called Tsuro, where our pieces are dragons, and the goal is to remain on the game board as it's built and also not run into one of the other players.

I had expected Vic to bring it up, so I'm surprised when Derek does.

"So what are we going to do about your little problem?" he asks, setting down a game board tile and moving his piece over it. I give him a sharp look and he holds up his hands. "I'm just saying. If one of my one-night stands showed up and started working at Blue Vista, I'd be kind of uncomfortable."

"It wasn't a one-night stand." Everyone stares at me. "It wasn't *supposed* to be a one-night stand." I glare at each of my friends in turn. "This is her dream job. So no one fucks it up for her."

WHY NOT BOTH?

They all nod.

"Before we knew who she was," Adalie says, "we were going to try to bring her into the group. She's technically one of the top staff at the venue now. Not one of the OGs." She fluffs her curly red hair before placing her game tile down and moving her piece. "But she'll have decision-making authority once her probation is over. We'd hoped to have her be more than just an employee. You still want to do that?"

It had always been a hope that whoever we hired as head chef would be able to mesh well with our already tight-knit team. We'd been running this business together for over five years now. While Mark, our last chef, had been a dick about how he'd left, he'd also never really clicked with us. I'd known it was only a matter of time.

My friends all know about my knack for reading people, and they watch me as they wait for what I'm about to say next. I turn one of the game tiles in my hand, tapping the edge of the tile on the table with each quarter turn.

"She'll mesh with us. I knew that the other night. She's the right person for the job."

"Good enough for me," Vic says.

Derek stands. "Who wants another beer?" Then he looks at me and I hold my breath, but he just says, "It's your turn."

The conversation is over. My friends trust me. They know I won't do anything to fuck up Blue Vista. Even if the woman of my dreams is going to be down the hall from me almost every day I'm there. As the event coordinator and the head chef, she and I will be working together more often than the others. I just need to figure out how I'm going to deal with that and not think about how her laugh made my pulse race, how her smile made me feel like the champion of the world, or how it felt to have my cock buried in her pussy.

I'm working at my desk the next morning when there's a soft knock on my door frame. Since everyone always just walks in, I already know who I'm going to see when I look up.

Lis is standing there, chewing on her lip, a black backpack in her hands. My eyes snag on it and I swallow, unable to prevent the sucker punch to the gut the sight of it gives me.

"What's up?" I ask. "Also, if the door is open, you don't have to knock. Just come in."

"I brought this back for you." She hands me my backpack. "I washed them both. Thanks. For letting me borrow this stuff."

All of a sudden, the office seems too small. I want to tell her I don't want it. I never want to see the hoodie again.

No. That's a lie. I *do* want to see it again. I want to see it on her. I want to strip it from her body before I make love to her all night long.

"You didn't have to bring it today," I say as I set the backpack on the floor, just to get it out of my hands. "There was no rush."

"I wanted to. You said it was your favourite. I'd never really intended to keep it."

I wish she had. I don't think I'll ever be able to wear it again.

"Well thanks. You got everything you need for today?"

Her eyes brighten with excitement at the thought of the upcoming event. "Yeah. It's just a corporate lunch. The staff seemed excited to work. So, I'm sure it'll go great."

"Absolutely. You'll be amazing. But if you need anything, just send a text. I'm only down the hall."

She smiles, finally a genuine smile that's just for me. The first one I've seen from her since Sunday morning—other than when she was grinning like a fool because of her kitchen. My heart hurts, and I resist the urge to rub my chest.

"You think you can keep up with me in the kitchen?"

"Fuck no. But I take direction pretty well."

Her gaze drops from mine and her cheeks flush pink. I wonder if she's remembering the directions she'd given me Saturday night, because I sure as hell am. I hadn't meant to reference it, but there it is, sitting between us.

"Anyway," she says, clearing her throat. "I better get to it."

I nod and when she leaves, I get up and close my door. We almost never close the office doors at Blue Vista, but I need a second to myself. I unzip the backpack and inside, neatly folded, are my t-shirt and hoodie. I pull out one, then the other, smelling them, inhaling the scent that has clung to my sheets for the past two nights. The smell of her and me together.

I shove the clothes back into the backpack and stride out of my office into Vic's, flopping into a chair.

"This is the worst day of my life."

She doesn't turn away from her computer when she says, "Two days ago, you said it was the best day of your life."

"I stand by both statements."

"And both statements are about the same woman?"

"Yes. Do you know what it's like to hold perfection in your arms, Vic?"

She stops what she's doing and slides her gaze over to me. I can see her considering. Finally, she says, "No." Then she sighs. "Maybe she'll change her mind."

"A man can dream."

"In the meantime, you guys can be friends like you and me or you and Adalie."

"No offense, but I don't have any desire to fuck you or Adalie."

"Good. Keep it that way." She turns back to her computer, typing something.

"That friend idea isn't a bad one, though. We had a lot of fun together Sunday morning. We made up this game—"

"You told me already," she interrupts. "Back on the best day of your life."

"Right." I lean forward, swiping the miniature Pride flag from the bi mug on her desk. Both were gifts from me to brighten up her otherwise black and white office. "Hey. Where were you Saturday night? I know I've been a bit preoccupied, but I noticed you didn't come home."

She lifts one shoulder in a shrug. "You had company, so I made myself scarce."

"You didn't have to do that. It's your place."

"You pay rent. It's your place, too." She continues typing.

"You didn't stay here, did you?" I ask, waving the flag in the direction of the staff lounge. "The couch is not the most comfortable of places to sleep. Trust me, I know."

"I didn't stay here." She's still not looking at me.

"So where did you stay, Vic?" I ask, dread coiling in my gut.

"None of your fucking business, Spencer," she responds.

"Noooo. Vic. You promised. We made a list. Do I have to get the list?" I turn my head toward the door. "Derek, Adalie, get in here and bring the list," I shout.

"Fuck you, Spencer," Vic says.

But it's too late. Derek comes into her office and slaps a piece of paper onto her desk. "I keep a copy printed out. Just in case."

Adalie follows him in with a sympathetic look on her face.

"Fifteen reasons not to call Emily," I say, pointing at the list with the tip of the flag. "Do we need to read them out loud?"

"No, we do not need to read them out loud," she says, grabbing the flag and returning it to where it belongs. "And I didn't call her. She called me."

I drop my head into my hands. "That doesn't make it better, Vic. Has she called or texted since?"

Her silence is answer enough.

"You know she's a bitch. You know she takes advantage of you. Don't let her do this to you," I plead.

"You're only saying this because you hate her."

"I only hate her because of how she treats you. If she made you happy, I would be on board. One hundred per cent. But she doesn't. She calls you in the middle of the night and you go to her, then you feel awful for days because she doesn't call again, and she leaves your messages on read."

"That's number three," Adalie says, pointing to the list.

"You deserve better than her," I say.

"That's number one," Derek says helpfully.

There's a soft knock on the door and we all turn to see Lis standing just outside, looking confused and worried.

"Was there a staff meeting I didn't know about?" she asks.

"This isn't a staff meeting," Vic says, standing. "This is three assholes not knowing when to mind their own business. And if you three don't want to get fired, you'll get out of my office and go do your fucking jobs."

I stand as well, catching Vic's eyes. "I've got your back, no matter what."

I hold out my hand, pinkie raised. She sighs, rolling her eyes, and links hers through mine. "Even when I fuck up." Then she sits and slides the list toward her.

Derek and Adalie file out of the office. I head out as well, feeling like the asshole she called me. So I turn before I'm out the door.

"Whatever you decide to do—"

"I know," she says, cutting me off. "Now get out of here and do some real work."

Lis follows me into my office, concern on her face. "Should I ask what that was about?"

"Probably not. Stick around long enough, I'm sure you'll figure it out. It's not something I should share, I think." I sit at my desk. "Did you need something?"

"I was going to ask if you guys wanted to try some of the things I made before we really get started on the menu for lunch."

I grin at her. "Why didn't you say so?" I get my phone and send a message to the team. Then I realize something. "You're not on the group chat," I say, making a couple quick updates. "There. Now you can text us any time you want someone to taste something."

I hadn't meant that the way it sounded. But fuck it if I don't enjoy the pink flush on her cheeks. I stand and follow her to her kitchen where the rest of the team meet us in a few minutes and we all get to taste the menu. It's fucking delicious.

The corporate client arrives and I get them settled. When everything is done and I'm no longer needed anywhere, I return to my office and spend the rest of the afternoon thinking of ways to invite Lis to be my friend. It's not exactly what I want from her, but at this point, I'll take what I can get.

Chapter 9

Lis

"Daisy."

I'm startled out of my work to find Spencer leaning on my door frame with a satisfied smirk on his face.

"Excuse me?"

He straightens and walks toward my desk. "Shut up. I'm making deductions. It's very exciting." He flashes me a grin and sits. "You have a tattoo of two flowers on your arm."

I look down as though I don't know exactly what he's talking about.

"I thought one was a lily, but I did a search for amaryllis after Vic mentioned it's a flower. I realized that's the other flower in your tattoo, so I started wondering: why would you get a tattoo of an amaryllis and a daisy? Then I remembered you said your sister's name, shortened, is Daze. After that, it was all very simple."

I bite my lips to keep from smiling.

"And why exactly did you do all this deducting?"

He shrugs. "I was curious. Anyway, about that favour."

"What favour?"

He stares at me for a long moment. "From the game. You owe me one favour for guessing *The Mummy* correctly. I owe you one for guessing *Firefly*. You also have twenty-four hours to guess the quote I said a few minutes ago."

I blink at him a few times. "I didn't—I thought—"

"You thought just because we're not going to date means you don't have to pay up?" He smirks at me with a mischievous glint in his eyes.

"What are you doing, Spencer? I thought we agreed."

He turns serious. "We did. But I figured, just because I can't date you doesn't mean we can't be friends. We work together. We're going to see a lot of each other. Vic, Derek, and Adalie are my best friends. I'd like to include you in that number. We had a lot of fun together Sunday morning. Let's just do more of that and, unfortunately, less of Saturday night."

My heart feels at once happy that I don't have to let him go, and sad that I can't have him the way I want. But I've made my decision—a decision rooted in logic and past experience—so I push the sadness aside. It was my choice, and I'm not going to change my mind.

"All right. Let's hear this favour."

He grins, the glint coming back to his eyes as though he'd just put it on pause.

"You're off tomorrow?"

I nod. I have the next two days off before I work all weekend.

"Me too," he says. "I was planning to go for a hike at Lighthouse Park with Derek, but he's bailed on me. He's going out with his sister. She's going to have a baby in a few months. Come with me? Keep me company on the hike?"

"I thought you said you hate running."

He shudders. "I do. But hiking and running are not the same thing. You could bring your little friend."

"Cerberus?"

He leans forward, placing both hands on my desk. "Your dog's name is Cerberus? Isn't he kinda small?"

"He's a corgi, so yes. And yes, his name is Cerberus."

He laughs. "I love it. Corgis have pretty short legs. Can he do a hike? Lighthouse is a pretty easy one."

"He can do Lighthouse. When do you want to go?"

"Oh. I usually take transit. Can you bring him on the bus?"

I shrug. "I'll just drive."

"You live and work Downtown and you have a car? What's the point?"

"Daze, Sophie, and I share it. My and Daze's parents live in Maple Ridge. So we use it to drive out there. Then sometimes to get groceries and stuff. One car to rule them all."

He gives me that mischievous smile again. "*Lord of the Rings.*"

"What? No. I didn't mean—"

"You quoted. I guessed. I get another favour."

"I was quoting the book," I protest.

He leans forward in his seat, fixing me with his clear blue gaze. I'm locked on it, my heart in my throat as I realize I could happily drown in his eyes forever.

"Tell me the truth, Lis. Have you ever read the books?"

"I read *The Hobbit*," I answer weakly.

"It counts. I win."

I narrow my eyes at him. "*Dr. Who.* I also win."

Suddenly I notice we've both leaned toward each other over my desk and his face is only a few inches from mine. My gaze drops to his lips and my pulse races. How did I get here? What am I doing?

I sit back, slowly, so as not to appear to be running.

"So tomorrow. I can pick you up. What time?"

He clears his throat as he sits back, the mischief gone. I wonder if he's as affected as I am.

"Nine? We'd get there by ten. The hike takes a couple hours. Then we can come back, eat lunch, and watch *The Dark Crystal.*"

"That sounds like a date."

"Nope." He stands. "Just two friends. Hanging out on a day off. I've got popcorn."

I raise an eyebrow. "If you're inviting me over to watch a movie, you better have popcorn."

His laughter floats back to me as he walks away, and I take much longer than I should to focus again on my tasks. I have a lot to do to get ready for a day off.

A couple hours later, Vic enters my office.

"You did great today," she says, sitting across from me.

"Thanks. It was fun. The catering company I worked for last had a lot of corporate clients, so this was the kind of thing I'm used to. And Tina's ready to take over for the next couple days."

"Excellent. I knew you'd have no trouble jumping in." She sighs. "I just wish Mark had given me more time. I lost an event last week because of him leaving so quickly."

"Damn. I'm sorry to hear that."

She shrugs. "Business. You have everything you need for the rehearsal dinner and wedding this weekend?"

I nod and motion to my computer. "I've been going over everything. It all looks doable. I checked the stock, and it's all there. So I think we're good."

"Excellent. You getting out of here?"

"Yeah. I was just closing up."

"Cool. I'll walk out with you and lock up." We gather our things and start toward the door. "Got any plans for tomorrow?" she asks.

"Uh. Yeah. I'm going for a hike with Spencer."

"How did he rope you into that?"

I laugh. "I don't mind hiking. And I'm bringing Cerberus, who's going to be in heaven."

"Cerberus?"

"My corgi."

Vic laughs this time as she locks the door behind us. "Cerberus the corgi. He doesn't have three heads, does he?" I laugh as well and Vic asks, "Do you take transit home?"

"If it's raining, I might. But it's still nice, so I'll walk. I usually walk along the Seawall."

"Do you mind if I come with you?"

"Sure."

We cross the street and walk, chatting about things we love in Vancouver like being so close to the beach, the restaurants, and the ease of getting around.

"Have you always lived in the city?" I ask as we near her apartment.

"Not always Downtown. Spencer and I grew up in Point Grey."

I miss my next step and stumble before I catch myself. "Point Grey. As in the most expensive part of Vancouver?"

"One and the same."

"You *and* Spencer grew up there."

"Yeah. Our parents are friends. Or were… before…" She shakes her head. "Anyway. We've known each other since we were kids."

Since before what? I want to scream. But it's none of my business. Just because I crave every scrap of information about Spencer doesn't mean I'm entitled to any of it. Besides, it might have nothing to do with him. Whatever she'd been about to say was their parents.

I still want to know.

Then we're at her building and she waves to me as she goes inside. I stand there for a moment, looking up at the third-floor windows on one side of the building, wondering if he's there, looking down at me.

Chapter 10

Spencer

When Lis arrives to pick me up in the morning, she's wearing a red tank top and black leggings and I remind myself to keep my hands to myself. They itch to touch her, the memory of those curves a constant buzz under my skin. Three hours later, when the clouds that have been threatening all day finally open up and pour, drenching us before we can get to the car, I am still reminding myself to keep my motherfucking hands to myself.

We get to the car and she pops the trunk, taking out a couple towels, and handing one to me. She uses the second to scrub Cerberus dry. It only works marginally. She gets him strapped in the back of the car and climbs in, starting it and cranking the heat, but she's shivering hard.

I hand her the towel.

"I'd offer you my shirt, but it's just as wet as yours," I say.

She takes the towel with a smile, wrapping it around her shoulders. She hadn't been wearing a lot of makeup, but her mascara has run. I find a napkin and tilt her face toward me, wiping away the black smears.

She laughs.

"I'm probably a mess. Pass me my purse."

I grab it from the floor where she'd tossed it after retrieving it from the trunk. She fishes out a packet and takes a wet napkin out. Flipping down the visor, she wipes away the rest of the makeup.

"Is the colour in my hair running?" she asks, tilting the visor down.

"I thought you said it was permanent."

"It is. It usually runs for the first few days, though. I didn't notice any when I went for a shower this morning, but I don't want to get colour on this shirt."

"You look fine."

She laughs again as she puts the car in drive. "I look like a drowned rat."

"A very cute drowned rat."

We chat on the drive back to the city, rain pouring on the car.

"I didn't think it was going to start raining until tonight," Lis says as we merge into the traffic heading over the Lions Gate Bridge. "I didn't bring any extra clothes."

"You can wear some of mine and we can put yours in the dryer."

"And Cerberus? He smells like wet dog. He'll probably just lay there. After all that exercise, he'll sleep for a few hours before he needs another walk. Those are pretty much his two settings, all out or sleep."

I glance back at the sleeping dog.

"He'll be fine. I talked to Vic about it. She said it was okay. What does he do while you're at work?"

"Sophie usually works from home. So I take him out for a walk or a short run in the morning. I give him his breakfast and Sophie takes him out to go to the bathroom a few times a day. Plays with him during her breaks. Then I take him out again when I get home. Usually to the dog park to throw the ball for a bit."

We're finally over the bridge and driving through Stanley Park. Traffic isn't bad, despite the downpour, so we make it quickly out of the park, through the city, and back to my apartment. I direct her to the underground parking lot where there are a few visitor spots, and we wake Cerberus to go upstairs.

Almost immediately, Lis starts shivering again.

"Are you all right?" I ask.

She nods. "Just cold."

"You weren't shivering in the car."

"We're not in the car," she says through chattering teeth. "And it wasn't hot enough in there to warm me up properly."

"Well, let's get upstairs so you can put on some dry clothes." I wrap my arm around her and she leans into my body as I lead her to the elevator, then into my apartment.

As soon as we get inside, Cerberus makes himself at home, trotting in and finding a spot on the floor by the heating vent in the living room to curl up and go back to sleep. I give Lis a quick tour, since she hadn't seen much of the place the last time she was here.

After I show her the kitchen and living room, she follows me into my bedroom. I find her a pair of sweatpants and my favourite hoodie, that I've now started thinking of as hers. Our fingers brush as I hand her the clothes, heat racing up my arms and tingling down my spine, hardening my cock. It doesn't help that my bed is right there, and I can easily remember us tangled together in the sheets.

I clear my throat. "You can get changed in the bathroom. When you're done, the closet between the bathroom and kitchen is the laundry. Chuck your clothes in the dryer and I'll get it turned on."

She takes the clothes and I'm certain she notices I've given her my *Evil Dead* hoodie again. I'm just emerging from my bedroom, dressed in clean, dry clothes, when I hear her start to laugh. I smile at the sound even though I don't know the joke yet.

"What is it?" I ask.

She just laughs harder before flinging the bathroom door open, arms outstretched to show off her outfit. Her wet hair hangs around her shoulders, which are swamped by my hoodie, the sleeves hanging past her fingers. The pants I gave her are staying up—probably because of the drawstring inside—but the pant legs go so far past her feet that I can't see them. Everything is a mile too big for her and she's laughing so hard tears are rolling down her cheeks.

Cerberus wakes up from where he'd parked himself and wanders over on his stubby legs to see what the commotion is about, the white tip of his tail wagging back and forth.

"How do I look?" Lis asks.

Beautiful. Gorgeous. Perfect. I say none of these because I know she doesn't want to hear about how much I'm falling for her. And I am. Every second I spend in her company, I fall further and further and I can't seem to stop the descent.

"I don't know what you're talking about. They fit perfectly."

She laughs again and I kneel to help her roll up the pant legs. She holds my shoulder for balance as she lifts one foot, then the other. I roll them up, revealing bright red toenails on each foot. My fingers brush her skin, probably more than is strictly necessary. I don't exactly care.

When I stand again, she stares at me with wide, green eyes. She is so hot, wearing my clothes, surrounded by me, my hoodie and sweatpants almost marking her as mine.

But she doesn't want to be mine.

"I thought you weren't supposed to wear nail polish in the kitchen," I say.

She blinks as though coming out of a dream, then rolls her eyes. "I don't cook with my feet, Spencer." She hands me a bundle of clothes. "Everything is soaked. Except my underwear, thank God." I take the clothes and shove them into the dryer with mine.

Then I notice a black garment still in the bathroom, hanging from the towel rack.

"What about that?"

She flushes pink and I'm overwhelmed with the need to kiss her for a moment, struggling to get it under control.

"My bra got soaked as well. But it has to hang dry."

My brain short circuits. She had been wearing a black, lacy bra. Now, she's wearing my hoodie and no bra. All I need to do is slide my hands under the hem along her silky skin. Just a few inches up to reach the soft swell—

I turn to the dryer, fiddling with the dials and pressing start, trying to contain the lust currently eating me alive.

"Okay," I say. "Time to make you lunch."

She follows me into the kitchen. "You know, I'm the chef. I should be making *you* lunch."

"Don't worry. I only know how to make one thing. So you can do all the cooking after this." I send her a wink over my shoulder as I get the ingredients I'd prepped this morning out of the fridge.

She leans against the counter out of the way, her arms hidden in the sleeves of my hoodie, and wrapped around herself. "What are you making?"

"It's a melted Havarti and prosciutto on brioche."

She presses her lips together, and I know she's fighting a smile. "You're making me a grilled ham and cheese sandwich?"

"Well, if you're going to take that attitude—"

"No. It sounds awesome." Her eyes are shining as I get everything ready, watching me.

"I admit, it's a little intimidating having a chef watch me cook," I say.

Finally, she laughs. "Why don't I go sit at the table?" She motions to the dining room on the other side of the pass-through. "You feel intimidated, and I feel awkward being in the kitchen and not cooking."

"Well, here. You can do this then." I grab the popcorn and hot chocolate from the cupboard.

She looks down at the packages with an eyebrow lifted. "You want me to make powdered hot chocolate?"

"How else do you make it?"

"From scratch," she says, but she moves to the microwave and gets the popcorn started.

"You'll have to teach me how to do that," I tell her. "But I doubt we have what we need."

"Where are your pots?"

I show her, bemused as she gets one and the milk from the fridge, pouring it into the pot with the hot chocolate mix, whisking them together.

"Do you have any chocolate chips, or vanilla, or cinnamon?" she asks.

"No, no, and yes. There." I point it out and she adds some to the pot. Then we continue working in silence, side-by-side. After a minute, she looks up at me with the sweetest smile and my heart clenches with the desire to take her into my arms and kiss her.

"That smells delicious," she tells me.

For a second, we stare at each other and I have a sudden vision of doing this with her, working side-by-side, building a partnership. I want it more than I've ever wanted anything. I blink and turn back to the pan with the sandwiches before I do something stupid.

Once we're done with the food and drinks, I get everything plated and poured and we bring it to the living room, settling on the couch while Cerberus snores in the spot he claimed on the floor. I'd already put the DVD into the player before I left this morning, so I just have to turn everything on, but as we sit, I notice Lis shiver hard.

"You still cold?" I ask.

She shrugs. "I'll be fine. It just takes me a long time to warm up."

I jump up and go to my room, grabbing the blanket off my bed. Then I sit in the corner of the couch and hold out my arms. "Come here."

She considers me and the blanket for a long time and I can see the debate in her eyes. Part of me wants to reassure her it's something I would do for a friend. The words would be true, but the intent behind them would be a lie. I want her next to me. I want her back in my arms. Even though it'll probably kill me.

Chapter 11

Lis

I eye Spencer suspiciously, but he just sits there, patiently waiting for my decision. On the one hand, snuggling with him while watching a movie feels very much like date territory. On the other hand, I'm still cold and he is very warm and I know that blanket is as well. I chew on my lip before sliding over the couch, snuggling into his side. His arm wraps around my shoulders and he tucks the blanket around me. His heat seeps into me, casting away the worst of the chill still clinging to me. I realize I haven't felt this warm since Monday morning before I told him we couldn't date.

He hands me a mug of hot chocolate and a plate with my *melted Havarti and prosciutto on brioche.* I lift the sandwich, Spencer watching me expectantly. I take the first bite and it tastes as delicious as it smells. He's grilled the bread to a perfect golden brown, the cheese melted around the prosciutto.

"Mm. Spencer, this is so good."

He grins and removes his arm to eat his own. "The secret is to cook it at a low temperature."

I snort. "Really? Tell me more about the secret to cooking."

He laughs, nudging my shoulder with his. I'm flooded with the desire to stay here forever, tucked into his side, listening to him laugh.

We finish our sandwiches and he removes the plates, replacing them with the bowl of popcorn, which he sets in his lap before turning on the movie.

"So what is this about?" I ask, taking a sip of hot chocolate.

"I'm not telling you anything. Just go into it blind."

I turn to him, about to call him a weirdo or a nerd or something, but when he smiles down at me, I lose my breath. I'm all too aware of the fact that I'm wearing his clothes, wrapped in his blanket and him. He completely surrounds me, and his lips are right there.

I suddenly wish I could go back to Sunday morning and just spend some more time in ignorant bliss. It occurs to me, if I'm wishing, I could wish to go all the way back to Saturday and not meet him, but just the idea of not having the memories of that night is enough to break my heart.

The movie starts, breaking the moment and I turn back to the television. It's a weird movie. Spencer quotes a few lines under his breath in time with it, including one he says with so much sadness I can't help but turn to him, but he doesn't look at me as he says it.

"We may meet again in another life, but not again in this one."

I tell him how much I love the character Aughra and he laughs, a rumbling sound I can feel from my place pressed against his side. We drink our hot chocolates and eat our popcorn, our hands brushing occasionally in the bowl. But just like when he held my hand Sunday morning, the touches feel natural and neither of us flinch away. I pull my feet up onto the couch, and he moves his arm to wrap around my legs, settling my knees over his lap. It's so comfortable, I don't complain, just burrow into the blanket and his warmth and enjoy the movie.

When it's over, I give him an appraising look.

"*This* is your comfort movie?" I ask.

He grins at me. "It was one of my mom's favourites. This one and *Labyrinth*. The one with David Bowie. Not *Pan's Labyrinth*, the Spanish one with the creepy vibes, though that's a good movie, too. Anyway, we used to watch it together all the time. Whenever she let me choose, I would choose this one."

"That sounds nice." I hesitate, noting the past tense and wondering if I should ask about it. I want to know more about him, but I don't want to pry.

He turns back to the television as the credits roll, his smile slipping away.

"She died when I was fourteen. Lymphoma."

My heart aches for the pain I can still hear in his voice.

"Vic mentioned your families were close before, but she didn't mention before what."

He nods, confirming my unspoken question.

"Will you tell me about her?" I ask softly.

"She probably spoiled me a little too much. She was always baking. Muffins, cookies, cupcakes. She always had something sweet for me. We read together a lot. When I was little, she would read me any book I brought her. No matter what she was doing, she would stop and read to me if I asked. When I got older, we would read the same book, then talk about it. Sort of like a book club. She got me to watch all these weird and cool movies. My father hated a lot of it. He thought I should focus on more serious things." He laughs a humourless laugh. "He still thinks that."

I'm about to say something—maybe something about how his mother sounds like she was wonderful, maybe something about how his father is wrong—but the front door opens and I'm prevented from saying anything.

"Hey Vic," Spencer calls. "Come meet Cerberus. He's got the shortest legs you've ever seen."

Except it's not Vic who comes down the hall from the door first. It's a regal blonde woman with cold grey eyes.

"Well, aren't you just the picture of hetero bliss," she says.

WHY NOT BOTH?

I would move away, except Spencer's arm tightens around my legs, keeping me in place.

Vic trails after the blonde woman. She and Spencer exchange a look loaded with meaning. Her eyes are begging him. His fill with annoyance then resignation.

"Emily. It's so nice to see you again," he says.

"Don't lie, Spencer," Emily says. "We all know the truth."

Vic steps around the other woman and smiles at me. "How are you, Lis? Did you have a good hike?"

"We did. We got caught in the rain at the end, but otherwise, it was a nice trek."

"Is this Cerberus?"

My dog gets up and stretches at the sound of the extra people. He pads over to Vic, who crouches down to greet him.

"Hey, pup," she says, giving him his required head scratches. He sniffs her pants and wags his tail as she continues to scratch him.

I notice Spencer and Emily still staring at each other with open hostility.

"Spencer?" I say, trying to diffuse the tension. "I should probably take Cerberus out and get home. Daze will be wondering where I am."

He turns to me, the hostility disappearing in a second. "I'll walk you out. Come on. Let's get your things."

He lets me go and I stand, following him to gather my clothes from the dryer and bathroom. I'm about to get changed when he says, "You can just wear those. Give them back later."

"Are you sure?"

"Yeah. They look better on you, anyway."

"Oh, gag," Emily says. "Can we please go to your room, Victoria? These two are revolting."

"Emily," Vic protests. "Stop it." But her voice is small. Not at all like the smart, decisive business woman I know her to be at work.

"Come on, Cerberus," I call, and he trots over to me so I can connect his leash. As I do, I tell him quietly, "Let's leave the old, mean lady alone."

Spencer helps me get my things into the backpack I'd used before, and as we're about to leave, Vic comes over.

"I'm really sorry," she says.

"Don't be," Spencer replies, holding up a hand with his pinkie extended. "When I come back up, I'll stay in my room."

Vic links her pinkie with his, grimacing. "I'll see you Friday, Lis."

I wave to her and we leave the apartment. Once we're outside, he opens an umbrella and holds it over us, linking our arms together so we're covered. The weather has eased from a downpour to a regular, heavy rain.

WHY NOT BOTH?

"I thought you were a Vancouverite," I say, pointing to the umbrella as we cross the street to the park between his apartment and the beach.

"Are you telling me you don't have an umbrella at home?" he asks.

"Of course I do. But I never use it."

He laughs and we come to a stop.

"Old, mean lady?" Spencer asks after a moment.

I shoot him a look as Cerberus sniffs around the grass, finding a place to do his business. "You weren't supposed to hear that."

"Trust me. I've called her worse."

"It's a quote, if you want to guess. Though I said it to Cerberus and not you, so I don't think it counts in our game."

He thinks for a moment and then shakes his head. "No clue what it's from."

"*A Hundred and One Dalmatians*. One of the pups calls Cruella that."

Spencer laughs, squeezing my shoulders in a half hug. "I love it. She would make a good Cruella, too."

Instead of linking our arms again, he leaves his arm draped around me.

"So, what was that pinkie thing about?" I ask.

"It's kind of like a secret handshake. It started when we were kids. I can't remember what the secret was, but she told me something and I pinkie swore not to tell anyone.

It kept going and eventually evolved to what it means today. I got your back, no matter what. Even if you fuck up. And we have both done our share of fucking up."

I smile, my heart warm from the story. "I'm glad you have someone like that in your life. Daze and Sophie are like that for me. What is the deal with Emily, anyway?"

He heaves a huge sigh. "I don't know. She's hated me since about a month after she and Vic started dating the first time."

"The first time?"

"Yeah. They break up and get back together. Sometimes they don't get back together and just hook up. Vic keeps taking her back."

"Why? She's an awesome woman. She doesn't need to put up with that."

"You tell her. Maybe she'll listen to you. Anyway. I think Emily might be a little bit jealous of me and Vic. She's always rude, but she doesn't antagonize Derek and Adalie like she does me."

"Anyone who's been around you two should be able to see you're not romantically interested in each other."

He tilts his head to the side. "I don't know. Maybe it's because we're really close, and I live with her. It's ridiculous, though. If Vic and I were going to get together, there were plenty of opportunities. There's nothing there between us." He shakes his head. "I don't want to talk about Emily. How are your feet?"

"My feet?" I blink at him, confused by the sudden topic change.

"Your shoes are still wet. You want to get back to your car so you can go home? I don't want you getting sick keeping you out here with wet feet."

We stand there for a moment, turned slightly toward each other. I wish I didn't have to go anywhere. Wish I could just keep walking with him forever.

"I probably should."

We get to my car and he waits for me to get Cerberus settled in the back.

"Maybe next week we can do another hike," he says. "The Grouse Grind should open soon."

"Ugh. The Grind? Please tell me you're not one of those masochists who like climbing that thing."

He grins. "I most certainly am. When it's open, I try to go once a week. Though transiting out there sucks."

I make gagging noises. The Grouse Grind is a two and a half kilometer hike up the side of a mountain. Practically all stairs. Absolutely awful.

He laughs at me.

"You will never get me to climb that thing. I refuse. However, if you want to do another hike next week, we could go out to Maple Ridge and do the easy one in Golden Ears Park. Then Cerberus can come again. Though I should warn you, if I go out to Maple Ridge,

I am contractually obligated to stop in at my parents' house."

"Deal."

He leans in like he's about to kiss me. My breath catches in my chest. Then he pulls back, smiles, and steps away.

"Have a good night, Lis. See you Friday."

"Bye." I get into my car, trying not to think about how breathy my voice is or the fact that my lungs still haven't figured out how to work right.

Chapter 12

Spencer

For the rest of the day Wednesday, all day Thursday, and since I woke up this morning, I think about how I almost kissed her and curse myself.

Friends. We're supposed to be friends. Yesterday morning, I stood at the front window and watched her run along the Seawall with her funny little dog. I'm watching for her again today. I feel like a fucking stalker.

Friends, I reiterate. We're friends and that's good enough. I have other girl friends. Vic. Adalie. I can have one more.

One more who I have been inside. Who I've seen naked and traced every line of her body with my tongue. Who took me so far into her mouth and milked my dick for all it was worth.

I close my eyes, but it doesn't stop the memories.

"Fuck," I say.

"What's wrong?" Vic asks, coming out of her room.

"Nothing. I'm fine."

"Liar. If you want to be with her so bad, ask her out."

"She wants the space, Vic. I need to respect her wishes."

"Right. So you're just going to watch her while she runs like a creeper. Think about her while you jack off in the shower. And act completely sane around her in person. How long you think that'll last?"

I thunk my head against the window, but I don't stop watching for her. "I get it. I'm a dumbass. Can we move on?"

"Sure." She holds out her pinkie to me and I link mine with hers without looking.

"Even when I fuck up," I say, resigned.

"Let's go to work."

"I can't. She hasn't run back yet."

Vic laughs at me and pats my head. "Poor boy. I'm really not sure if you're creepy or pathetic." She stands next to me.

I sigh as I watch Lis come into view from down the Seawall and run past back to her place. Just like on the way out, she casts a quick glance at my apartment building. "Both. I'm definitely both."

Once she's out of sight, I turn toward Vic and notice her scowling at a folder in her hands.

"What's that?"

She hands it to me. "Dad gave it to me last night."

She'd gone out for dinner with her parents the night before. Their relationship is tense at best, openly hostile at worst. I'd assumed, since she hadn't wanted to talk when she came home, something had happened, and she'd let me know when she was ready.

"What is it and why are you staring at it like you want to burn it?" I scan the report while she puts on her shoes.

"It's the company's quarterly earnings."

When she says company, she doesn't mean Blue Vista. She means Sterling Properties, her father's real estate company. It includes a portfolio of hotels, resorts, restaurants, and other venues throughout the province. It's a company Vic had every intention of joining when we were in university. A part of her still wants in, even though Blue Vista is doing so well. Since she was a little girl, she'd grown up believing one day she would work at the company with her father.

Right up until the day he told her he wasn't hiring her.

"These numbers look good," I say as I flip through the pages.

"They are good. They're great, in fact. And Dad gave all the credit to *Tanner*." She sneers as she says the name and I do everything in my power to suppress a grin, especially since she's staring at the white paper rose that she's kept for the last five years. It's sitting in its special vase on the China cabinet, where it hasn't moved in all that time.

"Was he at dinner last night?" I ask, handing back the report and getting my shoes.

"Yes. And he was his usual *cheerful* and *charming* self."

I don't laugh. I *do* remind myself how Tanner, Vic, and I had been good friends in university. She hadn't had a problem with his charm back then—though she'd always found his cheer a little annoying. Then I remind *her* who she should really be mad at.

"Look, Vic," I say, opening the front door and following her into the hall. "You're my best friend. You'll always be my best friend. So, when you decided you hated Tanner, I got on board. But if we're being honest here, Tanner just applied for a job and now he's doing it. Your father is the one who hired him instead of you."

"I don't need your reasonable opinions. I can hate whomever I want for whatever reason I want."

We ride down the elevator in silence, then step out the front door and cross the street to the Seawall.

"How was the dinner otherwise?" I ask and Vic tells me all about it.

She mentions how her brother skipped it again, in favour of going out to a club with his friends. Who goes clubbing on a Thursday night? Liam Sterling, the man who has his daddy pay for everything, that's who. I hate all of it for Vic—the obvious favouritism, the patriarchal drama, the fact her parents have never really gotten on board with her sexuality. They keep hoping she'll settle down with a "nice boy" and forget all the women she's dated. Which, I believe, is one reason she keeps going back to Emily: her parents hate her.

WHY NOT BOTH?

By the time we reach Blue Vista, Vic has run through the evening's events but seems as tense as before.

"Hey," I say. "I've got everything here. Why don't you go relax for a few hours? Go watch the seals."

She seems unsure. Vic's favourite place in the city is the underwater viewing area at the Vancouver Aquarium, where she sits on a bench and watches the seals swimming in circles. She always has an annual pass and every year, Blue Vista makes a sizable donation to the Marine Mammal Rescue Society.

"There's a rehearsal today," she says.

"I've handled rehearsals before. The wedding is the main event, and it's tomorrow. Go to the Aquarium, sit with the seals, relax, come back ready to help me kill it tomorrow. You put me in charge of event coordination for a reason."

"You put yourself in charge of event coordination," she reminds me, dryly.

"Yeah, when we came up with the business plan in school. When you made it a reality, you didn't change the business plan and you could have."

She rolls her eyes, but stares toward Stanley Park. It's still another thirty-minute walk to the Aquarium—longer if she walks through the park—but she nods. "Okay. Call me if you need anything."

I wrap her in a hug. Vic is not a big hugger, but I've always been able to tell when she needs one. "You are an excellent businesswoman. One day, your portfolio will look better than anything Tanner Marcus can create."

"That's not a fair comparison. He started with a pre-built company. I'm starting from the ground."

"Exactly. He cheated." I like Tanner, but I can still throw him under the bus if it makes Vic happy.

She huffs a laugh, and I let her go.

"Get out of here. I've got this."

She continues down the Seawall, taking the long way to the Aquarium as I knew she would. I unlock the doors to the venue and head straight to the staff lounge to start a pot of coffee. Derek and Adalie arrive, grabbing mugs—coffee for Derek, tea for Adalie—and heading to their offices. I stay in the lounge, but it isn't until Lis arrives that I realize I've been waiting for her.

"Morning," she says, pouring herself a cup of coffee and adding a bit of cream and way more sugar than should be necessary.

"Morning," I respond. "Ready for today?"

She straightens her shoulders. "Yes."

She's here much earlier than she needs to be—she doesn't need to cook anything until dinner. But I know she wants to get things sorted for tonight and tomorrow. It's her first wedding where she's the head chef. And even though we've only known each other a few days—not even a week yet—I know she wants it to go smoothly.

I follow her as she heads toward the kitchen, stopping at my office. "You'll let me know if you need anything?"

She turns to me with a small smile. "Shouldn't I go to Derek? Since he's the one who will get me what I need, if there's anything missing?"

"Right. I mean, just…" I scratch the back of my neck. "If you need anything from me. Don't hesitate." I am so lame.

Her smile widens a bit and I know she's laughing at me. I deserve it.

"I won't. Thanks, though."

She turns and heads into her kitchen and I am ashamed to admit, I watch her ass as she walks away. Then I go into my office and sit down, noticing the backpack with my clothes in it she must have left here before going to the lounge. I drop my head to my desk with a thunk.

"I am a creep and I am pathetic."

Chapter 13

Lis

The first thing that goes wrong is the bride brings two extra people with her. The second thing that goes wrong is the groom brings three. I have just enough to make their plates until the person cooking the chicken burns two of them. While also under-cooking the middle. I switch the person out, but the damage is done. I send a message to the group chat asking Derek if he can procure some more chicken in the next five minutes and he says he's on it.

Three dishes break while I'm plating, then Spencer arrives.

"I have good news and bad news," he says.

"I need some good news," I say, laying the chicken that's been cooked properly onto the plates.

"You no longer need the two chicken that were ruined."

I pause, turning to him. "Two people left?"

"No. Two people are vegetarians."

Everything in the kitchen pauses for a half a second before Tina yells, "Don't stop stirring that sauce."

I take a deep breath. "Please tell me the two people are two of the extras."

"No. It's two of the planned guests. The bride says she told me. I'll go through the notes later tonight, but I don't remember her telling me anything about vegetarians for the rehearsal or the wedding."

I tilt my head back and groan. "Tina, come finish plating." I rush to the fridge and take things out, eventually landing on a large head of cauliflower. I point to one of the cooks behind me. "Get that oven turned back on to four twenty-five."

I rush around gathering oil and the same seasonings we used with the chicken. I cut the cauliflower until I have thick slices, season them, and throw them in the oven.

"What do you need me to do?" Spencer asks.

"Stall them. These are going to take at least twenty minutes. I'd prefer thirty. The chicken won't last that long, though."

"We can bring these plates up in ten," Tina says, as she finishes with the sauce and moves on to the vegetables. "They'll last that long. Then we can have the wait staff set them out slowly."

"I can let them know the vegetarian dishes will be shortly behind," Spencer offers.

"No. I don't want them to notice they're coming out separately if they don't have to. If someone asks, we tell them then. Otherwise, just say nothing."

Spencer nods and leaves the kitchen to return upstairs.

My heart is pounding in my chest as I wait for the cauliflower to bake. There's really nothing else I can do other than stand there, wringing my hands. I'm supposed to be taking a minute between the dinner and dessert, but I'm just watching the time. The wait staff takes the chicken dishes and heads upstairs. Two plates are sitting on the pass, ready for me as soon as the cauliflower is done. I resist the urge to open the oven and check on them.

Do not open it, Lis. I tell myself. *You'll just let all the hot air out and slow down cooking. Relax and let the oven do its job.*

I check the time, watching as the second hand on my watch ticks around. I always wear the watch when I'm cooking, specifically for the second hand.

Finally, they're done, and I pull them out, plating quickly. A waiter is already there, ready to bring them upstairs. Just as he leaves with the dishes and I'm about to take a deep breath, a fire breaks out at the meat station—the one that should have shut down twenty minutes ago.

"What—" I turn and grab a pot lid, smothering the fire as quickly as I can, turning off the heat. "What are you doing?" I ask the cook sharply.

She's young and pale with fear.

"It's fine. Go start washing dishes. I'll finish up here."

I move off to the dessert station to check on the progress and find one person making a perfect caramel while the second is burning it.

"Turn the temperature down," I say. "And stir it constantly. Get rid of that and start again."

He does as instructed, and I go back to the pass.

"Are a couple of these people new?" I ask Tina as we set out plates for the dessert.

"Yeah. A few of the regular cooks left when Mark did. Adalie had to bring in some new staff. They came with good resumes, but I think we should talk to her about a few of them."

I don't want them fired. Probably not scheduled for a wedding in the near future, though.

Once the dessert is plated and served, I tell everyone to shut down and clean up. I help where I can, but each person is in charge of their own station. When they're done, I inspect it and tell them they can go. Tina hugs me before she leaves.

"You did great today."

"Thanks. I'll look at a few things for tomorrow and hopefully we don't have quite as many mishaps."

She smiles. "Even if we do, you'll handle them. Good night, Lis."

I consider going to my office and go to the staff lounge instead so I can lay on the couch. Kicking off my shoes and releasing the clip from my hair, I flop down, stretching my legs on the cushions. I'm dozing for a few minutes when I hear someone come into the room.

Through barely cracked eyelids, I see Spencer, who sits on the other end of the couch. I bend my knees to allow him space, but he just pulls my feet into his lap and starts massaging one. I try to sit up and he shoots me a look.

"Just relax. You've had a long night. Mine wasn't nearly as stressful as yours."

I do as he says, but I don't close my eyes again, watching him as he rubs my tired feet.

"Are all weddings like this?" I ask.

"No. Just the ones with bridezillas."

"How many of those do we have this summer?"

He thinks for a moment. "About four."

"I'll need to know which weddings those are so I can prepare."

He laughs. "I'll get the names on Sunday and let you know. We'll go over the details so you can figure out what you want to do about them. Also, I went through my notes. The bride never mentioned any vegetarians."

I snort and roll my eyes. "I'm not really surprised. That wasn't the first time I've had to come up with a sudden vegetarian dish not requested before the event. I'm just glad they weren't vegan or I wouldn't have been able to use the sauce."

Derek comes into the room and I try to tug my feet back, but Spencer continues massaging as though it's not strange at all he's doing it. My heart races as I wait to hear what Derek will say.

"You giving out free foot massages?" Derek says. "Because I'm next."

"You're not pretty enough," Spencer replies.

Derek flips him off before pouring a cup of coffee and sitting at the table.

"Adalie went home?" Spencer asks and Derek nods, stirring sugar into his cup.

"About an hour ago. I offered her a ride if she waited, but she wanted to do some painting before bed." He turns to face us, leaning against the counter. "Not bad today, Lis. There were a few pretty major snafus, and you handled them like a pro."

"Thanks," I say with a warm smile. "I'm going to go over the menu for tomorrow. If I want to add a few ingredients, when do you need the list so we can have them on time?"

He considers. "The earlier, the better. But I can get everything you need within a couple hours. So, whenever you want the stuff by, two hours before that."

"Okay. I'll get it to you first thing in the morning." I drop my head back again.

"You guys want to go out for a drink before heading home?" he asks.

I groan. "Not on your life. I'm going home to bed."

Spencer's hands pause their massaging, then continue. My heart rate kicks up for a second as well as I realize what I've said and what he thought of. Us. Going to bed together.

Then he breathes out a sigh and says, "Me too, man. I'm beat. Fucking bridezillas."

Derek laughs as he straightens, draining the last of his coffee. "You're the one who wanted to deal with the clients. That's why I work in acquisitions. I deal with you and Lis and people we're paying. You guys get to deal with the people who pay us."

"Not me," I say. "Spencer can do all that. I don't want to talk to people. People are idiots."

"Yeah they are," Derek says. He raises his hand and we high five.

I raise my hand and he slaps it, but I still don't open my eyes.

"Well. See you guys tomorrow. Get me that list as soon as you can, Lis."

Then he leaves.

"Come on, firecracker. Let's get you home. You want to take an Uber?"

WHY NOT BOTH?

"Seems a waste of money."

"It's late and you're exhausted. I'll pay for it."

I'm not sure what I'm going to say—possibly protest he doesn't need to pay for something I don't really need—but I end up saying nothing because he holds up a hand to stop me.

"Let me make sure you get home safe. Please."

My heart tugs at his concern.

"You can't pay for my ride home every night after work," I say. "It would be way too much money."

"Don't worry about my money, Lis. I can afford a few rides if it means you get home safely."

"And you do the same for Vic or Adalie?"

"Vic and I usually walk home together if we're here this late. Adalie takes transit. I know which bus she takes. It stops right at the corner here, then right in front of her building."

"So why don't you want me to take transit? The bus Adalie took from the corner goes right to my building as well."

"I know where you both live, and I hate to say it, but her neighbourhood is a little bit safer than yours."

I can't argue with that. It's Friday night and drunks often wander around the area, sometimes even throwing up on the sidewalk outside the building. It's a nice—and affordable—pet-friendly apartment. But the location leaves a lot to be desired.

"We can take transit if you want," Spencer says. "But I'd like to come with you, if that's okay."

"That's okay."

We stand and he tucks my hair behind my ear. I'm completely lost in his crystal blue eyes. Then he steps back and says, "You got a jacket?"

I grimace. "I forgot one. It's not a long bus ride. I'll be fine."

"Don't be ridiculous. You can wear my hoodie again." He moves off to get it from where I left it in his office earlier.

When he returns, I say, "I can't keep borrowing your clothes."

"Sure you can." He's already unzipping the backpack and pulling out the now familiar sweater.

I may or may not have slept in it Wednesday and Thursday night.

He shakes it out and slips it over my head, gently taking my hair out of the back. He's watching what he's doing, careful not to pull my hair, but I'm watching him, my heart expanding in my chest like it's about to burst with all the emotions I'm feeling.

"There. All cozy. Ready?"

I nod, dressed again in his clothes, and I wonder if he even really wants it back.

Chapter 14
Spencer

After the fiasco the previous night, everyone arrives early the next day. Vic calls us into an impromptu meeting first thing.

"Some weddings are like this," she begins. Then she turns to Lis. "I'm sorry this is your first. I promise they're not all shit shows."

The bride emailed me after the rehearsal to request a few extra things, including vegetarian options for the wedding buffet, and plate service for the head table. Lis takes these in without a word, scribbling some notes down on a pad of paper. Vic asks me to add another row of chairs to the seating area for the ceremony and if I have the tents ready in case it rains, while Lis continues scribbling on her notepad. Eventually, she rips the sheet off and hands it to Derek without looking, continuing to write.

Vic asks Adalie to call in two more people, if she can find them, and asks Derek to bring in another case of rum. Then we're dismissed and get to work. Lis takes Adalie aside to discuss something about the staff while I go to meet the groom and get him situated in a room where he can relax. The guests begin to arrive and find seats right before the rain starts.

I'd already started getting the tents set up, having seen the clouds this morning. People are stringing lights and adjusting seats to ensure everyone will be covered when the first drops land on my face.

I tell the staff to hurry and go to check on the rest.

The bride arrives and immediately says the flowers in the lobby are the wrong colour. Flowers *she* picked out. Flowers she saw last night and had no problem with.

"Would you like me to remove them?" I ask. "Because we don't have any more."

"I want them to be the right colour." Then she huffs, and says, "Ugh. It's too late now. They'll just have to stay."

She hurries to the room we keep aside for the bride to get ready for the ceremony. It's not long before I'm called back to the room because the champagne is wrong. I find Derek and ask if there was a mix-up with the champagne and he assures me there was not, but he'd grabbed a few extra bottles while he was out getting things for Lis.

I bring in the kind the bridezilla insists she had requested and find her complaining her bridesmaids' dresses are too short. Thankfully, that has nothing to do with me. I wait until I'm back in the hall before I roll my eyes.

WHY NOT BOTH?

When I check on the groom, I have to cut him off or else no one will get married today. Though maybe that would be for the best. I see couples sometimes and wonder what they're doing getting married. This couple makes me question if their marriage will last beyond a few months. In the time they've been here, including the rehearsal the night before, I've seen them competing, arguing, and now the groom is getting shit-faced before he says his vows.

I find my way into the kitchen where Lis is working on the appetizers that will be served after the ceremony.

"Got any coffee?" I ask.

She pauses, looking up from her chopping. "Coffee? Of course I do."

She jerks her head to one side, and I follow the motion to where a pot is waiting.

"What do you need it for?" she asks as I pour a cup. "Taking a break?"

"Not likely for this wedding. The groom is drunk."

She stops again. "Seriously? How do you get drunk right before your wedding?"

I shrug. "Some people get nervous." I set the cup on a tray with a small amount of cream and sugar.

"If you're so nervous that you have to get drunk beforehand, should you really be getting married?" she asks. "I thought it was supposed to be the happiest day of your life."

I pick up the tray and turn to her. "It's supposed to be. I've seen plenty of weddings where it is. When I see couples like this one, it just makes me more certain, when it happens for me, I'll be completely sure it's the right thing. I'll be nothing but excited. Otherwise, what the fuck am I doing?"

"You don't think you'd be nervous at all when you get married?"

I consider her question. There's no way to know for certain until it's happening, but after a couple seconds, I shake my head.

"If I ask someone to marry me, it would be because I want to spend the rest of my life with them. I wouldn't ask unless I was sure. It wouldn't make me nervous at all."

"You asked me to marry you," she says with a smile, quirking an eyebrow. "We'd only known each other a few hours. You don't think that would have made you nervous if I'd said yes?"

What do I say to that? I hadn't exactly meant it then. I also wouldn't have taken it back. I've often wondered in the last week, if she'd said yes, if she'd meant it, would we be together now? Or would she still have cut off our relationship when she started working at Blue Vista?

Eventually, I say, "You didn't say yes. So I guess we'll never know."

Chapter 15

Lis

For the rest of the wedding and all day on Sunday, I replay Spencer's words over and over.

You didn't say yes. So I guess we'll never know.

Had he *wanted* me to say yes? The idea is absolutely insane. Though he'd tried to play it off like a quip, he hadn't been able to keep the edge of sadness out of his voice.

If I'm going to be honest with myself, there had been a part of me that wanted to say yes. Throw caution to the wind and figure it out later. But I'd also thought we'd have time.

I shake myself out of my thoughts Monday morning as I finish dressing and gathering what I'll need. When I head into the living room, Daze is just putting on her jacket to head out to work.

"So, you're taking Spencer to visit Mom and Dad today?"

"No. I'm taking him hiking in Golden Ears. We're also stopping by Mom and Dad's because I'll be out there."

She snorts. "Whatever you need to tell yourself. You staying out there for dinner?"

"Obviously. I've already talked to Mom. I'm making beef and broccoli."

"Right," she says, drawing out the word.

"Spencer and I are just friends."

"I didn't say anything."

"Ugh. Go away. Go do something productive."

Daze smiles and kisses my cheek. "Have fun with your *friend*."

She leaves and I say goodbye to Sophie. Then Cerberus and I drive to Spencer's house. He meets us downstairs in just a couple minutes. I'd given him his hoodie back on Sunday and he's wearing it now. I haven't actually seen him wear it before. He's always given it to me to wear.

The fabric stretches over his strong shoulders, and his hands are shoved into the front pocket. He looks so comfortable and I admit; I want the sweater back. Especially now that it'll smell like him again.

He slides into the passenger seat with a smile. "Hey. I figured, if it's an easy hike, jeans would be okay. I didn't really want to wear sweatpants to your parents' house."

"Jeans are fine. Though my parents wouldn't care if you wore sweatpants."

I pull into traffic and start the long journey out to Maple Ridge. Thankfully, rush hour is in the opposite direction from what we're travelling, so once we get onto the highway, it's a pretty fast drive.

We talk about movies and future hiking adventures. I staunchly refuse to hike the Grouse Grind next week, telling him I'll only do it if he runs the Seawall with me. He pouts, but lets it go. We pass my parents' street and I point it out, continuing on to Golden Ears Park. It's actually quite a drive to get there.

"You can go camping here?" Spencer asks as we pass the signs pointing to the campgrounds.

"Yeah, but it fills up pretty fast. We went a bunch when we were kids. Daze and Sophie like to camp. If they're close enough, I visit them for a day."

"Not a camping person?" he asks with a smile.

"I like sleeping in a bed. If I had an RV, maybe. But I'm not sleeping on the ground."

He laughs. "Fair."

"Though camping cooking presents a fun challenge."

"I'm certain you make gourmet meals, even when camping."

I flash him a smile as I slow to cross a rickety, single-lane bridge. "Of course I do."

Just after the bridge, I turn into a parking lot and we get out. Cerberus hops out, wiggling his excitement as he sniffs the air, starting off in a random direction.

I laugh, catching him and clipping his leash to his harness.

"Excuse me, sir. Just where do you think you're going?"

Spencer and I put our things in the trunk.

"I have to confess. It's not really much of a hike. More like a walk. But it's one of Cerberus' favourites."

He grins at me and I just stare at him, lost for a moment in his captivating smile.

"No problem. He guards the gates of the Underworld. The least we can do is take him on his favourite walk. So you grew up in Maple Ridge?"

"Yeah. My parents still live in the same house I grew up in."

"Why did you move to Vancouver?"

"For school, initially. I went to the Pacific Institute of Culinary Arts. After I graduated, I went to work at a restaurant in Burnaby for a while. Then it ended kind of badly, and Daze was already living there, so I moved in with her and found a new job in Vancouver. I can't imagine living anywhere else now."

Cerberus stops to sniff a tree stump on the side of the path for a moment before we continue.

"Was it always a dream to live and work in Vancouver?"

"No. The original dream was to open my own place somewhere. Probably *not* in the city since it's so expensive. But," I shrug. "Dreams change."

"Why did yours?"

WHY NOT BOTH?

"The business side doesn't appeal to me. I just want to cook. Blue Vista is almost my ultimate dream job. To be in charge of my own kitchen. The only thing that would make it perfect would be to have creative control over the menu. I figure, if I prove myself on this menu, I can convince Vic to let me have more control in the future."

As we walk, he asks me about what kinds of things I would change on the menu and I tell him some of my favourite things I've created, like the smoked salmon croquettes and a braised chicken my mom loves.

After a while, he groans. "Stop. You're making me hungry."

I smile and pull a granola bar from my pocket, handing it to him.

He bursts out laughing.

"Feeding people is my love language," I say.

He just laughs harder. Eventually, he says, "That probably won't cut it. I want to try some of those things you were talking about. I'll wait."

I slide the granola bar back into my pocket. "Enough about me and my dreams. What's yours?"

"I'm living it," he says. "Amazing friends, a job I love, an awesome apartment on Sunset Beach. What more could I want?"

"So that's it? You wouldn't change anything?"

He's silent for a few minutes and I let him think about my question.

"Maybe. I don't know. Vic's talking about expanding and if she does, I'll probably take on more responsibility. The four of us discuss all that quarterly. I guess I've just been living my life one moment at a time."

He falls silent again and I can see he's thinking.

"I never really thought about it before," he finally says. He's looking ahead, but I know he's not really seeing the trees or the path we're walking. "I honestly love my job. I don't think I want to do anything else. If we decide to expand Blue Vista and I get more responsibility, that would be fine. But I don't need more there."

"You say that like you might want more somewhere else in your life."

"I guess." He hesitates.

"It's okay to want more, Spencer. You can be happy in your life and still want more from it."

He glances at me and the look in his eye has me wondering what he's thinking.

"Can I think about it and get back to you?"

I almost want to laugh at the question. "It's your dream, Spencer. You don't need to tell me what it is. You just need to figure it out for yourself."

"I want to tell you." Then he gives me his signature grin, blinding me with the brightness. "You've just thrown me into an existential crisis here, woman. You deserve to know the outcome."

Chapter 16
Spencer

We make it to the waterfall at the end of the first part of the path. Lis tells me she's never bothered to continue on and so doesn't even know where the rest of the path leads. Most people only hike to the lower falls and turn around. I want to see where we could go from here, but Lis says Cerberus wouldn't be able to do much more, so we head back.

We talk about our childhoods. Lis tells me about growing up in Maple Ridge and I tell her about growing up in Vancouver and going to private school with Vic. If she notices my lack of family anecdotes, she doesn't mention it.

She's pretty observant. I'm sure she notices.

But I don't want to talk about my family. Especially not now I've realized that's what my dream is. I told Lis I wanted to think about it, but the truth is, as soon as she asked the question, I knew.

I want a wife and kids.

I'd tried so hard to build a family for myself with Vic, Derek, and Adalie. We love each other and have each other's backs. But when it comes right down to it, I want the thing I never had growing up. I want to be the man my father never was. And, since I'm in the mood to be completely honest with myself, I want to see if Lis is the person to do that with.

We've only known each other a short time, but I feel like we connect in all the right ways.

We reach the car and Lis spends a few minutes cleaning Cerberus' feet while he gulps down some water. Then she gets him buckled in and we leave the park.

"So, what did you think?" she asks. "I know it's no Grouse Grind, thank God. But it's a nice walk."

"It's gorgeous. I looked it up and there are some harder hikes here, too. Maybe one day we can leave Cerberus at your parents' place and do a difficult one."

"Sure," she says. "I'd have to check if they're working, but we can probably plan something. And if it means I'll be out here for a visit, Mom will agree in about 0.2 seconds."

I laugh. "You're really close with your parents, then?"

She nods, telling me another story about her childhood and growing up with two parents who loved her and her sister to the point of distraction. I'm smiling as I listen, but the closer we get, the more nervous I am.

WHY NOT BOTH?

Lis doesn't want to date me right now. I feel like I might be able to change her mind eventually. But if her parents hate me, that will never change.

Cerberus dozes in the back seat until Lis turns off the main road onto a side street. He picks up his head and sniffs. Then he stands and starts wagging his tail and vibrating with excitement.

"He knows where we're going?"

"He does. And he knows they're going to spoil him rotten."

She pulls into the driveway of a nice, two-story house on a quiet street. It's blue with a white door and white trim. The front lawn is neatly mowed and there's a rhododendron with bright pink flowers to one side of the front stoop. She doesn't bother with a leash for Cerberus, partly because she lets him out of the car and he races straight to the front door, pawing at it and looking back at us like we need to hurry.

His excitement eases something in me. No one who can make a dog this excited can be bad. I mean, no one who could raise a woman like Lis could be that bad either, but there's something different about seeing it from a dog's point of view. He's staring at us, wiggling and waggling in his impatience to get inside.

Lis just laughs as she opens the door, calling out, "Mom. We're here."

Cerberus takes off into the house, up the stairs. We remove our shoes and follow him. At the top, there's a woman crouched down, smiling, giving Cerberus a treat.

"That's enough, Mom. You're going to make him fat."

"Don't be ridiculous. Until I get some human grandbabies, I just have to spoil my fur grandbaby."

"Mom!"

I grin as I watch Lis' face turn red.

Her mother doesn't even acknowledge us until after Cerberus has eaten his treat and received plenty of head scratches. Then she stands and turns to us with a smile.

"Mom, this is Spencer. A friend from work."

"A friend or *friend*?"

"Mom!"

I stretch out my hand to shake hers. "It's a pleasure to meet you, Mrs. Stone. I feel like we're going to get along great."

"Please. Call me Linda. Would you guys like some coffee or tea? Your father should be home in about an hour, so we can sit and chat for a bit before he gets here."

"Coffee would be amazing," I say.

"I'll make a pot," Lis says, then heads into the kitchen. I follow Linda into the living room, where we sit down.

"Tell me about yourself, Spencer. You work with Lis at Blue Vista?"

I tell her about what I do at the venue. Cerberus jumps onto the couch and snuggles up with her. Lis brings out the coffee. She hands her mom a mug, then gives me one. She's already added cream and sugar. I take a sip and it's exactly how I like it.

I don't remember telling her how I take my coffee. Given how much sugar she adds to hers, I'm impressed she only put a small amount in mine.

We chat for a while. Lis tells her mom about the wedding this weekend and I jump in with commentary and praise for Lis' quick thinking and impeccable planning.

"That's my Lis," her mom says with a proud smile. "She always wants everything to go perfectly."

Cerberus lifts his head and hops down from the couch, his butt wiggling as he looks up at the women with a doggy grin.

"Does he need to go out?" I ask.

"No," Lis says. "Dad's home and he knows he's about to get another treat. He keeps them in his car just in case we come over while he's at work."

As soon as she says the words, the front door opens and a male voice calls, "Where's my grandpup?"

Cerberus takes off, all excited wiggles. They take their time coming back.

"That's my cue," Lis says, standing.

"Cue for what?" I ask.

"To start making dinner."

"I thought the point of going to your parents' place for dinner was *not* having to cook?" I say. "I mean, I don't have a lot of experience myself, but that's what Adalie and Derek are always telling me."

"Lis is very territorial of the kitchen," her father says as he comes up the stairs, Cerberus walking beside him looking up adoringly. "She always has been. Hello, Lissy."

"Hi, Dad. This is Spencer. A friend from work."

"Friend or *friend*?"

I burst out laughing.

"You guys," Lis says, exasperated. "Can't a woman and a man be just friends?"

"Of course they can," Linda says. "But a mother can hope. You two would make adorable babies."

"I'm sorry, Spencer. My mother is baby crazy. Daze and Sophie have stated outright they won't be having kids until after they're married, and they're not even engaged yet. So I bring a man home, it's all Mom can think about."

"It's not a problem," I say, grinning. "I think she's right. We would make adorable babies."

She rolls her eyes, but I notice the blush creeping along her cheeks. Then she turns and escapes into the kitchen. I'm not sure if I should follow her or stay with her parents. Her father decides for me, holding out his hand.

"I'm Dan. Nice to meet you, Spencer."

We shake and he sits next to his wife with a bit of space between them, which Cerberus happily jumps right into.

WHY NOT BOTH?

"I don't want to pry," Linda starts, then stops. "Well. Maybe I do. May I ask what you meant about not having experience with dinners with your parents?"

Shit. I'd said that, hadn't I? I sigh, deciding to answer, but keeping it short. "My mother passed away when I was young, and my father and I are estranged."

"I'm so sorry to hear that," Linda says. I notice her eyes are a little brighter than they'd been before.

Dan puts a hand on her knee. "Linda wants to be a mother to everyone. She's taken in a bunch of Daze's friends. Some of them came out to their parents, and it didn't go so well. So Linda would always try to be their surrogate mother."

I smile at that. "Every kid deserves a mom like that. I think you and my mom would have been good friends."

"So, what is the real relationship between you and my daughter?" Dan asks, changing the subject. Though this one isn't any easier.

There's a crash in the kitchen and Lis appears, waving a wooden spoon. "Just because I'm in another room doesn't mean I'm not listening. You leave him alone. No third degree." She walks up to me and takes my hand, glaring at her parents. "In fact, Spencer, why don't you join me in the kitchen? I can protect you better in there."

I laugh again but follow her.

"I don't need protecting. Your parents are pretty great."

"They are. But they like to tease. And they like to push buttons and ask hard questions." She huffs as she gathers a few ingredients and starts cutting and mixing. She moves around the kitchen, finding exactly what she needs in the first place she looks.

"You learned to cook in this kitchen, didn't you?"

She flashes me a smile over her shoulder. "I did. This one and my granny's. She taught me how to make cabbage rolls. It's one of my favourite things to make, though it takes forever. I usually make a huge batch and freeze a bunch. There's some in my freezer at home. I can bring some to work this week for you."

I love how she casually throws out that she's going to bring me food. Feeding people really is her love language. "I'd like that."

She whisks something and sets the bowl aside.

"Your mom and granny taught you to cook?" I ask.

"And my dad." She organizes some meat in a pan, pouring the stuff from the bowl over top. "I used to spend nights with my granny, and she would tell me stories and we'd cook. She had this ring I loved. It had a blue stone that would sparkle in the dining room light whenever we sat down to eat. That sparkle always reminded me of family dinners."

"Where's the ring now?"

"She left it to my mom. It's not really Mom's style, so she keeps it safe somewhere." She waves a hand toward the rest of the house. "I think it was those family dinners that really fostered my love of cooking. Feeding people, bringing them together."

When dinner is done, she sets out the food and her parents and I sit at the table. They start filling their plates—and it all smells awesome—but Lis still putters around the kitchen.

"What are you doing?" I ask. "Come eat."

"I just have a couple things I need to sort out first," she says.

"She's always like this," Linda says. "Never sits with us until the kitchen is clean."

"Can't she do that after she eats? Her food will get cold."

"You try telling her," Dan says, pointing his fork in her direction.

I twist in my seat to see she's putting dishes into the sink and loading it with soapy water.

"Nope," I say, standing. Then I go to her, lift her, and literally carry her into the dining room.

"Spencer! Put me down."

I do as she says, setting her in the chair next to where I'd been sitting. Her parents are laughing, but I don't look at them.

I lean toward her, one hand on the back of her chair, caging her in the spot at the table. "Dishes are patient as fuck. They will literally wait forever. Right now, you're going to sit and have that family dinner you love so much. While the food is hot. Or else."

She glares at me. "Or else what?"

"Or else I'm not going to eat until it gets cold. Then I'll put the food in the microwave to heat it up."

"Ooh," Linda says. "I never thought of threatening her with that."

Lis' eyes widen. "You wouldn't."

I sit back, my arms crossed, eyebrows raised, waiting.

"I will help you with the dishes after dinner," I say.

Finally, she rolls those beautiful eyes—she's been doing that a lot today—and picks up her fork.

"Sweetheart," Linda says. "You need to marry this man."

Lis chokes on her first bite.

"I actually asked her to marry me, Linda. I think we'd known each other for about twelve hours."

"What did she say?" Dan asks, as though he's asking about the weather.

"If I remember correctly, she didn't say anything. She just laughed at me."

"Great," Lis mumbles under her breath, staring hard at her plate. "Now there's three of you."

Chapter 17

Lis

I sink into the bath with a sigh. The water is far hotter than most people would probably like and it's turning my skin pink. The bubbles smell like lavender, the music is soothing, my white wine is cold. Everything is perfect. I close my eyes and relax. Three weeks after I'd brought Spencer to dinner with my parents, I have another few weddings under my belt, and I feel like I'm on a roll.

After the first wedding from hell, the rest of them have been pretty easy in comparison. But this past weekend had two weddings—one on Saturday and another on Sunday. So today, my big plans are to relax. I'd taken Cerberus out for a run in the morning, did my laundry in the afternoon, and now I have my eyes closed as I consider whether to read a book or watch a show on my phone. Until it starts ringing.

I answer it without checking who is calling.

"What is it?" I ask in a sing-song voice, assuming it's my sister.

"What are you doing right now?"

I sit up quickly, sloshing water around the tub, when Spencer's voice comes through the speaker. We haven't gone on any more hikes since the event season started picking up, but he's walked me home every time it was a nice enough night.

"Nothing," I say.

"Lis. Are you in a bath?" he asks, humour lacing his voice.

"None of your business. What do you want?"

"I just need a second to scrub the image of you naked in a bath from my mind. No, wait. Image stays. Anyway. Derek just told me he forgot to invite you out tonight. He's hosting his monthly game night. Last Monday of every month. You started at Blue Vista on the date of the last one."

I blink, trying to keep up with everything he'd said. "Game night?"

"Yeah. I think we're playing Cards Against Humanity tonight. If Daze and Sophie are free, they're welcome as well. Unfortunately, Cerberus is not invited. Abyss would probably take him out in about three seconds."

"Abyss?"

"Derek's cat. So, are you coming? Or are you going to stay in your bath? Because honestly, I'm not sure which is a better option."

"Staying in my bath is more relaxing. Which was my plan for tonight." I pause, thinking. Spencer waits. "Where does he live?" I ask, resigned.

He tells me and I groan.

"I'm going to have to drive."

"Or you can take an Uber. We can share one back. There'll be drinking tonight."

I look at my glass of wine. "There fucking better be. All right. Give me an hour to get ready and get there. I'll ask Daze and Sophie, but they work tomorrow."

"No worries. See you in a bit."

We hang up, and I drain the tub with a small pout. But if the rest of them are at Derek's house for a night of fun, I want to be there, too.

After I'd been fired for dating a co-worker, I'd tried not to involve myself at all in my next job. As a result, I never created any rapport, and it ended almost as badly as the previous job. I'd managed better with the next one, and I was determined to do the same with Blue Vista.

As I suspected, Daze and Sophie are going to have an early night. I get dressed, take Cerberus out for a quick walk, then order an Uber while I finish getting ready.

When I arrive at Derek's house, I knock, and he opens the door.

"Lis! You came. Sorry I didn't mention the game night. Everyone else knows. It's a standing thing. You've blended so seamlessly, I completely forgot you hadn't been to one before."

He ushers me inside, and I remove my coat and shoes. Loud chatter and laughter resounds from deeper in the house.

"It's no problem. I didn't have any plans."

"Spencer said you were just relaxing."

"I was. I brought the wine I'd planned on drinking, plus an extra bottle. Just in case. Can I get a glass and put the rest in the fridge?"

"Right this way," he says with a grin.

He leads me to the right into his galley kitchen and gets me a glass.

"Bathroom is on the other side of that wall," he says, pointing as he pours my wine for me. "Everyone else is over there in the dining room. Living room is over there as well." He nods toward the other end of the kitchen. "That's pretty much my place. Upstairs is my bedroom and office. Another bathroom. Further up is the rooftop terrace. We'll spend more time up there in the summer. It's a bit cold now."

"A rooftop terrace sounds so cool. This place is great."

Then I look down as a black, fluffy thing winds around my legs with a nudge and a purr.

"Well," he says, handing me my glass. "You are officially Abby approved."

"Abby or Abyss?"

"Either. Both. Her name is Abyss, but I call her Abby just as often." He bends to pick up the cat. "Or your majesty."

She's pure black with long, soft fur and bright yellow eyes.

"She's so pretty," I say, petting her head, making her purr louder. She leans into my caress, accepting it as her due.

"She's the queen of this house. I'll take you up to the roof later to see her outdoor space. Spencer helped me build it two summers ago, just after I moved in."

Derek is always sort of charming in that ready-to-have-a-good-time kind of way. But in his own house, holding his fluffy black cat, talking about the outdoor space he built, I feel like I'm seeing the real Derek for the first time. His charismatic exterior is just a front for a marshmallow-soft interior. Someone who likes to do things for the people he loves, even if that *person* is actually a cat.

We move into the dining room where everyone is seated around a table, drinks and snacks laid out, the black box of cards in the middle. My eyes are drawn immediately to Spencer, who has his back to me, an arm along the back of one of the empty chairs, legs stretched out in front of him under the table.

"Lis! You're here!" Adalie says, jumping up to wrap me in a hug.

She's usually much more reserved at work, so I'm surprised, until it occurs to me I'm seeing all these people for real for the first time. These four are best friends, have known each other for years, and are fully comfortable with each other in the same way I'm comfortable with Daze and Sophie.

"Derek really dropped the ball on this one," she says.

I hug her back, feeling like part of the group and my heart constricts in my chest. I realize I want to be one of them, one of the Blue Vista Crew, included in game night and other outings. Then Spencer's eyes find mine over Adalie's shoulder. The look he gives me is full of promise and heat and damn, I want that, too.

He turns back to the table and Adalie returns to her seat, dragging me with her and forcing me into the spot next to Spencer. His arm drops from the back of the chair, and he offers me a smile. His expression has cooled, so I no longer feel like sliding into his lap and making out with his face. But the idea is there, just under the surface.

Derek hands me a pile of cards, and we begin. Or at least, I begin. Everyone else has been playing the whole hour I was getting ready. Adalie is a little drunk already and Vic explains she's a lightweight and has been put in time out. In this setting, even Vic has loosened up. She always seems to be on, never letting herself have a moment to decompress.

"So, what did we pull you away from, Lis?" Derek asks after he reads out his black card and everyone decides what to give him.

"I wasn't doing anything. Just trying to figure out if I wanted to read a book or watch a show."

My glance drifts to Spencer, waiting for him to announce I'd been in a bath when he called. He says nothing, focusing much harder on his hand of cards than he needs to.

"You've been doing an awesome job at work," Vic says, handing over her card. "You've really hit the ground running."

"Drink!" Adalie says with a grin.

Vic rolls her eyes and drinks from a can of craft beer.

Adalie turns to me. "Since we work together, it's easy to fall into work discussions. So if anyone brings it up, they have to take a drink."

"Fair rules," I say, taking a sip of my wine. "What do you guys talk about instead?"

"Anything goes," she says. "Nothing is off limits."

"Nothing? I can ask super rude and personal questions?"

"Anything," she confirms.

"But," Spencer says, bringing my attention back to him. "Anything you ask, be prepared to have it asked back to you."

Our gazes linger on each other for just a moment longer than I probably should have let happen. Then I snap back to the rest of the group.

"Well, let's start with an easy one then," I say, selecting a card and handing it to Derek. "How long have you all known each other?"

"You know Spencer and I met when we were practically babies," Vic says. "These two joined us during university."

"We did our MBAs together," Derek says as he picks up the cards, shuffling them. "Became friends during one of the classes."

"*One* class?" I ask.

"It was intense," Adalie says.

We pause in the conversation as Derek reads out the options people have given him. Spencer wins and adds the black card to his massive stack.

"Do you win every round?" I ask him. He just smiles, but everyone else groans.

"It's all about knowing your competition," he says, leaning toward me conspiratorially.

Adalie is next, selecting a black card and reading it out for us.

"It was a group class," Adalie says, continuing the conversation from before. "At the beginning of the semester, we selected a group, and together had to come up with a business plan. Vic and Spencer were always going to be together, but the groups needed three to five people. To learn how to work well with others. Spencer selected me and Derek. In fact, I was already part of a group and I remember Spencer coming up to me and saying, 'You're in the wrong group.'"

"What did you do?"

"I wasn't going to do anything. I was going to ignore him. Then he said the magic words."

She pauses, smiling, waiting for Spencer to say them now.

He leans his arms on the table and says, "Do you want to get an A or not?"

Adalie fans herself with a dreamy sigh.

"You see," Spencer says. "Just like this game, it was all about knowing people. With Derek, just going up to him made him curious enough to join our group. But with Adalie, I knew she was an overachiever. *Is* an overachiever. Of course, then I had to ensure I backed up my claim."

"I switched groups then and there," Adalie confirms. "Turned out, we were the only group to get an A. We worked so well together that when Vic decided to start the business we'd come up with, she invited us all to be part of it."

"You came up with the idea for Blue Vista at university?"

Everyone nods.

"What happened to the group you had been with at first?" I ask.

Adalie bursts into laughter. "They ended up in counselling and barely passed."

Everyone joins her laughter. She reads out the options and selects Spencer as the winner again.

"How do you do that every time?" I ask, pulling a black card from the stack.

"I told you. It's about knowing who you're playing with. Knowing what the person receiving the white card will find funny and knowing the kind of card the others will offer. Then choose the card that beats them."

Before I read out the black card, he selects a white one from his hand and sets it down in front of me with a smile.

"Like this one."

I'm so tempted to just flip it over, but I read the black card first, something about never leaving the house without whatever is on the white card.

As everyone else selects their choices for me, I watch Spencer, who is just looking back at me, full of confidence.

"There is one card in this game that is an automatic win for me," I say. "And it's not even that funny."

"That's it." He taps the card. "I've been saving it for you."

I have all the cards now and I'm supposed to shuffle and read them out. But I just want to read Spencer's card.

"Go ahead," Vic says, resigned. "It's the one you're going to choose, anyway."

I flip over the card and laugh. All it says is "puppies." I hand him the black card.

"You're right. That's my automatic win. How did you know?"

He shrugs, but he's smiling.

The game moves on.

"Okay. You asked us a question," Derek says. "Our turn. Spencer mentioned you grew up in Maple Ridge. What made you decide to move to Vancouver?"

"A series of unfortunate events," I say, realizing too late everyone would want to know more, and I don't really want to talk about it. I blindly hand Spencer one of my white cards. They're all waiting, though. So, I tell the story.

"After I graduated culinary school, I started working for a company in Burnaby. I wasn't quite in the thick of Vancouver, but close enough to be able to get out here whenever I wanted."

No one is looking at their cards now.

"I started dating this guy, and it was going well. I got a promotion at work, my boss really liked me, I was moving up. Then my boss found out about my relationship. The guy I was dating was his sous chef, and it was apparently against the rules. Except the sous chef never mentioned that to me. I've actually wondered if it was even a rule or if the chef was just being a dick. He'd asked me out a couple times and I'd turned him down. Anyway, I was fired. The sous chef was not. I'd worked there for almost three years, been dating the guy for four months. When I was fired, he broke up with me and I had to start all over again. Daze had just moved to Vancouver and so I moved in with her."

I don't say how much I needed to be with someone who loved me back then. Someone who I knew wouldn't betray me. Daze had been my rock when everything was falling apart around me.

I look up to find everyone staring at me like they don't know what to say, which I get. They all know Spencer and I slept together. They know I decided not to pursue a relationship with him. Now, everyone knows why.

I stand, finding a smile. "I'm going to get more wine. Anyone else want something from the kitchen?"

I don't wait for an answer before going to the fridge, pouring my glass of wine, and standing at the counter for a minute.

"I'm sorry that happened to you," Spencer says.

I'm not surprised he's followed me.

"It wasn't you, Spencer," I say, staring at my wine. "I wanted…"

"I know."

He wraps his arms around me, and I lean into him.

"I just can't go through that again. I can't. I'm so close to where I want to be." Tears fill my eyes and a hard lump forms in my throat.

"I know. It's okay." He kisses the top of my head, a gesture he's been doing lately as we hang out more often. It feels so warm and safe in his arms and I wish I could stay there forever. He sighs. "You know, Burke. I don't know which species is worse."

I snort, my face still buried in his chest. "Who's Burke?"

"Guess."

I shake my head. "Not tonight. You can win this round. Just tell me."

"It's from *Aliens*."

"So humans are being compared to aliens who eat people?"

"Something like that. It's a commentary on how shitty humans can be. You ready to go back? No more hard questions. If anything comes up you don't want to talk about, shift your wine glass toward me and I'll change the subject."

"Promise?"

"I promise."

I take a deep breath and step back, grabbing my glass and heading back to the table. Spencer follows me with a couple beers, handing them out and asking Adalie to tell him about her latest art project.

She launches into an animated explanation of a painting she's creating.

Later, when we're on our way home, we all share an Uber. It drops Adalie off first, then me. I'm about to get out of the car when Spencer mentions I don't have a jacket.

I laugh. "I'm only going up the elevator."

He follows me out of the car, telling the driver he'll be right back and pulling his hoodie off, slipping it over my head.

"You're ridiculous," I tell him, but I also feel so cared for that I don't complain any more than that.

"I don't want you to be cold," he says, walking me to the door.

"Well, thank you. And thanks for changing the subject earlier."

He shrugs. "It's easy. You can always count on Adalie if you need to change the subject. Though Vic and Derek totally saw through it. Probably Adalie, too."

"I still appreciate it."

He wraps me in a hug, warming me to my toes. "I'll see you on Wednesday, firecracker."

Then he presses a kiss to the top of my head and holds the door open for me to go inside. When I get to the elevator, I turn back and wave at him where he's standing, watching me through the door. He waves and goes back to the car where Vic and the driver are waiting.

Chapter 18

Spencer

As is my usual routine these days, I stand at the window looking down at Sunset Beach with my coffee when Vic emerges from her bedroom.

"Has she run past yet?" Vic asks, deadpan.

"I don't know. Because I am not a stalker."

She snorts and goes to pour herself a cup of coffee as well, coming to stand next to me to look out the window as well. She's taken to doing this for me, so I don't feel like such a creep. I love her for it.

"There's something I've been thinking about lately," I say after a few moments of silence.

"What?"

"I think it might be time for me to find my own place."

In my peripheral vision, I see her turn toward me. "Why?"

I consider how to answer her for a moment. Then, I say, "I don't really have anything that's just mine."

She doesn't argue with that. Instead, she says, "I like having you here."

She says it in her small voice, her I'm-letting-you-see-something-that-might-hurt-me voice.

"I like being here. But I think it's easy. It's safe. For both of us." I turn to face her. "Do you think Emily is your person?"

"I don't know."

"Maybe me being here is stopping you from figuring it out."

She lifts her eyebrow. "You hate her."

"Yep. But I will love her if you do."

"You'll love her, huh?" she asks, disbelief lacing her tone.

I roll my eyes. "Fine. I'll tolerate her. What do you want in life, Vic? Because neither of us has been in any kind of serious relationship in the last seven years. If I keep staying here, that's probably where we're going to be in the next seven years as well."

I turn back to the window, resting my head against the glass.

"So you're moving out."

I snort. "You know what the market's like here. It'll take some time. I should have got in when you did."

"You had your reasons. In fact, didn't they have something to do with *not* wanting a serious relationship?"

"I'm starting to think it might be okay with the right person."

"Is that her?"

WHY NOT BOTH?

At first, I wonder if she's referencing my statement. Then I see Lis and Cerberus running along the Seawall back to her apartment.

"Yes." I sigh. "That's her." And now I'm not sure which *I'm* referring to: the statement or her physical presence outside my building.

Probably both.

"Now you know why she wouldn't date you, can't you do something about it?" Vic asks. "Tell her Blue Vista isn't like that other place. I'm not like that. Neither are you or Derek or Adalie."

I shake my head as I turn, and we get our shoes and jackets. "I don't think it's something I can just say. I think it's something she has to believe. After what happened before, I don't really blame her if she never does. She's worked really hard to get to where she is. Do you know how many female head chefs are in Vancouver?"

Vic gives me a sympathetic look. "I just know how much you like her. And, while I don't know her as well as I know you, I'm pretty sure she likes you just as much. I wish it could work out for you guys."

We walk to work and I sit in my office, making phone calls, checking emails, and making sure everything that needs to be scheduled is. I check on what needs to happen for the weddings this weekend—one on Saturday and another on Sunday. Both are ceremony and reception weddings, so we're hosting rehearsals as well. Everything has to move like clock-work.

The corporate client arrives, and I get them situated in the hall for their seminar, but there's not a lot for me to do during these events.

By the time lunch rolls around, I need a break from all the planning and rearranging, so I open a new tab on my computer and pull up a real estate website. I set my parameters and search the listings. Something I've done a few times over the past few weeks.

"What are you working on?"

I look up to find Lis leaning against the door frame. She is gorgeous with her hair twisted up in one of those clips she likes and her red chef jacket on. She has a few different ones—a white one with black piping, another white one with red piping, a black one—but this red one is her favourite.

"Nothing. Just checking out some condos for sale."

She comes into the office and sits down in the chair she usually sits in.

"You're thinking of buying a place?"

I laugh. "For the last seven years."

"You don't want to live with Vic anymore?"

"I love living with Vic. It's been great. But you were right when we went on that hike a few weeks ago. There's something missing in my life and I think part of that is I want my own place. I'm thirty years old, for fuck's sake." I lean back in my chair, folding my hands behind my head.

"I'm sure she doesn't mind having you," Lis says.

"She doesn't. But it was always supposed to be a temporary solution. Seven years isn't feeling very temporary."

"Oh. I didn't realize you meant you'd been there that long. I just assumed you'd lived with that woman I saw at the bar."

I have to think for a minute to remember who she's talking about. "Lucy? No. I never lived with her. Or anyone else besides my parents and Vic. There was a time between when I lived alone."

"Why did you move in with her, then?" She props her cheek on her fist, elbow on my desk. She looks at me with curiosity, like she wants to know everything about me. And I want to tell her everything. Even things I don't normally share with anyone.

I sit forward, leaning toward her. "My girlfriend at the time asked to move in with me."

Her brows draw down in confusion. "So?"

"I ended up breaking up with that girl and moving in with Vic right after. That way, no one could ask to move in with me again. If someone asks me to move in with *them*, it's easy enough to say no."

"Why is that an issue? Do you have some fear of commitment?"

I shake my head. "Not exactly. Do you know what the common-law laws are in Canada?"

"Vaguely. I know Daze and Sophie are common-law. It's pretty much like they're married."

"Exactly. If you live with someone for a year in a conjugal relationship—the law's words, not mine—you're effectively married in the eyes of the government. What's yours is mine and what's mine is yours."

"And you have something."

I nod. "My mom left me an inheritance. It's a fair chunk of money. I've invested it and it's grown a bit over the years. I try not to use it because I'd intended to use it for a down payment one of these days." I hesitate, wanting to tell her the rest. Only three people in my life know about my money.

She notices my pause and says, "You don't have to tell me anything more, Spencer. It's none of my business."

"I want to tell you. We're friends and the rest of my friends know." Still, I hesitate. *This won't change anything*, I tell myself. *If it does, she's not the woman I thought she was.* "I also have a trust fund. I don't use it. Don't even have access to it. There are certain stipulations attached I refuse to agree to."

"What kind of stipulations? Getting married or something?"

I snort. "My father doesn't care if I get married. He won't release it unless I join his company or start my own *approved* business."

"Approved by who?"

I arch an eyebrow and say nothing.

She smiles wryly. "That was a pretty stupid question. What happens if you don't?"

I shrug. "Nothing. I won't fall in line. He won't give me the trust fund."

"How much is it worth?" Lis asks, then immediately bites her lip, her eyes sliding away. "I'm sorry. You don't have to tell me. I've just never met anyone with a trust fund before."

I laugh. "Well, now you know two. Me and Vic. Vic has hers, though. That's how she started this place." I consider for a moment, then tell Lis what I think is in my trust fund. It's been a while since I last checked.

Her eyes widen at the number and her mouth drops open. "And you don't care that you don't have access to it?"

"Why would I? I don't think of it as real money. I mean, of course it *is*. But unless my father takes the stipulations off, I'm never going to see it. So it just sits there and collects interest and I work a regular job for regular money and get to be a regular guy."

She gives me a slow smile. "Well, I kind of like the regular guy."

A bit of tension eases. I've known a lot of women who found out who my father is and wanted to be with me, even though I don't have anything from him. I'd even accused Lucy of it at the bar the night I met Lis. I'd been certain Lis wouldn't be like that, but it's nice to be proved right.

"So," I say, motioning toward the computer, "do you see any you think I should check out?"

She stands excitedly, coming around the desk, and positioning her chair so she can look at the screen with me. "I love looking at houses. It's so fun to see all the different layouts. And I admit I spend more time than I should critiquing other people's kitchens."

She offers me a cute smile and I fight not to lean closer to press my lips against it. Over the last few weeks, I've gotten pretty good at keeping the urge to kiss her in check, partly made easier since I started kissing her head and cheek frequently. More frequently than maybe I should.

"You want to stay Downtown?" she asks, as we finally turn our attention back to the screen.

"I was thinking about it. It's nice to be able to walk to work. And all my things are here. Besides. Why would I want to leave Vancouver?"

She grins at me. "Can't think of a reason." She turns back to the computer. "There's a place for sale in Vic's building. Fuck. Look at those prices. You can afford that?"

"That one is a little high, but I could probably swing it. Vic's apartment doesn't allow pets, though."

"You're thinking of getting a pet?"

Shit. It would be weird if I told her I'd been thinking of Cerberus. Lis is just my friend. But I'd been thinking, if I ever had her over for a movie night, she could bring him. And maybe, deep down, I still hope we can work something out. As the idea of buying my own place grows, so does the desire to find something she might like.

"Uh," I say, clearing my throat. "Not right now. But I want to keep my options open."

Right. That makes sense. Perfectly reasonable.

"Ooh, I like this one," she says, and I check to see what she's looking at. "That *kitchen*."

It's bright and open, with a large island and a gas stove.

"I assume kitchen would be your number one priority when finding a place to live?" I ask.

She tilts her head to the side. "Well. Tied with allowing pets. Having a parking spot would be important, too. I need a car to get out to visit my parents."

"What else?"

She gives me that smile—the what-are-you-up-to smile. "Shouldn't this be more about what *you* want?

If you're planning to spend over a million dollars on a condo, it should be about you. Not me."

I lean back, trying to be as nonchalant as possible. I'm not certain I pull it off. "Just getting ideas of things to look for."

"What do you want in a place?" she asks me.

I think about it. "It would be nice to have at least two bedrooms. A gym would be awesome. Or at least close to one."

"I thought you liked hiking?"

"Grouse Grind is closed during the winter. And I can't go hiking every day."

"Thank God."

I chuckle. "Two bathrooms would be good as well. Near the Seawall. Some kind of outdoor space."

She turns back to the screen and clicks on another listing. She clicks through the information on it.

"I think this is the winner then," she says. "It allows pets, two bed, two bath. *Look* at that kitchen. And it's got those big sliding glass doors so you can almost open the living room right onto the patio. The building even has a gym."

She gets more and more excited as she talks, pointing out everything I've just mentioned.

"It's also a bit below my budget." I watch as she scrolls through the pictures.

"*That's* your budget?"

I check again to be sure, then nod. "Yeah. I could manage that. I've already run the numbers. Does it say what the maintenance fees are?"

We keep scanning the listing. It's definitely one worth checking out in person. It's a little smaller than I was hoping for, but not by much. And it comes with a parking space. Though I would maybe rent that out until I need it.

"Fuck. That view, though," she says wistfully, stopping on one of the pictures. "There's an open house on Sunday."

"We're really busy this weekend," I say. "Two full weddings."

"I don't start until three on Sunday. I know you have to be here for set up, but maybe we could meet there around two and do a quick walk-through? If you don't mind me joining you. It's only a ten-minute walk from here."

"You want to come with me?"

She turns back with a sheepish smile. "If you want."

I don't tell her I want her to like any place I consider. I don't wonder if I'm setting myself up for heartbreak. I just say, "All right. Sunday it is."

Chapter 19

Lis

Once all the food is served and the cleanup is done, I stay behind to prep for tomorrow's rehearsal dinners. We're doing two, one for each of the two weddings this weekend. By the time I'm done, the corporate clients have left and so have Vic, Derek, Adalie, and all the rest of the staff. Spencer and I are the last ones.

I stop by his office.

"Hey. I wondered if we could go over this weekend again. I just want to make sure I have everything ready."

"We can do that. I'm hungry, though. You want to order something?"

"Sure." I take out my phone, about to ask what he wants to order, when it rings. "Sorry. Daze is calling. Hello?"

"You're still at work?" she asks without preamble.

"Yeah."

"Are you done? Come out for dinner."

"I was going to have a meeting with Spencer about this weekend. We have two weddings."

"Sophie and I are across the street. Both of you come. It'll be nice to finally meet him. You can have a *meeting* after dinner."

I roll my eyes at her tone, but don't comment on it. "I thought you guys were going out for your anniversary today."

"We are. But since we're across the street, we want you to join us."

I sigh. "You're not going to let this go, are you?"

"Nope. Now get your little ass over here." She hangs up on me, not letting me protest anymore.

"They're at the restaurant across the street. You want to get dinner and we can talk about this weekend after?"

"If you want to go with them, I can wait until after."

"She said to bring you, and you're hungry. Come with me. I don't know why she wants me to go, anyway."

We leave the building and go across to the restaurant. I spot Daze and Sophie immediately and make my way over to them.

"Shit," Spencer says as we sit down, his head swiveling between us. "You guys are identical."

"I told you that," I say.

"It's one thing to know it. It's another thing to see it."

I give him a nudge with my elbow, then turn to my sister. "Well, you got me here," I say. "Spit it out. I know you want to say something, so let's have it."

Sophie and Daze exchange a look, then Daze turns back to me, her face alight with joy. She holds up her left hand, showing me a ring that hadn't been on her finger yesterday.

I slap my hand over my mouth. "Are you engaged?" I ask through my fingers.

Daze's grin grows even wider as she nods, gripping Sophie's hand.

I jump up and circle the table, pulling my sister into a tight hug, tears flooding my eyes. "I'm so excited for you guys."

I hug Sophie next. Then ask to see the ring again, before I'm back to hugging Daze. The server has come over a couple times by the time we're settled enough to order.

"Congratulations," Spencer says once the server is gone. "Have you guys thought about where you want to get married? Because I know a pretty great place with an extremely talented chef."

I smile at his compliment.

"I would love to get married at Blue Vista," Daze says. "On the rooftop with the ocean right there. But I don't think it's in our budget."

Spencer shrugs. "Come to a meeting. I'll introduce you to Vic. You let us know what your budget is, and we can see if we can work something out."

"Tell me all about how it happened," I say, vibrating with excitement.

"Sophie told me to take the day off today. She had something special planned for our anniversary. In hindsight, I probably should have suspected then, but I didn't."

Sophie laughs. "You can be a little oblivious to things sometimes. I really wanted to do it at sunrise, but I knew that would be tricky because I'd have to get her to take the day off."

A twinge of pain steals over me, a feeling that reminds me I don't have what they have. My sister and Sophie are so cute together. Sophie always does little things for Daze like making sure she has coffee ready when Daze gets up and drawing her a bath when she's had a long day. They make their bed together every morning.

"So I take the day off and she wakes me up at way-too-early-o'clock, and we drive out to Queen Elizabeth Park—"

"Where we had our first date," Sophie interjects.

"—And there's so few people around—because it's so early—and Sophie got down on one knee."

They share a look of pure love and happiness, and that stab of envy flares again. I hate the feeling. I should only be excited right now. But I also want what they have. I want it so much and it's never happened for me. The relationships I've been in never felt like the perfect fit, the sense that this is where I'm meant to be.

The feeling I had in those few hours with Spencer.

I have such a mix of emotions inside me and I'm not entirely sure what I mean when I shift my water glass toward Spencer. I'm not even sure he'll understand the gesture since it was a few nights ago and I don't exactly want to change the subject. I just want to move on from this moment so I can feel excited, and only excited.

"So how did you two meet?" he asks.

And the moment is broken. The pain in my chest eases because I know this story. It's one I've heard a dozen or more times. I lived part of it. It's cute and funny and I help tell it. How they'd met at a small Christmas party five years ago through a mutual friend, but both had been seeing someone at the time. They became friends and broke up with their girlfriends sometime between Christmas and Valentine's Day.

"Yet neither of them realized they'd done it because they wanted to be with the other," I say dryly.

Our food arrives as Sophie continues. "Finally, Daze asked me out, and we went on our first date. We went to Queen Elizabeth Park intending to go for a walk before getting some dinner. It started to rain, so we went into the Bloedel Conservatory to stay dry. Have you ever been?"

"A really long time ago," Spencer says. "I went in high school with a science class. We had a unit on birds."

"So you know it's a pretty short walk around the path. We probably went around that place ten times, just talking. A year later, on our first anniversary, we got these." She rolls up her sleeve to show off the silhouette tattoo on her left wrist of two birds on a branch turned toward each other. Daze pushes up her sleeve to show off her matching one, placed right below the daisy and amaryllis tattoo matching mine. "Since Daze asked me out first, I decided a while back I wanted to be the one to propose. I'm glad I got to do it and make it a surprise."

They smile at each other again.

"So wait. You guys were engaged at sunrise?" I ask. "Before I even left for work this morning?"

"Yes," Daze says. "Then we went for breakfast and walked around the park for a while. Then went to Bloedel since it opens at a reasonable hour." She casts a sidelong look at Sophie.

"I wanted to do it at sunrise. A lot of people choose sunset. But it's the beginning of our life together, not the end of it."

Daze and I clap our hands to our hearts from how adorable that statement is. And the envy is back.

"Okay, guys," Spencer says. "You're giving me a toothache from all the sweetness."

The joke is so well-timed that I find my way back to only being excited.

"You've been engaged all day," I say. "Who have you told so far?"

Daze gives me a secret smile. One we've shared since we were kids, when we were the only two people in the world who knew everything about each other.

"So far, we've told you and Spencer."

"I'm the first to know?"

"Of course you are. You think I'd tell anyone else before you?"

Tears spring to my eyes and I hate myself for all the jealousy I've been feeling.

"I'm going to ask this, to make it official, even though it should go without saying," she says, reaching across the table for my hand. "Will you be my maid of honour?"

I take her hand and roll my eyes. "That's a stupid question. If you tried to choose anyone else, I'd have a duel. Pistols at dawn."

"I have to warn you," Sophie says, "dawn is pretty early these days."

Chapter 20

Spencer

After dinner, Lis and I walk back across the street to Blue Vista. Daze and Sophie are going to stop in next week to talk to me and Vic about what their budget is to see if there's anything we can do for them.

When we get back, I lead Lis into my office. Everything is quiet. I know she's in her head about something, but I can't figure out what.

"Are you okay?" I ask.

She freezes, lifting her eyes to search mine. "What do you mean?"

"You're upset about something. I don't think it's the engagement. But you shifted your glass closer to me, so I thought you wanted me to change the subject."

She stares at me for a long moment and doubt flashes across her features. "I am so happy for my sister," she says. "I know how much she loves Sophie and how much Soph loves her. Their wedding is going to be spectacular and their life together is going to be perfect."

"But..."

Her shoulders slump and she looks up at me with damp eyes. I want to wrap her in my arms and take away whatever she's feeling that's making her sad.

"After the initial excitement wore off, I felt jealous. Then I felt guilty for feeling jealous. I should be able to be happy for her without anything else interfering."

"It's okay to feel two conflicting emotions at the same time, Lis."

She wraps her arms around herself, and her gaze drops to the ground. "It's not just that."

The weight of everything that happened between us settles in the room. I want to know what she's thinking. Is she regretting not giving us a chance? If she is, do I want her to make that decision based on what she's feeling right now? I'd rather she come to it on her own, because she knows, like I do, that we're right for each other.

I wonder if it matters. As long as she gets there, does it matter how she did?

All at once, I'm certain the answer is yes. I don't want to be her choice because she's feeling lonely. I want to be her choice because she realizes we belong together.

I clear my throat. "Should we get to work?" I ask.

She looks back up at me, blinking, and I wonder again what she'd been thinking. What has that doubt still marring her expression? Then she nods.

She sits in one of my office chairs, and I move around my desk, turning my computer on. I shake myself out of the thoughts of Lis, and we focus on work. When we're done thirty minutes later, she has a list that she leaves on Derek's desk for the morning.

"You going to take transit home or walk?" I ask when she returns, getting my jacket on.

"I was thinking of walking. I brought your hoodie for you, but since I didn't think I'd be here this late, I assume you're going to make me wear it."

I grin. "Absolutely. Come on. I'll walk you home."

While she pulls the sweater over her head, I catch sight of the flower tattoo on her arm.

"Why the left arm?" I ask when we're walking along the Seawall.

"What?"

"You and Daze have your tattoos on the left arm. Her and Sophie have their matching tattoos also on the left arm. Why?"

"Because that's the heart side."

I nudge her shoulder with mine. "Are you just as toothachingly sweet as Daze and Sophie?"

She flips her hair behind her back, nose in the air. "I prefer to think of it as romantic."

We walk in silence for a bit before I ask, "So how are you feeling now?"

She gives me a small smile. "I'll be fine."

But her tone doesn't match her words. She's still in her head, still thinking about something making her unhappy.

"You know I'm here to listen if you want to talk about it," I tell her. "Sometimes just saying it out loud helps you figure it out."

She opens her mouth, then closes it again. We walk in silence for a few steps before she finally says. "Did you know I haven't had a serious relationship since the one that got me fired?"

I glance at her in shock. "Really?"

"Yep. After it happened, Daze and Sophie helped piece me back together. I got a new job, and I didn't let myself get close to anyone. So when there were some layoffs, it was easy for them to let me go."

"Fuck."

She shrugs. "It's fine. I understood it was more about needing fewer employees than me actually being bad at the job. They gave me an excellent reference letter. So I got my last job, and I had to figure out how to be friendly without being too friendly. I worked there for three years and made my way up through the ranks until I was second in command. I knew I could never go further there. The head of the kitchen is also the owner."

She takes a breath and I have a feeling we're coming to the heart of what she's been thinking about for the last few hours.

"After I was fired, when I thought about dating again, I just couldn't. It was all tied so closely to what had happened. I'd felt like I was on a good path until it was suddenly ripped away. I figured it was better to focus on one thing at a time, so I focused on my career. And I don't regret that." She says it like she's trying to decide if the statement is true. "I know I'll have it all one day, the whole future I want. For now, I guess I'm just a little envious Daze found her person so young. She was only 22 when they met."

"Practically still a baby."

She nudges me this time, and we walk in silence for a few steps. I figure it's time to change the subject.

"How do you think your parents are going to react to the news?"

She laughs. "I actually hadn't thought of that, but it's quite a perk for me. Mom and Dad are going to be so overjoyed about the wedding, they're going to stop bugging me about relationships and grandbabies for a while. Well. Maybe a date for the wedding. But the grandbabies part? They are going to be all in, begging Sophie and Daze to get to work."

I smile at her sudden lightheartedness. "Do they plan to have kids right away?"

"I don't think so. I know Daze wanted to be married. I think Sophie wants to be married for a year at least."

"I've actually been thinking about what you asked when we went on that hike a few weeks ago," I say. "About what my dream is. I know what it is, if you're interested."

"Of course I am."

I swallow. She'd been open and vulnerable with me. I could be the same with her. "You know my father and I aren't close."

"I believe you've used the term estranged before."

"He wasn't an easy man to grow up with. I guess I've always kind of wanted to prove him wrong. To show him... no, to show *myself* that it's possible to be successful at business and family life. I want a wife. Family. Kids. That's what I'm missing."

"Yeah?"

I nod, trying to seem casual despite my racing heart.

"I guess I've always known it was something I wanted, but I just haven't really thought about what that means."

"And now?"

I glance aside at her, but she's not looking at me.

"Well, now I need to buy a place. I figure the first step is to remove Vic as my safety net, then figure it out." I don't tell her I want her to be that wife, that I want her to be the mother of my kids. Especially since I've never even asked her if she wants kids. Which, now I'm thinking about it, I really want to ask. It would be weird, though.

WHY NOT BOTH?

She sighs and answers the question I haven't asked. "A husband and kids. It's such a pretty dream."

"You want those things, too?" I ask.

"Yeah. I mean, getting married isn't as important to me as it is to Daze. But then, it's never been illegal for me to marry a man. And I definitely want a kid one day. Maybe two."

"I want at least two."

She smiles up at me. "So we agree on two, then."

"Would you want to wait a bit? After you're married? Like Daze and Sophie."

"I don't know. I think it'll depend on the guy and our relationship. Maybe a little on how old I am. I don't want to have kids past thirty-five. I know I can, and lots of people do. It's just not for me."

"You still have lots of time."

"Do I? I'm twenty-eight, Spencer. And I'm not in a relationship at all. I still need to meet someone, fall in love, decide to get married, and *get* married, before I even think of having kids. I don't want to rush any of that just because my biological clock is ticking."

Something inside me eases as she lays to rest the fear I'd had earlier about her wanting me only because I'm here and she's lonely. Lis is not the kind of person who would enter a relationship that way. If she does, she'll do it consciously. Once she makes a decision, she goes all in, just like I do. Except I usually make my decisions fast with little thought and all instinct. Lis takes her time. Time I'm willing to give her.

I grab her hand, tugging her to a stop. "You don't need to rush anything. You could meet the person of your dreams tomorrow." *Or a month ago.* "Worrying about it won't help you."

She steps closer to me. I immediately wrap her in a hug, giving her the comfort she needs. I take the opportunity to kiss her head because that's the only way I can kiss her right now.

Chapter 21

Lis

I hurry down the street toward the building where the open house is, checking the time again. This place is only a fifteen-minute walk from my apartment and I'd left with way more time than I needed, but I still don't like to be late. And I know Spencer will be anxious about leaving work on a day when there's a wedding happening.

Sure enough, he's waiting for me outside, seeming tense.

"Everything okay?" I ask.

"Yeah. I left Adalie in charge. Everything's in good hands. It just feels weird."

"Let's go up then." I link my arm through his and tug him along.

There's a person at the front door to let us in and he gives us a fact sheet on the apartment. As we ride up the elevator to the sixth floor, I read the sheet over Spencer's arm.

"The maintenance fees are pretty high," I say, pointing.

"They're not bad. Considering the rooftop garden and the gym. I've seen worse. And since there's one here, I'd get rid of my current gym membership."

The doors slide open and a woman in a skirt suit smiles at us.

"You're here for the open house?" she asks.

I smile back. "We are."

The realtor holds out her hand. "I'm Sam. Can I show you around?"

"Please."

We follow her inside and she says just to leave our shoes on. She points out the in-suite laundry and how both bedrooms have attached bathrooms. The master has a walk-in closet that almost makes me swoon.

"Do you think the bedroom is big enough for your king-sized bed?" I ask.

Spencer nods. He seems thoughtful as he looks around. "This bed is a queen and there's still plenty of space."

"The bathroom has a double vanity *and* a separate shower and bathtub."

Sam laughs. "Are you trying to do my job?"

"It's a really nice bathtub," I say with a shrug.

Spencer sends me a mischievous smirk. "I know how much you like baths."

My face heats as Sam leads us into the open-concept living room/kitchen. As soon as I see the kitchen, I come to a dead stop.

"Are there two ovens?" I ask.

Sam offers us a smile. "Why, yes, there are. You like to cook?"

"I'm a chef."

I go into the kitchen, trailing my fingers over a pristine, white counter. It's not stone, but I don't really like stone counters, anyway. They can be porous, they require special care, and if they get damaged, they're expensive to repair. This counter is much more practical as well as being pretty.

I open one of the ovens, peering inside.

"What are you looking for?" Spencer asks.

I turn to him with the most serious look I can muster. "It's important to check inside your oven." Then I move to the refrigerator and open it as well.

I know Spencer is fighting to keep from laughing at me. But kitchens are serious things.

"Check all the cupboards, firecracker. Make sure there's enough space."

I flash him a quick smile. "Don't worry. I was planning on it."

As I'm checking through every single cupboard and drawer, Spencer and Sam discuss the space including the patio and the living-dining area. They discuss the building in general, including the rooftop garden and the gym. They talk about how to access them and if

Spencer is allowed to invite guests to join him in the gym. Apparently, he and Derek work out together often.

I spend a lot of time checking out the kitchen, so when I'm done, he's already looked at everything else.

"So?" he asks. "Is it your dream kitchen?"

I laugh. "Hardly. You couldn't fit my dream kitchen in a condo in Downtown Vancouver. That's why I work at Blue Vista. That said, I could be happy with this kitchen and so I think you could also be happy with it."

"May I remind you, I don't actually cook," he says.

"Save a mean melted Havarti and prosciutto on brioche? I know. But you need to have a good kitchen if I'm going to come over and cook for you."

"Oh, you wouldn't be moving in as well?" Sam asks.

Spencer's smile slips a bit. "No. Lis and I are just friends. She offered me her opinion. And there's no one whose opinion I'd trust more when it comes to kitchens."

"What did you think about the rest of the place?" I ask, trying to get the conversation away from our relationship status. Or lack thereof.

"It's great. The view is stunning. I kind of wish we were a few floors up and facing the other way, though. I'd prefer a view of the water instead of the mountains. Otherwise, it's got pretty much everything I want."

"But what do you *feel* about it?" I ask. "You want to buy a place that can feel like home. Not just a place that checks off all the boxes."

He considers for a moment. "I think this place could feel like home."

"Well, we should get to work," I say.

Spencer shakes Sam's hand again. Then he does something surprising. "I wondered if you're open to new clients?"

Sam grins and hands him a business card. "Certainly. Call me and we can discuss what it is you're looking for."

He pockets the card and we leave the apartment.

"So, what did you think of it, really?" I ask as soon as we're outside again.

"I don't know." He seems lost in thought as we walk to Blue Vista.

"Feeling a little overwhelmed?"

"Maybe."

"Have you looked at places before?"

"A couple times." He shrugs. "Never had anything stick out enough for me to jump on it."

"So maybe this isn't the place for you then, either. You only just started looking. You liked Sam, though?" I'm watching him as we walk, but he's focused ahead.

"We clicked. I've always been good at telling if a person is going to mesh well with me or not. She's the right realtor for me, I think."

"Do you always make such snap decisions?"

"Yes. I trust my instincts. They've never steered me wrong before."

"Well, then I'm sure you'll know when the right place comes up."

He smiles down at me. "You're right. Thanks."

I smile back and we continue toward work, but as we walk, I think back on what he said. He makes snap decisions. He trusts his instincts. And his instincts were to be with me. It hadn't been my instincts that had led to me putting a halt on things between us. It had been past trauma. So what if I'd been wrong?

Chapter 22

Spencer

I contact Sam and, while the apartment I'd gone to see ended up with an accepted offer quickly, she gets me a list of other condos that meet my criteria. I don't tell her or Lis that I've included the things Lis thought were important.

We go to see a few places, but it's instantly clear how picky I am. I'd thought I didn't have any must-have items on my list, but the more condos I see, the more I decide, I do. Sam starts giving me fewer listings to check out, but every one is *almost* perfect. There's just something off about each.

I keep thinking back to the one I saw with Lis and wishing I'd jumped on it sooner. I'm still thinking about it four weeks later when I should be working. There's a wedding rehearsal tonight that I force myself to focus on, getting chairs set up with white slip covers and pink bows on each. The pergola has matching fancy pink gauze draped over it with strategically placed flowers in the gathers of the material.

After some pretty nasty June-uary weather for the last couple weeks, today has blue skies far off into the distance. I have the tents set in the back of the area in case we need to set them up in a hurry.

Then I check on the progress in the hall where dinner will be served later tonight and tomorrow for the wedding. While I'm heading down, I check the weather app on my phone to make sure no rain is forecast.

"Spencer," someone calls. I turn to see Nessa, the bride for tomorrow's wedding. Thankfully, not a bridezilla.

"Hey. How are you doing?"

She's followed into the hall by her fiancé and two women, one older, probably her mom, and one around her age.

"Excellent. Is everything ready?"

"Just about. Everything for the rehearsal is ready upstairs. We're just finishing up down here for the dinner. Once they're done, you can do the rehearsal dinner at the top three tables."

"You remember Carter," she says, holding her fiancé's arm and looking up at him adoringly.

"Of course." I hold my hand out and we shake. In addition to being a groom at our venue, Carter is also Derek's mechanic. Adalie takes her car to him now, too.

"This is my mom, Deb, and my best friend and maid of honour, Annie. Everyone, this is Spencer, the event coordinator for Blue Vista. Are Vic, Adalie, and Derek around?"

I shake everyone's hands as I'm introduced. Annie holds the handshake just a second too long.

"Not tonight," I tell Nessa. "They'll be here tomorrow for the main event, though. If people are starting to arrive, I'd better get someone stationed downstairs to make sure they all get to the right place. You can find your way to the roof?"

Nessa gives me a nod and starts toward the stairs. Annie lingers.

"Hi," she says.

"Hello."

"Will you be here all night?"

"Yes. Tonight and tomorrow. It's my job to make sure everything runs smooth."

"So we're like co-workers then?" she asks, fluttering her eyelashes at me.

I admit, it's not the first time I've heard that line from a bridesmaid.

"I guess so."

"Well, Spence, if you need me for anything," she says, stepping closer. "Anything at all. Just let me know. I'll be happy to assist."

I grit my teeth at the use of my shortened name. I hate it when people call me Spence, especially when it's used to create a familiarity that doesn't exist. Smiling politely,

I remind myself Annie doesn't know I hate it, and she's a guest.

"I prefer Spencer," I say. "I think we have everything under control. But thank you. If you'll excuse me."

I turn before she can respond, escaping downstairs, hoping the retreat lets her know I'm not interested.

It doesn't.

Two hours later, the rehearsal is wrapping up and the guests are starting toward the hall for dinner. I've staved off Annie's advances as best I can without being outright rude. If we'd met at a bar, I would simply tell her I'm not interested. But I can't be rude to a guest. Especially when the guest is part of the bridal party. At least she hasn't called me Spence again.

When I've had enough, I tell Nessa and Carter I'm going to check on the dinner even though I'm certain Lis doesn't need my help.

I'm right. She doesn't. She's plating the first of the dishes when I enter the kitchen, standing near enough that I can talk to her, but out of the way so I don't mess up her rhythm.

"What are you doing here?" she asks, barely looking up from her work. She's plating all twenty, moving around a large table with Tina as they get everything ready to leave the kitchen at once. Wait staff stand by to take the plates on four trolleys as soon as they're done.

"Hiding," I tell her.

"From your job?"

"From the maid of honour. She keeps hitting on me."

She gives me a startled look and I think I see a flash of jealousy cross her features before she concentrates on her task again.

"Poor baby. Some chick wants to bone. Whatever are you going to do?"

"I keep trying to let her down easy. She's not getting the message."

"Tell her you have a girlfriend," Lis offers as she places the last piece of roast beef on a plate.

"I have. She doesn't seem to care." I'd mentioned it when she tried to grab my ass. I don't tell Lis I'd been thinking of her when I told the lie.

She sets down the tray she'd been carrying and pats my shoulder before picking up a pot of red sauce to drizzle over the meat. "I'm sure you'll be fine."

"Your vote of confidence is overwhelming," I say, deadpan.

She pauses in her plating and fixes me with a look, one eyebrow raised. "You must be having a bad night if you think a *Princess Bride* quote is going to stump me. Even a more obscure one. There is no line from that movie you can recite that I won't guess."

I manage a smile. "Inconceivable."

"You keep using that word. I do not think it means what you think it means."

I huff a laugh and straighten. The plates Lis has put sauce on are now being loaded onto the trolleys. She only has a few left. "I guess I better get back to it. Wish me luck."

"Have fun storming the castle," she says without looking up.

As I climb the stairs with the wait staff that won't fit on the elevator, I wonder if it's weird I'd rather trade quips with Lis than be hit on by an admittedly beautiful woman.

I know weddings bring out the loneliness in some people and they act in ways they wouldn't normally. But Annie's behaviour is more of a turnoff than a turn-on and I try to ignore her while dinner is served. Wait staff top up glasses of wine and people start eating.

After everyone is settled, but before I can make another quick departure, Annie stands and catches my arm, keeping me in place.

"Weddings are so lovely, aren't they?" she asks.

"They are," I respond, gently extricating myself from her touch.

She's saying something else when I catch sight of a rainbow-haired siren coming up the stairs. Instead of paying attention to the guest, I watch Lis' sure steps as she makes her way toward us, eyes fixed on me.

Annie must notice she doesn't have my attention anymore because she's watching Lis approach as well.

"Hey babe," Lis says as she slips an arm around my waist and rises to her toes. I tilt my head down so she can brush my cheek with her lips. The whole interaction is so smooth, it's like we've done it a million times instead of never. My arm settles around her waist, keeping her against me, and every part of me relaxes.

"I just came up to check on things, see if we're still on schedule for dessert."

She didn't have to come up for that. She could have texted me. In fact, she *should* have texted. It would have taken a lot less time. She came up to see this woman who wouldn't leave me alone and had taken it upon herself to help me.

"Running like clockwork. Everyone loves your food. We should be ready for dessert in about twenty minutes. Maybe bring it up in fifteen?"

She checks her watch, noting the time and, even though coming up was a ruse, I know she's going to have the dessert here in exactly fifteen minutes from this moment.

"Sounds good." She reaches her free hand out to Annie. "Hi. I'm Lis, the head chef."

Annie shakes her hand, her gaze darting between us.

"I'm Annie. The maid of honour. So, you and Spencer..." she trails off.

Lis turns to me with a bewitching smile, and I catch myself before I kiss it off her lips. "How long has it been, babe? A year almost? Time sure flies when you're as madly in love as we are."

"It sure does," I respond, slightly bewildered at this amazing firecracker.

"Well, I should head back downstairs to the kitchen. Will you come down in about ten minutes to help get everything onto the elevator?"

She lifts onto her toes again, to give me what I'm certain is supposed to be a quick peck on the lips. But as soon as our lips touch, sparks shoot through me and my arm tightens around her, pulling her closer. She responds in kind, her hand grabbing a fistful of my shirt. The kiss, that was probably meant to last half a second, turns into three seconds, which turns into five. I don't deepen it, but fuck, I want to. Though they've become like the Charlie Brown adults, I know twenty guests surround us, including Annie, who is right fucking there, ruining what would have otherwise been me pressing Lis into a wall and taking her lips in a searing kiss that leads to—

We draw apart, Lis' eyes darkened to green and heavy-lidded. I keep my arm around her to steady her.

"As you wish," I whisper.

I don't know what I'm saying. Am I teasing her? Drawing out the *Princess Bride* joke? Or have I just told her I love her? Because I'm not sure how far from the truth that might be.

WHY NOT BOTH?

Annie clears her throat, and the moment is broken. Lis steps back, and I let her go. I can't stop from staring at her retreating back as she hurries down the stairs and I'm left to deal with Annie on my own again.

Chapter 23

Lis

The rest of the night flies by in a blur. The feeling of that kiss lingers on my lips the whole time. Tina and I get the desserts out and onto the trolley. Spencer arrives as I'd requested—a request that was supposed to just give him a legitimate reason to leave the party and escape Annie. Once we deliver dessert, we clean up and do some prep for the dinner tomorrow. I double and triple check everything, filled with a nervous energy I don't exactly understand.

His whispered words come back to me almost as frequently as that kiss. He'd been teasing me. Of course, he'd been teasing. He couldn't possibly have meant it the way Westley meant it in the movie.

I'm the last one in the kitchen, scrubbing a spot that doesn't need to be cleaned as the kiss and his words play on an endless loop in my brain.

"You know, I'm pretty sure you can't scrub the counter away."

I jump at his voice and turn. Then I chuck the rag into the bin where we keep our soiled laundry.

"You all done for tonight?" I ask.

"Yep. Heading home. It's a nice night. Want to walk together?"

I hesitate. Do I want to be alone with him while those words are still circling my thoughts like sharks? While wearing his hoodie, which I've long since stopped trying to give back to him. He always puts it right back on me, anyway.

It is a lovely night and we've had a week straight of rain, so eventually, I say, "Sure. Just give me a few minutes to get changed."

I retreat to my office and quickly change out of my chef jacket and pants and back into leggings and a t-shirt. I take the clip out of my hair, letting it down and running my fingers through it to ease the tension in my scalp. Then I pull on his sweater and grab my purse.

"Nice hoodie," Spencer says with a smirk when I come out.

I arch an eyebrow at him. "If you won't take it back, I'm going to keep using it. Someone ought to."

He gives me that look. The one that never fails to set butterflies fluttering in my belly. The one that tells me he thinks I'm beautiful. I wonder if he's remembering the kiss upstairs. His whispered words, *As you wish*.

"I'm not Buttercup," I say. "And you're not Westley."

He searches my eyes for a moment, but I start toward the door, leaving him to catch up.

"What do you have against Buttercup and Westley?" he asks when he does.

"Against Westley, nothing."

He locks the door behind us after we exit into the cool June night. We're the last two again.

"He falls in love with Buttercup and basically does everything he can to prove it," I continue. "He goes to seek his fortune, becomes the Dread Pirate Roberts, rescues her from Vizzini, and on and on. But Buttercup? She gives up on him. Again and again."

We cross the street and start along the Seawall toward home.

"In Buttercup's defence, at first she thinks he's dead."

"I'll give her that one. But she just goes along with Prince Humperdink. She could have said no to him. Did she think once they were married, she wouldn't have to put out? Because I assure you, she would."

"Well," Spencer says, drawing out the word. "Not really. He was planning to kill her the whole time."

"She didn't know that."

I steal a glance at him. He's smiling and I know he's laughing at me. I turn forward again.

"Then Westley finds her, and she tells him, point blank, *I will never doubt again.* Then she does! Almost immediately after. If I ever told someone I'd never doubt them again, I'd fucking mean it."

"This has got you really fired up."

"It's just… Westley spends the whole movie doing everything he can to get her back, and she never does anything to help him. I never thought it was fair."

"Think of it this way. Westley knew, from the very beginning of the movie and even before then, he was in love with her. That what they had was real and could last forever. Not everyone has that kind of instinct. Buttercup had to have proof. And she went with Humperdink the second time to protect Westley."

"You don't think Buttercup is an idiot?"

He shakes his head. "I think if she was, Westley wouldn't have fallen in love with her."

The night is chilly, even with his hoodie on, and I shiver.

"Are you cold?" he asks.

"Unless it's scorching hot, I'm probably cold. It's a curse. Ask me next month. I'll be warm then."

He walks a little closer, wrapping an arm around my shoulders. His heat sinks into me. I wrap my arm around his waist because it's the best way to keep my balance while he's walking so close to me. And because he's warm and I'm cold. Not at all because I want to be closer to him. His blond hair is a little messy from running his fingers through it all day. His crystal blue eyes smile down at me. There's a smirk on his full lips.

The kiss flashes through my mind again, and I look away before I do something stupid.

I clear my throat. "So, does it happen often? Getting hit on by bridesmaids?"

He chuckles. "Why? Jealous?"

"What would I have to be jealous of?"

"I don't know, firecracker. What would you have to be jealous of?"

I don't have an answer.

"You'd be surprised how often it happens, actually," Spencer continues, letting me off the hook. "Me *and* Derek. And Derek doesn't even deal with the guests very often."

"I actually wouldn't be surprised. You and Derek are both really hot."

"You think Derek's hot?"

I give him a sweet smile and flutter my eyelashes at him. "Why? Jealous?"

The dark look in his eyes gives me the answer.

I laugh. "Hot or not, Derek isn't my type."

"But I am?"

My laughter dies and my steps hesitate. He stops as well and we just look at each other for a minute. I'm searching his eyes.

"Spencer…" I say, but I don't know how to finish.

WHY NOT BOTH?

He tugs me forward and we keep walking. "What are you doing Monday? Want to do the Grind with me?"

I make a gagging noise and he laughs.

"Come on. You said you'd do it with me. And we haven't been hiking in a while."

"I'm pretty sure the caveat is you go running with me."

"We can go running another day."

I glare up at him. "It sounds like you're trying to get me to climb that fucking mountain with no intention of holding up your end."

"I would never!" he says in a falsetto voice, a hand over his heart.

"Hey. Get your own quotes."

He grins down at me, and I have the startling realization that walking home with him was a bad idea. I'm only torturing myself with what I've decided I can't have. Why can't I have it again?

"I can't on Monday. Daze and I are going to our parents' house. We'll be there most of the day."

"Tuesday then?"

"Why do you want me to do it so much?" I ask.

"Maybe I want to see if you can keep up with me."

"Of course I can't. I run, not climb stairs. And you have longer legs than I do. You're like a foot taller than me."

"I don't think I'm that much taller."

My eyes scan him from the top of his head to his feet and back up. When I reach his face again, he smirks at me.

"Like what you see?"

I roll my eyes and don't respond. We turn onto my road and in no time at all, we're at my door and I have to let him go. It feels like tearing my arm off, but I release him. We stand facing each other, neither making a move to leave.

I heave an aggravated sigh. "Fine. I will come with you to do the Grouse Grind on Tuesday."

He grins. "Excellent."

"I'm going to regret this, aren't I?"

He just keeps grinning. Then he leans forward and places a kiss on my head in a brotherly gesture that does not make me feel sisterly toward him at all.

"Good night, Lis. See you tomorrow."

Inside, I push the button for the elevator. When the doors open, Spencer is still there outside the glass front doors, waiting for me to get on. I wave at him and step in.

As the elevator starts up, I wonder what the fuck I'm doing. I'd created a line I wasn't supposed to cross. But the longer I spend in Spencer's company, the blurrier that line becomes.

WHY NOT BOTH?

It doesn't get easier to see the line the next day, either. Even when I'm busy ensuring everything gets started on schedule, the kiss remains in my mind on an endless loop. I avoid Spencer during the day, and when I notice a problem, I seek out Derek instead.

I find him on the roof, leaning against the railing with his arms crossed, watching as guests get settled for the ceremony.

"Hey," I say. "I didn't think you watched the weddings."

"I don't. But Carter's my mechanic, so I thought I'd hang out for this one. Something wrong?"

"The cake hasn't arrived."

I don't bake if I can at all avoid it, which is fine because Blue Vista partnered with a highly admired baker in the area. Usually they're prompt getting the cake here first thing in the morning.

"Shit." Derek straightens and gets out his phone. "I'll call them. Find out what's going on."

He moves away to place the call and I wait for him to get back. I spend the time checking out the ceremony. Since I'm usually downstairs cooking, this is the first time I've had a chance to see one, and it's honestly breathtaking. The groom is at the front already with the officiant. They're standing under an arch covered with a blush pink gauze, caught in various places and tied with silver ribbons and bunches of white flowers. In the background, the ocean sparkles out to the horizon.

I'm about to turn to see if Derek is finished on the call when music starts and the groom looks down the aisle. Annie comes down first in a pink dress with a silver belt. She smiles at the guests, walking sedately to the altar. When she gets there, the music changes and "A Thousand Years" by Christina Perri begins. The bride starts down the aisle.

She's wearing a gorgeous lace dress, fitted to her curves with a long train embroidered with silver filigree. I notice her groom watching her with tears in his eyes. When I refocus on the bride, Spencer stands behind her. He must have come up with the bride because I hadn't seen him on the roof.

I forget all about the ceremony as our eyes lock. Distantly, I hear the officiant begin, but I don't know what he's saying. I feel the phantom memory of Spencer's kiss, hear his whispered words. I can't look away. Then the groom begins to speak.

"A long time ago, I was coming home from a graveyard shift, and my life changed. A woman tripped over a rug and fell into my arms. At that moment, my heart woke up and said, 'It's you. It's going to be you.' If I had to wait ten years or a thousand, it was always going to be you."

Tears fill my eyes and I can't exactly explain why. The groom's speech is sweet, but the way Spencer is looking at me, like he agrees with every word, makes my heart expand in my chest. I want to take a step toward him, but my feet are frozen. The bride speaks next.

"I told myself I couldn't fall in love with you," she says. "It wasn't in my plan. But from the moment we met, whether I intended to or not, I started to fall in love with you, anyway. Leaving you was the hardest thing I've ever had to do. You will never know how grateful I am that you loved me enough to wait until I was ready."

I blink to prevent the tears from falling as my heart cracks. Spencer takes one step forward.

Then Derek touches my elbow. I turn to him, swallowing past the lump in my throat.

"The cake is on its way," he says, his voice pitched low so as not to interrupt the ceremony. "Ironically, they had car trouble. It should be here in about fifteen."

I nod. When I turn back to Spencer, someone has pulled him aside, so I return downstairs to the kitchen. Since Tina has everything under control, I go into my office for a second to gather my thoughts.

There had been a reason I'd decided we couldn't be together. The logical part of my brain tells me I don't want to mix my career and personal life. I've been down that road, seen other women go down that road and had it blow up in their faces, just like it had mine. This job is important to me and I can't forget that.

I pull myself together and return to work, focusing on what I need to do, even though my emotions are a jumbled mess. I'm finished long before Spencer and so I take transit home. We don't see each other much on Sunday for a retirement party and, again, I take transit home. I don't know if Spencer suspects I'm avoiding him, but I need a little distance to figure out exactly what it is I want.

On Monday, when I wake up with an ache in my chest, I realize it's because I won't see him at all today. It's ridiculous since I specifically avoided him yesterday and the day before, and I'm going for a hike with him tomorrow. I feel it anyway.

I shake it off, telling myself I'm stupid and I need to get over this. He's just a man. An insanely attractive man who is also kind and funny and smart and overall, pretty much perfect, but just a man. And even better, we're friends.

Right. Better.

Daze drives us out to Maple Ridge and we arrive at our parents' house in the afternoon.

"Mom, Dad," I call. "We're here." Cerberus runs ahead of me and by the time I catch up, he's chowing down on a cookie Dad has given him.

Cerberus thunks his tail against the ground as he swallows the last of his cookie and waits expectantly for a second.

"No more," I say. "You can spoil him more later."

WHY NOT BOTH?

We sit in the chairs around the outside table and Mom and Daze start talking about wedding plans. Daze has a few places she's thinking about. Unfortunately, after talking with Vic and Spencer a few weeks ago, she and Sophie had decided they couldn't afford a wedding at Blue Vista. It's also already fully booked for next summer, so even if they'd wanted to, they would have to wait until the year after. They're trying to find something that will work for about a year from now.

Then Mom turns to me. "And how is Spencer?"

"Yes, Lis. How *is* Spencer?" Daze says, taking a sip of her sparkling water.

"He's fine." I roll my eyes. "You guys. We're just friends."

"Right," Daze says, turning toward Mom. "They went on a date, you know."

I want to strangle her.

"That was before I started at Blue Vista. It was one date and we're just friends. I don't date people I work with. Not anymore."

Mom's and Daze's smiles slip. They remember how devastated I was when I'd been fired and subsequently dumped.

"Oh, honey." Mom pats my hand.

"Is there a policy against dating at Blue Vista?" Dad asks.

I sigh. "No. But I didn't think there was one before either. It's just… It's better this way."

"Sure it is," Daze says, unbelieving. I admit, I'm not sure how much I believe the statement anymore, either. "You're just crazy about each other. But it's better this way. Did you know he walks her home almost every night?"

I give her a look that I hope she knows means I want to strangle her.

"He's just being nice. It's not like it's really far. His place is only fifteen minutes from ours."

"Which he has to pass, then backtrack to. And he's somehow convinced her to hike the Grouse Grind tomorrow."

Forget strangulation. I'm going to stab her. Especially when Mom looks at me with delight.

"I recall you saying you'd never do that hike again."

"It's awful," I say. "My legs were killing me for a week last time."

"That's an exaggeration," Daze says.

"It's what I remember," I say haughtily, even though I'm certain she's right. I think I was only sore for a day. I should have thought of that before I agreed to do it with Spencer when I have to work the next day. "Can we change the subject, please?"

Mom takes pity on me and tells us about her pottery class she started a few weeks ago. Then she gets up to check on dinner, which she started before I'd arrived to ensure I didn't take over, and I follow her while Daze and Dad talk about work.

"How are you really doing, honey?" Mom asks when we're alone. She hands me a bag of carrots so I take out a few and begin peeling them.

"I'm fine."

She just looks at me.

"What?"

"Your sister is getting married."

"I know that. She told me before anyone else."

"Mhm. She's your best friend in the whole world. I know how happy you are for her, but I also want to know how you're doing."

Of course my mother would know everything wasn't all sunshine and roses.

"I guess I'm a little worried things are going to change. I've known this was coming, even if I wasn't sure when. And maybe I'm a little bit jealous that she gets to have the dream now and I don't. I mean, I've been on a couple dozen dates in the last year and all of them have been awful. I finally find a guy worth considering—more than worth it, if I'm being honest—and he's my boss' best friend. It would just be so messy and complicated. I don't know that it's worth it."

"All the best things in life are difficult, Lissy. And they're all worth it. If there's no policy against it, maybe you should give it a chance. There are other jobs."

I grab a knife and start slicing the carrots into circles, all exactly a quarter inch thick.

"There are other jobs, but this one is exactly what I've wanted. I'm in charge. If I stay here for a while, prove my worth, Vic will let me have creative control over the menu. It's what I've been working for."

"Why can't you have both? Why not the dream job *and* the dream boyfriend?"

I scoff as I scoop the chopped carrots into a bowl. "It's never worked out that way before. What's going to make it work out that way now?"

I season the vegetables, add some oil, and toss them before spreading them on a pan and sliding them into the oven.

"Because this job and this man are different from before. Maybe they're the right ones."

We stare at each other for a long moment before Mom says, "Either way, I want you to invite him to dinner next time you come out."

"Why?"

"Because he's your friend, and he needs a family dinner every once in a while. And because he doesn't have a mother to give it to him."

I look at her for a moment before nodding.

WHY NOT BOTH?

When dinner is ready, we sit down to eat and Daze says, "You're actually going to sit with us and not putter around in the kitchen for half an hour before eating?"

"When Spencer was here, he forced her to eat," Dad says.

I groan.

"What? What did he do?" Daze asks, her gaze darting around the table at each of us.

"Please don't."

Mom chuckles. "He lifted her over his shoulder and sat her in the chair. Then he threatened to let the food go cold and microwave it."

"He didn't!"

Everyone laughs at my expense.

"Why are we back to bugging me? Bug Daze for a while."

"There's nothing to bug her about yet," Dad says. "She's getting married. Once she's married, we'll start bugging her about grandchildren. Don't you worry. In the meantime, we're going to bug you about being single."

"Well, I'm not looking anymore," I say. "Apparently, my standards are too high. Because I can't find anyone worth dating." Except Spencer.

"What are your standards?" Dad asks. "We can help you figure out if they're too high."

I roll my eyes but list the things I've decided are essential. "He has to make me laugh. He has to be kind and like my dog and get along with Daze and Sophie and you guys. Someone who likes a lot of the same things as me. Someone who can keep me warm. Someone I can steal hoodies from and play games with, who's tall and—" I stop myself from saying the rest because I know I'm just describing Spencer.

The way my family looks at me, they know it, too.

"Anyway. I'm done for now. I'm just going to focus on work and getting through wedding season and eventually I'll get back out there."

After dinner, I load Cerberus into the car with his farewell treat from Mom. The fifth one he's received today. Daze drives us home. We're about halfway there when my phone buzzes with a text from Spencer making my breath catch in my throat. I want to open it and read it immediately. But I also consider that we're supposed to just be friends, and this is not the kind of reaction one has when a friend texts them.

I read it anyway.

Spencer:

You ready for tomorrow?

WHY NOT BOTH?

Me:

> Ugh. Yes.
>
> I was recently reminded that the last time I did the Grouse Grind, my legs were sore for a week. I swore I'd never do it again.

Spencer:

> You'll be fine.

Me:

> I'm sure I will. But I may need a massage after.

Spencer:

> I'm certain that can be arranged.

Chapter 24

Spencer

It would be weird if I called. Friends don't call each other in the middle of the night. Especially friends who have plans to see each other the next day. I check the time. It's too late to call, anyway.

I pace my room. Her text about needing a massage after the hike has been causing fantasies to plague me all night. I haven't seen her today, and it feels like there's a part of me missing. I want to call her. I want to hear her voice. Ask about her day.

I send a text.

> Me:
> **Are you awake?**

The reply comes almost immediately.

> Firecracker:
> **Yes**

> Me:
> **Do you want to chat?**

WHY NOT BOTH?

The dots appear and disappear five times before the response comes through.

Firecracker:

> Sure

I take a deep breath, tapping the button to call her instead of text.

"Hi," she says after half a ring.

"Hi," I say. Shit. What do I say next? Why did I want to call? There should have been a reason.

"How was your day?" she asks.

Right. Conversation. I also wanted to ask about her day.

"It was good. I did pretty much nothing, so that was nice. Adalie and Vic were busy, so I was the only one at Derek's. We played some video games and watched a movie."

"What did you watch?"

Her voice is soft, like she's trying not to be too loud. I wonder if she doesn't want anyone to know we're talking. Or maybe she just doesn't want to wake people. It's late. I should have just gone to bed. I'm going to see her tomorrow.

"*Alien*," I tell her.

"I was going to suggest we watch *Evil Dead* tomorrow after the hike. It's been a while since I saw it."

"We can do that."

"You made quite an impression on my parents, you know."

I can hear the smile in her voice as I sit on the edge of my bed, finally relaxing enough that I think I can sleep tonight.

"Oh yeah? How so?" I ask her as I strip out of my clothes and pull back the covers.

"They regaled Daze with the story of how you forced me to eat dinner."

"Mm. Sorry, not sorry."

"Mom wants me to invite you to dinner next time I go out there. She said you need a family dinner once in a while."

"Is that something you want?" I ask quietly.

She takes a while to answer, finally whispering, "Yes." Then, louder, she says, "Spencer—"

I'm not ready to hear the end of what she's about to say, so I interrupt. "Your mom is amazing, Lis."

She hesitates before accepting my change of topic. "She is. She'd be better if she didn't spoil Cerberus so much. He's in a food coma now."

I chuckle. "Just wait until you have kids."

"Oh, not you, too. They go on and on about how much they want grandbabies." Her words and her tone are at odds. She seems to love the good-natured teasing. Probably because she knows how much her parents love her.

She yawns. "Sorry. It's been a long day."

"You're right. It's late. I shouldn't have called."

"No. It's fine. I said you could."

Had she wanted to hear my voice as much as I wanted to hear hers? What are we doing? Why aren't we together?

"You need to sleep if you're going to keep up with me on the mountain tomorrow."

She groans. "Don't remind me. I'm trying to pretend it's not going to happen. You are going to owe me so hard for this."

"You have a few favours saved up. What would you like me to do?"

Some of the things I'm thinking are certainly not things friends would do for each other. Like a full-body massage. Her soft skin beneath my hands. Fuck. Now I'm hard.

"I'm sure I'll think of something." She yawns again.

"Go to sleep, firecracker. I'll see you in the morning. You'll pick me up at about nine?"

"Yeah. I'll see you tomorrow."

We say goodbye and hang up. I'm left more relaxed and more tense, my dick telling me he's annoyed with me.

He's still annoyed with me in the morning, after dreams of rainbow hair spread on my pillow, soft skin beneath my hands. I take a shower that makes us both feel a little better, then get dressed and pack a couple things into my backpack. In the living room, Vic is sitting on the couch with Emily.

"Good morning, ladies," I say as I go over and kiss the top of Vic's head. "Emily. So lovely to see you."

"You're lying again, Spencer," Emily says.

"Nope. I am happy enough right now, not even you can ruin it. Vic could tell me you're moving in, and even that couldn't spoil my mood today."

Vic smiles up at me. "Going to see Lis?"

"I convinced her to hike the Grouse Grind with me." My phone buzzes. It's exactly nine o'clock. "In fact, that's probably her now."

"Have fun."

I hurry downstairs and we drive out to Grouse Mountain. What's usually a two-hour bus ride is only a thirty-minute drive, and we're there in no time. The weather has turned again, foreboding clouds rolling in overhead. Though it hasn't started raining yet. I pay for parking—since the hike was my idea—and we walk to the trailhead, stopping by the signs at the fence.

"No downhill travel for safety reasons," Lis reads. "So once we start, there's no turning back."

"Adventures beware: Do not begin unless you intend to finish."

Lis turns to me, an eyebrow raised. "There better not be any *Jumanji*-esqe adventures on this trail. Climbing a mountain is bad enough." She warms up with some high knees. "I just want to start this by saying I hate you. And if it starts to rain on us, I might have to kill you."

I grin. "It'll all be worth it in the end. Just think of the view at the top."

She scowls. "If I'm in it for the view, I could just take the gondola up."

Now I'm laughing. "Where's the fun in that? Come on. I'll race you."

"Absolutely not. No racing. Let's just get this over with."

I scan my timer card—only people who regularly climb the Grouse Grind get them—and we start. The beginning of the hike isn't too bad. The trail is wide enough for us to walk side-by-side and not too steep so we can talk while we walk. We discuss favourite movies and Lis staunchly refuses to choose one.

"There are so many. How can I just pick one? Maybe one night I'm feeling more like a romance and the next I'm feeling like a fantasy. Or an action movie. You can't make me choose."

"Okay, how about this? Top five right now, off the top of your head. They don't have to be your favourites. Just the first ones you can think of."

She looks up at me through her eyelashes. "Fine. *The Mummy, Princess Bride, The Fifth Element, Penelope,* and *Stardust.*"

"I don't think I've seen the last two."

"Oh my god, you have to. They're both excellent movies."

"They must be if they're on your list. Do you want to watch one today?"

"Nah. Next time. We'll watch *Evil Dead* tonight. So what's your list?"

I love the casual way she says we'll watch more movies together. We've been pushing the line of "friends" a little further each day. The memory of the kiss at the rehearsal floats through my mind, followed by the supercharged moment at Nessa and Carter's wedding. The moments give me hope that she's going to change her mind about us. I shake the thoughts off and I answer her question.

"Well, *Evil Dead*, of course. Though if I can only choose one, it would probably be the last one."

"*Army of Darkness*."

"Yes. Then probably, *Alien*, *Princess Bride*, *Star Wars*—but if I have to choose one, *Empire Strikes Back*—and *Commando*."

"What's *Commando*?"

"Are you kidding me? Arnold Schwarzenegger as John Matrix trying to rescue his daughter. Classic."

She gives me a bemused smile and shakes her head. "Never seen it."

"You have to. We'll start a list." I get out my phone and find the notes app, typing in the three movies.

"Spencer," Lis says, bringing my attention back to her. "What does that sign say?"

I look at where she's pointing. "It says one quarter."

"Are you telling me we're only a quarter of the fucking way?"

"Yep."

She stops walking, shifting off the path in case anyone comes up behind us, then fixes me with a glare. "You seem a decent fellow. I hate to kill you."

I know what the next line should be. Everyone who loves *The Princess Bride* knows what the next line should be. But there's a better one. "We are men of action. Lies do not become us."

She laughs. "You're right. I'm going to enjoy killing you for this. I'm very good with knives, you know, and get kind of stabby when I'm angry."

Unable to stop myself, I wrap my arms around her, pressing a kiss to her temple, which is sweaty beneath my lips. I don't care at all.

"Come on, firecracker. You can make it. Besides. That marker is actually the elevation. Not the distance. We're further than a quarter of the way distance-wise."

We continue walking, my arm around her, urging her forward.

"I still hate you and I'm still going to kill you."

I have to let her go. We can't walk like that on this trail. As much as I wish we could.

"How long does it usually take you to get to the top?" she asks.

"Usually an hour and a half. I pushed once to see what I could do and managed it in an hour, but I don't like going that fast."

"I feel like I'm going to take longer than an hour and a half."

"We'll go your pace. There's no rush. Besides, when the trail gets narrow, you can walk in front. I will happily follow you up the mountain."

She lifts an eyebrow at me. "Are you implying you're going to stare at my ass?"

"Yes." I give her an unrepentant smile.

"Well, then I think it's only fair we take turns," she responds primly.

"You want a chance to stare at my ass, then?"

"And your shoulders. You have nice shoulders."

We stop for water. Lis does a few stretches. We continue. The trail gets harder and we don't talk as much, climbing stair after stair, some built, some formed from the mountain itself. When we reach the three quarter sign, Lis stops, bending over with her hands on her knees.

"Fuck. This is awful. You do this for fun?"

"Yes," I say, grinning. "You're doing great. And the worst is behind us now."

"I think the whole thing is the worst. I think you're the worst for making me do this. I am never doing this again."

"Yes, you will. You're going to get to the top and the endorphins are going to flood in and you're going to beg me to take you next time I come up here."

She snorts. "Sure. And you can hike up the mountain and I'll take the gondola. I'll have a nice leisurely breakfast and you can reach the top all sweaty."

We keep going, climbing the final quarter faster than the last while. When we reach the top, we find the timer station and I hand Lis my card.

"Want to do the honours?"

She grabs it and swipes it, letting out a huge breath.

"Come on," I say, grabbing her hand and tugging her with me. "Let's get a selfie."

"You're insane if you think I want my picture taken looking like this."

"It's just for me. Here." I pull her to a stop with the view of North Vancouver in the distance.

She pats her hair, trying to smooth it down. It only marginally works. Then she scowls at me as I take a picture. I love it.

"No social media," she says. "I don't want people thinking I like hiking."

I laugh. "No social media. Just my own reference. You want something to eat?"

"Hold it," she says. "After that whole hike, I'm at least going to enjoy this view. Wasn't that the point?"

We turn and she props her arms on the railing, leaning on them as she gazes into the distance. I've seen it a million times, and I'd rather watch her, but eventually, I turn as well. There's North Van stretching right to the edge of the water of the Georgia Strait. Some tanker ships float near a harbour. In the far distance, mountains jut against a sky filled with grey clouds. Thankfully, those clouds have held off raining, though I'm certain it's going to start sometime today.

Lis points. "Is that Vancouver Island or one of the other islands?"

"I think it's Vancouver Island. The Gulf Islands would be too small."

"Okay. I could come up here for another look at this view." She turns to me with a glare. "Without the hike. I'll take the gondola up next time, and *you* can hike by yourself."

I laugh and guide her away from the railing, my hand hovering over the small of her back. "Come on, firecracker. Let's get something to eat."

I buy her lunch from the cafe and we sit.

"So, do you still hate me and want to kill me?" I ask.

She chews on a fry, contemplating, her chin propped on one hand. "Maybe a little less than I did before. Now that it's over, my hatred is waning. Not because I'm

WHY NOT BOTH?

thinking it was fun. Just. The immediacy of wanting to shove you off the side of the mountain has passed. No promises for if you make me do this again."

"Obviously."

"So what are our plans for the rest of the day?" she asks.

I can't contain the smile when she says *our plans*.

"I figure you need to get back to your place for Cerberus. I brought *Evil Dead* if you still want to watch it. Or something else. Whatever you want."

"Sure. I don't need to hurry back to him. Sophie's at home, so she's probably already taken him out. But we can go to my place and watch it there. Should I get the gondola tickets down since you paid for lunch?"

"I figured I'd pay for everything since I dragged you here."

She arches an eyebrow at me. I'm beginning to love that I-have-a-feeling-you're-up-to-something-but-I'm-not-going-to-do-anything-to-stop-you look. "Does that mean when I take you running, I get to buy you lunch?"

"Fuck yes. I am not running anywhere unless I get a reward at the end."

Her eyes sparkle, more blue than green right now. "You remind me of Cerberus. He's also very food motivated."

"I've been compared to worse things. At least you think he's cute."

"I do."

I want to ask if she's talking about me or the dog, recalling her comment about watching my ass and shoulders climbing up the mountain. I just smile at her.

Then I pay for our tickets and we ride the gondola back to the parking lot.

Chapter 25

Lis

"So this is it," I say, unlocking the front door. As soon as he hears the door open, Cerberus gets up from his bed, his tail wagging. I kick off my shoes. "Sophie, we're here," I call. I walk past the closet and give Spencer the stand-in-place tour. It's a nice apartment, though a little small. I point to the two doors on the left. "First one is the bathroom. Second is Daze and Sophie's bedroom. This is the living room and kitchen. On the right is my bedroom and there's another bathroom in there."

I turn to see he's now scratching Cerberus behind the ears. He straightens when Sophie emerges from her bedroom.

"Hey," she says. "He was just out. I'll be in here until four."

"Hungry?" I ask. "I'm going to make popcorn."

"No, thanks. I just had lunch."

"We'll keep it down."

"No worries. I've got my headphones." She gives us a smile and goes back into her room to keep working.

"I'm going to change," I say. "Your hoodie is there if you want to change out of your shirt." I point to the coat hooks where I've hung it in case he wants to take it with him. I'm almost certain he won't.

"Are you trying to tell me I'm smelly?"

I arch an eyebrow at him. "Yes. I am."

He laughs and takes his backpack off. "I brought an extra t-shirt and pants. Partly because I wasn't sure what the weather was going to do today." Then he takes off his shirt.

The man should be arrested for pulling a stunt like that. How am I supposed to do anything with his abs just sitting there? My eyes trail up his chest, and over the shoulder where the orange and red bird looks like it's about to take flight. He wears mostly long-sleeved button-up shirts at work, so I haven't seen much of it since that night two months ago. I move closer as though in a trance, my fingers reaching up to trace the bright tattoo.

"It's beautiful. I guess I didn't really pay attention before…" I trail off and my eyes flick up to his. I hadn't meant to reference our night together, but there it is. He's watching me now, his eyes filled with heat. "A phoenix?" I ask unnecessarily.

He nods.

The head rests on his shoulder, one wing over his heart and the other on his back. Almost like it's giving him a hug. The tail feathers trail down his arm toward his elbow. My hand stays on his arm, his skin hot beneath mine, and I want to slide my hand up to hook around his neck.

"How long ago did you get it done?"

He takes a shaky breath, making me want to step a bit closer. "I was twenty. My father hates tattoos. He says they're not professional. So when I cut contact with him, I got a nice big, bright one. Though, he must have still been in my head a bit because I can easily cover it with a shirt." He shrugs.

"You have another one," I say. "On your back."

His face loses the usual easy smile he wears, and he blinks, his gaze falling from mine. I've shattered the moment somehow and I'm not sure what I've said.

He turns, and on his back is a quote and a small symbol. I skim my fingers over the words as I read them. "'We may meet again in another life, but not again in this one.' That's from *The Dark Crystal*." I remember him quoting it when we watched the movie, the sadness in his voice as he said the words.

He turns back around and slips the t-shirt over his head. "Yes."

He doesn't offer any more and the look in his eyes makes me want to wrap my arms around him. I want to ask him what's hurting him so much so I can know how to take the hurt away. But I can also see he doesn't want to talk about it right now, so I move on.

"I only have the one. Got it a couple years ago with Daze. I've been thinking about a second, but I'm not sure what I want to get." I give him a small smile, trying to bring his back. He finds one for me, but it's strained. "I'm going to get changed. Make yourself comfortable. Get the DVD into the player." I motion to the living room.

Hurrying into my room, I strip off my clothes, quickly changing into clean ones. In the bathroom, I note that my hair is a god-awful mess. I leave it for a minute and just wash my face. Then I grab my hairbrush and return to the living room. Spencer is sitting on the couch, rummaging through his backpack.

"How long has my hair been like this?" I ask.

He looks up at me, confused. "Since about the halfway point?"

"And you just let me walk around with my hair all over the place? Took a picture of me like this? I look like I stuck my finger in a light socket."

A smile is forming, the sorrow fading from his eyes. "I think you look cute."

"Ugh. Men." I remove the clip from my hair, letting it fall, shaking my head so it untwists. I notice his focused attention as it releases.

"Are you wearing pyjamas?" he asks.

"Yes. Do you have a problem with that?"

He presses his lips together. "Nope. No problem at all."

"Come on. Let's make some popcorn." I pull the brush through my hair as I go into the kitchen and twist it up, clipping it back in place. Then I gather what I'll need.

Spencer follows me, watching as I get out two pots, some measuring cups, and all the ingredients.

"What are you doing?" he asks.

"Popcorn and hot chocolate," I say, sending him a look. "The right way."

He folds his arms over his chest and my gaze lingers as his t-shirt stretches tight over his shoulders. Then I move back to my tasks. I start the hot chocolate first, since it'll take longer. I feel Spencer watching me as I whisk the milk, cocoa powder, and sugar together, adding chocolate chips a little at a time. Once all the chocolate is in, I add a splash of vanilla.

"What's that?" Spencer asks.

"The vanilla?"

"But it's brown."

I turn to him, pausing in my whisking. "Of course it's brown. What colour did you expect it to be?"

"White. Vanilla is white."

"No. Vanilla *cake* is white. Vanilla *ice cream* is white. *Vanilla* is brown." I return to the hot chocolate and remove it from the heat. Then I start the popcorn. "Actually, vanilla beans are almost black."

"Vanilla comes from a bean?" he asks.

I turn again. "Are you serious right now?"

"Yes. I don't really know anything about cooking. Aside from my melted Havarti and prosciutto on brioche."

I suppress my laughter. "Are you sure you're a functioning adult?"

"Only mostly."

I get the popcorn started and go to the cupboard, putting everything away and selecting the slim container with three vanilla beans inside. I hand it to him before finding the mugs and a bowl.

"This is not what I expected vanilla to look like," he says, turning it around in his hands. "You use these for something?"

"Those are specifically for a cheesecake I plan to make. You can use them in other things, though." I pour hot chocolate into the mugs and shake the pot with the popcorn, listening carefully as the kernels pop.

"Who is this cheesecake for and am I invited to eat it?"

I give the pot another shake and take the beans back, replacing them in the cupboard. "Sophie's birthday is next month. They were on sale. Vanilla beans are expensive."

"And am I invited to eat it?" he repeats.

"I can maybe try to save you a piece. No promises."

"What if I cashed in a favour?"

WHY NOT BOTH?

The popping slows down, so I give the pot a final shake, then grab the bowl. "You're going to use up all your favours if you keep running through them."

"What's the point of saving them?"

I pour the popcorn into a bowl and hand it to him, followed by his mug of hot chocolate. He takes them to the couch while I quickly clean the pots and set them in the drying rack. Then I take my mug to the living room as well.

"Shit!" Spencer says. "This is delicious."

I watch as he takes another sip of the hot chocolate, his eyes closing as the sweet drink touches his lips.

I bite the inside of my mouth to keep the smile contained. It's insane how happy it makes me that he likes something I made.

"I told you so," I say, sipping my drink before sitting on the other side of the couch.

"Legs up," he says, pointing to the space between us.

"Excuse me?"

"You said you needed a massage after the hike."

I roll my eyes. "There's a hot bath and some yoga in my future. I'll be fine."

"I'm offering."

The idea of his hands on me, rubbing my legs, sends tingles to my core. I'm left in a fifty/fifty split on whether I should let him or not.

"It's fine," I say, eventually.

"Okay," he says. "You're sitting too far away, then. How are you supposed to keep me warm from way over there?"

I arch an eyebrow at him. "You want me—the icicle—to keep you—the human heater—warm?"

"Yes. Get over here."

Alarm bells go off in my head. Flashing neon lights scream, *Warning! Warning!* This is not how friends act. This is flirting 101.

But since the kiss a few nights ago, that line has become more and more blurry. Plus, I am cold, as usual, and it'll be easier to share the popcorn if we're closer. I move until my body is pressed along his—fully aware I'm just coming up with any justifications I can to do what I want—then I pull the blanket off the back of the couch. We spread it over our laps, and I trade my mug for the remote. Before I can start the movie, Spencer grabs my hand. He's silent for a moment and I notice the sorrow has returned to his eyes.

"About before," he says. "The tattoo."

"You don't need to explain anything, Spencer."

His eyes meet mine. "I want to." Then he looks away, seemingly lost in memories. "It was the last thing my mom said to me. It happened really fast. One day, everything was fine, then she was sick, then she was gone."

Without thinking, I interlace our fingers. He looks down at them as though confused how it happened.

"I was at the hospital, and we knew it was the end. She said she'd rather I wasn't there when it happened, so I gave her a hug and a kiss and I told her I loved her and she said she loved me, too. Then she said, 'We may meet again in another life, but not again in this one.' Then my dad's assistant took me home."

A hole opens up in my heart and a tear slides down my cheek. I don't bother to brush it away. Then I blink.

"Wait. Your dad's assistant?"

He nods, still staring at our entwined hands.

"Where was your dad?"

He snorts. "Where he always is." He shakes his head, finally looking at me again. "Sorry. I didn't mean to get all dark and gloomy." He wipes the tear from my face with his thumb. "I don't really think about that tattoo very often. I never see it. So when you brought it up…"

"I didn't mean to—"

"You couldn't have known. I just needed you to know I wasn't mad or anything."

That sadness is back in his eyes. I climb onto my knees on the couch so our eyes are level. I want to say the exact right thing, but what can I say? Nothing can erase a hurt like that. So I just wrap my arms around him, pulling him into me. His arms come around my waist and he buries his face in the crook of my neck. He takes a shuddering breath.

When he sits back, the sadness is still there, but less. "We should get started." He tilts his head toward the TV.

I settle next to him, my legs tucked under me, my knees resting on his thigh. He keeps an arm around me. My thoughts are spinning, telling me this is not the way friends sit. I tell myself I stay because he's sad and I want to offer comfort. But I know the truth: I don't want to move. I want to sit in his arms where I feel safe and warm.

Just before I press play on the movie, he reaches up and steals the clip from my hair, letting it fall. He runs his fingers through it and my breath catches.

"There," he says. "Isn't that more comfortable?"

I swallow past the lump in my throat, lost in his eyes as I nod. He sets the clip down and turns back to the TV like he hasn't just made me want to jump on him and tear his clothes off with a simple touch.

We drink our hot chocolate, eat our popcorn, and watch the movie. It tries to be scary but ends up being funny. When the first person is possessed, I cringe and turn my face into his chest as she stabs someone in the ankle with a pencil. "Have I mentioned I'm not usually a fan of horror movies?" I say.

Spencer laughs, his arm tightening around my waist. "Then why did you suggest we watch this?"

I peek up at him. "I make an exception for *Evil Dead*. There's only a few parts I don't like. And I've been wearing a hoodie lately that advertises it."

I don't mean to be snuggled right into his chest, but by the time the hands pop out of the chests of the possessed people at the end of the movie, that's where I am. When I jump, I end up moving even closer, helped in small part by the arm he keeps around me. He's watching me as the movie ends—his clear, blue eyes bright with laughter, his lips tilted up in a mischievous smile.

"Wanna watch the next one?"

"Not today."

His head shifts closer to mine and my eyes drop to his mouth. I don't need to move much and I'll be able to take another kiss. The kiss at the rehearsal dinner was so brief and has been on my mind so often in the last few days. The friendship line would be destroyed. But it's blurred so much, I'm not entirely sure I remember where it is, or why I put it there in the first place.

Then the spell is broken as the front door opens and Daze comes in. I move away from him and feel cold.

"Hey, Daze," I call. "How was work?"

She comes down the hall. "It was fine. What were you watching?"

"We just finished *Evil Dead*," I say.

She shudders. "No, thank you. I'm going for a shower. Are you making dinner?"

"Just about to put it in the oven."

"You're a peach."

She goes into her room, closing the door behind her. I have a feeling she's not going to be heading into that shower immediately.

"Do you want to stay for dinner?" I ask as I go into the kitchen and turn on the oven.

In the half second before his answer, a war wages in my brain. I want him to say yes so I can spend more time with him. But I also want him to say no, so I don't have to constantly remind myself why we're supposed to be just friends.

"I would, but I have plans with Derek. Another time?"

"Sure. Do you have to leave now?"

"Pretty quick. Unless you need help with something?"

"No." I grab a casserole from the fridge that I'd made previously. "It just needs to heat for about an hour."

He gets himself ready to leave, and I follow him to the door.

"Admit it," he says. "You had fun today."

"I will never admit that. You can't make me. But I hope you know next time, we're running the Seawall in Stanley Park."

"The whole thing?"

"You made me hike up a fucking mountain. I'm making you run around Stanley Park."

"How long is that?"

"Only about ten kilometers."

"Ten?" he says weakly.

WHY NOT BOTH?

"Just be grateful I'm not making you do the whole Seawall."

"Don't even joke about that." He gathers me against him in a hug, pressing a kiss to my hair. "I'll see you tomorrow, firecracker."

Then he's gone. I stand at the door for a lot longer than I should, replaying the feeling of his arms wrapped around me, his lips on my head, too far away from my own lips. The oven beeps telling me it's ready for the casserole. I turn and grab the hoodie he's left behind again, holding it for a moment before I pull it on.

Chapter 26

Spencer

In the middle of July, I'm working on my outline for the following day's wedding. Our corporate client lunch is wrapping up and I've already sent the clean-up crews to get started.

Something has changed in the last few weeks since the Grouse Grind hike. Lis and I flirt more, sharing more quick touches and hugs. Though she still hasn't let us cross the line she put between us, we've certainly made our way closer to it.

I went running with her around Stanley Park a few days ago, complaining way more than she did during the Grouse Grind. She laughed at me the whole time, barely breaking a sweat on the hour-long run. She took me out for tacos after, then we watched *Stardust* at her place since the run had been too long for Cerberus and his tiny legs. It was really easy to convince her to sit next to me, my arms wrapped around her.

WHY NOT BOTH?

I'm trying to think of something else we can do together, how I can keep this momentum going, when Derek walks into my office.

"Okay. I've had enough," he says, settling into one of my guest chairs.

"Enough of what?"

"You. Spencer, my friend, the best way to get over someone is to get under someone else."

I roll my eyes and turn back to my computer. "You're such a whore. Who are you even talking about?"

"I'm talking about Lis. I hate seeing you so moony-eyed over some chick who won't date you."

I turn back to Derek, surprised at the sudden anger welling up in me.

"Stay out of it, Derek," I warn, and he must get the message that he's overstepped, because he holds up his hands.

"I'm just trying to look out for you, man. You're practically dating her, except you have no exclusivity and you're not sleeping with her. She could start dating someone else at any time."

"It's my choice. If I want to wait around until she's ready, that's what I'm going to do."

"I just don't want to see you getting hurt." He holds my gaze for a moment before dropping it to the side. "I remember what it was like. I'm worried you're going to get your heart broken."

Derek has never told me about the woman who broke his heart. Every once in a while, statements like that one slip out. The four of us are usually nosing into each other's business, but when it comes right down to it, we never make each other talk if the person doesn't want to. And Derek has never wanted to.

I sigh and lean back in my chair. "It's my heart to break."

He considers me and finally nods. "Fine. We're still going out tonight."

I turn back to my computer. This part of the conversation doesn't need my undivided attention. "I work tomorrow."

"We have an early night tonight and a late start tomorrow. The wedding is reception-only, so we don't have to be here until three to set up. And the next two weeks are going to be a gong show. We're going out."

He has a point. We're booked solid for the next two weeks. It's going to be all hands on deck pretty much all day every day as we get through these events.

"Fine," I say, returning my attention to him. "Two conditions: We're not out past midnight and we invite the others."

"You're going to invite Lis, aren't you?"

"She's part of the others now, isn't she? If I wasn't interested in her, would you invite her?"

"Of course I would. She's our head chef."

"Then invite her. Or I will."

He chuckles as he leaves my office.

Later that night, I meet Derek and Adalie at the bar where they already have sleeves of beer, with an extra one for me.

"Vic still at the office?" Derek asks as I slide into my seat.

"Yeah. What about Lis? Did she say if she was coming?"

Adalie tilts her head toward the bar. "We didn't know what she likes, so she's getting herself a drink."

I ache to turn and find her. But I stop myself. Friends. We're just friends. And the last spot at the table is the one next to me, so I'll see her in a minute. I don't stop myself from turning when she gets to the table, though, and I drink in the sight of her. My gaze slides up the smooth skin of her legs to the hem of a silky red dress, over curves my hands itch to touch, to lips coated in a red lipstick that matches the dress. Her blonde and rainbow hair is caught up in a cascading ponytail. Over the last few weeks, I've started stealing her clip, loving the way her hair tumbles down her back when I do. The colours aren't quite as bright as they had been at first, but are still just as distracting. Tonight, she hasn't put the big claw clip in her hair, securing it with some kind of hair tie instead. I want nothing more than to untie it, so it'll fall.

I clear my throat in order to get my voice to work. "What did you get?"

"Mojito," she says, taking the seat next to me.

I lose track of the conversation as I wonder: if I were to kiss her, would she taste like mint? I may also glance down as she sits and notice the skirt of the dress riding up her thighs.

"Toasts!" Adalie says. She leans toward Lis. "When we go out, we always start with toasts. Everyone has to make one, but it can be anything. I'll start. To new friends and old ones." She points her beer to Lis first, then to me and Derek. We clink and drink.

"To random Friday nights," Derek says.

"To beer and mojitos," I say.

Lis turns to me with an evil smirk and my heart is pounding as I wait for her toast.

"To dancing," she says. We finish the last round of drinking and she turns from me to… Adalie. "Come dance with me?" she asks.

Adalie grins and the women get up and make their way to the dance floor, laughing, linking arms, and leaning close together to talk. I watch them walk away, then quickly turn back to the table.

"Son of a fucking bitch," I mutter.

"What?"

"She's wearing those shoes."

"What shoes?"

"The ones she wore that first night. When I took her home. Her fire engine red fuck me shoes."

I can't help looking at her again on the dance floor. She's laughing at something Adalie has said, head thrown back. And fuck if she isn't the most gorgeous woman in the bar. I want to be out there with her, but she asked Adalie instead, so I remain in my seat and drink my beer.

"You're going to be pining all night, aren't you?" Derek asks.

I turn back to him. "Self-imposed torture. I'm a masochist. Who knew?"

He lifts a hand, indicating he'd known, but doesn't say the words. "By the way. Isn't that yours?"

He points to a black garment slung over the back of Lis' chair. He's right. Instead of bringing a jacket, she brought my hoodie. She has completely stopped trying to return it by now, wearing it without me telling her to. It's been a delightful form of torture, seeing her in my clothes and not being able to take it off her.

"It might be mine," I finally say.

"Well, it was nice knowing you, man."

I laugh, but I also realize I'm okay with it. The longer I spend with her, the more I'm certain: Lis is the woman of my dreams and I just have to wait for her to be ready. She'll get there.

The women return from the dance floor. We finish our drinks and order more. We laugh and tell stories. And

Adalie and Lis continue to dance together, never inviting me or Derek to join them. We talk about crashing their dancing party, but neither of us does anything about it. Derek, because he's checking out our waitress. Me, because I want to a little too much.

I'm maybe a little bit drunk as the night gets closer to midnight—my previously decided curfew. Derek and I are finishing our beers when I notice a couple of guys hitting on Adalie and Lis. My blood turns hot and I'm about to get up when Derek reaches over and stops me.

"Not yet," he says.

We wait to see if the women are interested. They are technically single, after all, even if I already think of Lis as mine. They shake their heads at the men, but are still smiling, still dancing. We watch as the smiles disappear because the men aren't taking the hint.

"Now," I say. This time, Derek agrees.

Without needing to discuss it, he moves toward Adalie and I stalk to Lis. She sees me coming a moment before I reach her and I scoop her against me like I've wanted to do since I first saw her tonight.

"Hi," I say.

She tilts her head back, her hands on my arms, a slightly dazed look in her eyes. Damn the darkness of the bar. I can't tell if they're blue or green right now.

"Hi," she says.

"Hey man," the guy who had been hitting on her says.

WHY NOT BOTH?

I send him a cold look and he takes in the way she's plastered against me, still looking up at me like I'm a fucking knight in shining armour.

"Nevermind," he says and turns away.

Derek hasn't been nearly as dramatic—he only has one arm draped over Adalie's shoulders—but he's gotten the point across to the other man as well.

"I'm taking Adalie home. You guys want to share a ride?" he asks.

I look down at Lis, the question in my eyes. She gives the tiniest shake of her head.

"We'll stay for a little longer," I tell him, and he waves before leaving the bar with Adalie.

The beat of the music slows and suddenly we're dancing together like we did that first night. I know we're both a little drunk. Maybe a little more drunk than I'd intended to be. But watching her all night has done something to my brain and I can't seem to make it function.

I could tilt my head just a tiny bit more and I would finally know if she tastes like mint.

"Hey," I say, "You're not usually this tall."

She gives me that sassy smile I love so much. "Well, the air is so thin up here. Honestly, it's a wonder you survive."

I laugh, my insides melting, all defenses falling. "I—"

I clack my teeth together, physically preventing myself from saying those three words. Even drunk, I know I can't tell her. But in the darkness of the bar, with her pressed against me like a second skin, I feel it. I've only known her for three months, but I'm as sure as I've been of anything in my life.

I am in love with Amaryllis Stone.

Instead of terrifying me, the thought excites me. I feel keyed up, like suddenly everything makes sense.

"You what?" she asks when I don't continue.

"I was starting to get jealous of Adalie," I say, coming up with anything else I can say. "You kept asking her to dance and not me."

She pats my cheek like I'm a cute puppy. "Poor baby. You don't have anything to worry about, though. I'm not into women. Thought about it for a bit when Daze came out, but it's not for me."

"That's a relief. You're going to be cold going home," I say.

"I brought a sweater. This silly man refuses to take it back from me. So I've decided to make use of it." She leans closer, lowering her voice like she's sharing a secret. "It's the warmest thing I have."

"You don't own a winter coat?"

"I do. But this particular hoodie is magic."

"Is it?"

"It has the essence of the owner sewn right into the fabric, and he is the warmest person I've ever had the pleasure of touching. I wear that hoodie all the time now.

WHY NOT BOTH?

When I'm walking home in the cold. When I'm sleeping. All. The. Time."

An image of her sleeping in my hoodie, surrounded by me, flashes through my mind and I tighten my hold on her waist. I dip my head a fraction closer to her.

Her eyes drift closed as she waits for me to finish closing the distance. One arm stays wrapped around her waist, but my other hand slides up her body, cupping the back of her head. Her arms twine around my neck and she parts her lips, inviting me in.

She does taste like mint. And rum and lime. And I have missed these lips. I kiss her again and again. There is no way I could ever get enough. She kisses me back just as feverishly, pressing her body into mine, our tongues caressing, teeth nipping. My dick is straining to get out of my pants and just fucking into her.

"Spencer." My name is a sigh on her lips I can barely hear over the pounding beat of the music.

Then I say the hardest words I've ever had to say in my life.

"If I take you home with me, will you regret this in the morning?"

Her eyes blink open, hazy with lust, and I want to take the question back. But I think it might kill me if she regrets it, so I wait.

"I—I don't know."

I nod, grateful she didn't try to lie to me or to herself.

I press a gentle kiss to her lips again. Then one more. Because I won't be taking her to bed tonight and I need just a little more before this night is over.

"I'm sorry, Spencer," she begins, but I stop her.

"Don't be. I want you, Lis. But I'm willing to wait until you're sure."

I entwine our fingers and tug her with me back to our table. I order us an Uber and finish the last gulp of my beer while she does the same with her mojito. Then I pick up the hoodie from the back of the chair and slip it over her head, loving the weirdly erotic feeling dressing her in my clothes gives me.

We go outside and the car I ordered takes us to her place first. I ask the driver to wait a moment while I walk her to her door. The rules have slipped for tonight, so instead of the kiss on the head or the cheek I've been limiting myself to for the last few weeks, I kiss her properly, sliding my tongue along hers in a caress she returns.

When I end the kiss, she watches me with green eyes.

"Sleep well, firecracker. I'll see you tomorrow."

I've been walking her home almost every night we've worked together. I'm not sure she realizes I wait for her to finish sometimes—I don't mention it, and neither does she. Every time, when we arrive at her building, I wait for her to get inside and onto the elevator before I leave.

Tonight, I don't. Because if I don't leave right now, I'm not sure I'll be able to.

Chapter 27

Lis

As I ride the elevator up to my floor, drunk off the mojitos and Spencer's lips, I think I've made a huge mistake. Though whether that mistake was kissing him or not sleeping with him, I have no clue.

Thankfully, the wedding keeps me so busy that kissing Spencer plays in the background of my mind instead of the foreground until I leave for the night. The cooking and cleaning is all done by nine, but he has to stay until the event is over. I consider briefly going to find him to say goodbye, but I'm not sure what to say. Or what I'll do. I find Vic instead and tell her I'm leaving.

"You're not coming in tomorrow, right?" she asks.

"Right. Since there's nothing going on tomorrow or Monday, Tina and I are going to come in Monday and do an inventory and some prep for the upcoming events."

Since Sophie's birthday is tomorrow, I'd already cleared it with Vic to move things around so I could have the day off.

"I want to thank you again for agreeing to work these next two weeks straight," Vic says. "With all the people coming through here for the Pride events, weddings, and the Celebration of Light this next little while, I'm glad we'll have our head chef on hand."

"Of course," I say. "I've loved the events. And I'm excited to see the fireworks from the rooftop deck this year. These last few months have been exactly what I was hoping they'd be."

"So you're liking it here, then?"

I laugh. "I love it here."

"Good. Spencer mentioned you'd like to make some changes to the menu."

I falter, blinking. "Oh. I, um… well, yes. I think the menu is good. Great, actually. It's just not mine."

"I understand. Let's finish off this wedding season. When it's all calmed down a bit, you can tell me what you'd like to change."

"Really?"

"Yeah. It's your kitchen, Lis. I hired you for a reason. You've proved you know what you're doing. We'll set up a meeting in September and figure out what you want to do."

I squeal and wrap my arms around her in a squeezing hug. Then I jumped back. "I'm sorry. I should have asked to hug you first."

Vic laughs. "It's fine. Get out of here. I'll see you on Monday."

I walk home, excitement still thrumming through me, and after a shower, I pull on Spencer's hoodie and my comfiest pyjama pants and go back into the kitchen. Daze and Sophie are out for the night with their friends to celebrate Sophie's birthday. I'd been invited, but I knew I wouldn't want to go out after working, especially with all the days I'd be on coming up and the cake I still need to bake.

I take Cerberus out for a quick walk to the dog park and back. When we get home, he flops down on his bed and falls asleep. I turn on some music, get out the ingredients I need and my stand mixer, and start working. While I measure and mix, my mind strays to what I haven't let it think about all day. Spencer's arms around me, his lips on mine, his heat sinking into me. I'd felt the erection pressing into my belly as we danced and kissed.

Then his question, *Will you regret this in the morning?*

I still don't know the answer.

My class at the culinary institute had been made up of almost fifty per cent women. Yet, of that class, only a handful of us have found positions in Vancouver where we actually lead a kitchen. And many of us, myself included, had our reputations called into question after relationships had soured in the workplace. If that happened again, I'd have to start all over. I think of Vic's offer to let me change the menu. I'm so close to exactly what I've been working toward. I can't mess it up now.

On the other hand, no one has ever made me feel the way Spencer does. After a few months working with him, I'm not sure how much longer I can keep up the "just friends" façade. He's never once pushed me for more, letting me set the pace. Which just makes me want him more.

I'm carefully pouring water into the roasting pan with the cake in its spring-form in the middle when my sister and Sophie come home.

They change and Sophie says good night, but Daze meets me in the kitchen as I wash dishes.

"How's it going?" she asks, sitting on a chair at our little dining table and pulling her knees up to her chest.

"Not bad. Cake needs to bake for another sixty minutes. Then cool for about thirty. I'll get the mousse and whipped cream made tomorrow."

"Thank you for making it. I know how much you hate baking."

"I don't mind when it's for someone I love."

She watches me for a while, then says, "You're wearing the hoodie again."

I glance down at it, though I'm not sure why. I know exactly what she's talking about, though I'm wearing an apron over top.

After the dishes are done, I wipe down the mixer and the counter. Daze waits me out.

"I kissed him last night. Or maybe he kissed me? We'd been drinking. It was… It shouldn't have happened." I catch my lower lip between my teeth, biting down hard enough it hurts. "He asked me if I would regret it if we slept together again and I said I didn't know."

"And now that you've obsessed about it all day? What do you think?"

I cast her a look. I don't ask how she knows I've been obsessing about it. Then I sigh. "I still don't know. What if we get together and it goes bad? The four of them are so close, it would be awkward and terrible. Today, Vic said we can set a meeting up in September, after wedding season is over, to discuss if I wanted to make changes to the menu. She said it's *my* kitchen, Daze. Mine. If word got out I was sleeping with him, people would think I only got the job at Blue Vista because of it."

"You don't know that it would go bad. As for the rest." She shrugs. "Fuck what people think. If you like him, I say go for it." She stands. "You going to bed now?"

I check the time. "The cake still needs another twenty minutes to bake. Then it needs to cool."

"Let it cool in the fridge."

I look at her, aghast. "If I put it in the fridge before it cools, it'll crack."

"Will it still taste good?"

"I don't know. I've never been a heathen who puts it in the fridge before it cools. Go to bed. Leave the baking to the professionals."

She laughs and gives me a hug. "All right. You've got this. But just one more thing? I think the only one standing in the way of you and Spencer is you."

The birthday dinner with my and Daze's parents is fun. Sophie's parents live on Vancouver Island and don't make it to Vancouver often due to the cost of the ferry. She and Daze have a trip planned soon to visit them, to celebrate Sophie's birthday and the engagement.

The cake turns out perfectly and with only five of us, we each get a piece with three left over for me, Daze, and Sophie.

I bring my extra piece to work the next day.

Tina and I work on inventory and when I tell her to take a break for lunch, I go to Spencer's office. He's here doing a similar thing to what Tina and I are doing, making final preparations for the next two weeks. Other than Tina and Vic—who both left for lunch recently—we're the only ones on site today.

I'm feeling jittery with nerves at seeing him again. The memory of his soft lips and hard body pressed against mine makes me stop for a moment and catch my breath.

"Hey," I say when I get to his door.

He looks up from his computer, a smile breaking out on his face.

"Hey, firecracker. What brings you here? I thought you were doing inventory."

"I am. We just stopped for lunch. I brought you something." I pull the cake from behind my back with a flourish, setting it on his desk. "Voilà. I have to say, it's a masterpiece. My best work yet."

"Really?" He takes the fork from me but doesn't move to take a bite. "Where's yours?"

I wave his concern away. "I had mine last night. This is my extra piece. You said you wanted to call in a favour to have some, so…"

He gets out of his chair and moves around his desk to sit in one of the guest spots, motioning for me to take the other. "Then we have to share."

"I only brought one fork."

He gives me a patient look. "I've had your tongue in my mouth. We can share a fork."

A frisson of heat races through me as I sit down, watching as he takes his first bite, while also remembering our kisses at the bar.

"Oh my god, this is amazing," he says, sliding the fork into the cake for a second bite.

"I thought you said we were going to share."

"That was before I tried it."

I roll my lips together to keep my smile from getting too big. I love feeding people. Their reactions to my food is my favourite part about cooking. He fills the fork for a third time, holding it out for me. I open my mouth and he feeds me before I can think about what's happening. The intimacy of the situation settles in me as he pulls the fork from between my lips. I'm watching him for his reaction.

Though his eyes burn with desire, he doesn't say anything about it and just takes another bite.

"Spencer," I say, not entirely sure where I'm going. "About the other night."

"Nope."

"No?"

"I said I'd wait, and I will. So unless you're going to tell me to fuck you against my desk right now, not another word."

He holds out the fork for me again.

I can't breathe as the image of us fucking against his desk plays in my mind. I'm suddenly hot and I'm certain my panties are now drenched. My mind is screaming at me that we're alone in the building. I open my mouth and he feeds me a second bite of cake.

The vanilla mousse is sweet and fluffy mixing perfectly with the creamy tanginess of the cheesecake. It really is one of my best creations. He takes his next bite and I watch as his eyes close, savouring the taste before swallowing. I'm gripping the arms of the chair so hard my hands hurt. I just sit there and wait for him to give me another bite of cheesecake, my whole body vibrating with tension.

He only looks at me when he's feeding me, but I can't take my eyes off him. We're down to the last couple of bites and he holds the fork out for me, turning so his whole body is facing me. I note the way his cock is pressing into his zipper. He's not as unaffected as he's trying to seem.

"If you keep looking at me like that, I might fuck you against my desk anyway," he says, sliding the fork out of my mouth.

I swallow. "Looking at you like what?"

"Like you think I taste better than this cake," he says, before eating the last bite.

"You do."

The words are out before I can stop them, but I don't try to take them back.

He sets the fork down with exaggerated care, then stands, pulling me up with him. His hands skim up my arms to cup both sides of my face gently. Then he leans toward me, very slowly, his eyes searching mine the whole time. I don't move away. When he kisses me, it's with the same exaggerated care he used to set the fork down. Like he's holding onto his control with an iron grip.

We don't hold each other. We don't melt together. Fuck, I want to.

He ends the kiss as slowly as he began it, dragging his thumb along my lower lip.

"Go back to work, firecracker," he says, his voice husky. "Thank you for the cake."

I don't move, my heart hammering in my chest. His hands are still on me, one thumb caressing my cheek. He asks the question with his eyes. If I lean in now, if I wrap my arms around him and kiss him the way I want to, he'll take me here, on his desk, maybe against the door.

"Hey, Lis. You ready to get back to it?" Tina calls.

The moment shatters. Spencer turns away from me, passing me the plate and sitting behind his desk once more. Tina leans into the office just as he sits, sending me a questioning look.

"Yeah. I'm ready." I turn away from him and walk back to the kitchen, the heat in his eyes keeping me warm for the rest of the day.

Chapter 28

Spencer

The morning of the first day of the Pride festival is busier than I anticipated. I receive a phone call first thing, which leads to an emergency meeting with Vic. Once the meeting is over, I place another phone call.

"Hello?" Daze answers when she picks up.

"Hey, it's Spencer."

"Spencer?"

"Spencer Cole."

She takes a breath. "I actually didn't know your last name, so that's not exactly helpful. But I only know one Spencer. I'm just confused why you're calling."

"Well," I say slowly, dragging out the moment, "how would you feel about getting married in seven weeks?"

"Excuse me?"

"We had a cancellation in the middle of September. They've lost their deposit. I already talked to Vic. We have a lot of stuff already ordered for this wedding. We won't be getting our deposits back on any of it. We've hired people to work it so we'll have to pay those people whether or not they work. Vic agreed to offer you the date first for the remainder of the fees."

"How much?"

"You'll be getting a fifty per cent reduction in price. We'll have to make sure Tina is good to run the kitchen that night. I have a feeling our head chef will be busy."

"This is… I can't believe… I'd have to talk to Sophie."

I grin. "Of course. Talk to Sophie. Think about it. You're coming by for the party tonight?"

"Yeah. Lis gave us the tickets."

"Come a bit early and we can show you what we have. If you want to make any changes, we can discuss what that will do to the cost. I know it's short notice, so you may not want to take the date what with dresses and everything. Vic said you can have until Sunday night to decide. Monday, we'll release the date for other potential events."

We finish the call, and I get back to the preparations for the party. About an hour later, my phone rings. I answer it, half expecting to hear from Daze. Instead, it's Sam, my realtor.

"Hey, Sam. Got another condo for me to consider?"

"I do. And I think you'll be happy about this one."

"Where is it?"

"Remember the condo where we met? You said you really liked it, but you wished it was a few floors up and facing the water? How would you feel about the tenth floor?"

I go into my office and close the door, leaning against it.

"Are you serious? South-facing, tenth floor?"

"Yep. Same layout, just inverted. All fittings are the same."

"Sam. I want it. Put the offer in."

She laughs. "You don't even want to look at it first? At least learn the asking price?"

"No. Just write it up."

"I will. But there's an open house this weekend. They're not accepting offers until next Tuesday."

"They want a bidding war."

"Everyone does," she says regretfully. "The market is hot."

"What can we do?"

We discuss a few options, including how much over asking price I'm comfortable offering. We decide to do a home inspection on Monday before the offer goes in to keep it out of the conditions.

"I also heard from their realtor they'd like a fast closing," she says.

"We can close tomorrow if that's what they want. I don't fucking care."

"You don't need time to give notice to your landlord?"

"No. My landlord is my best friend. I rent a bedroom from her."

"Okay. I'll get the home inspection booked and let you know what time. Will you be available for it?"

"Yes. I'll make sure I am. Just let me know when."

I hang up with Sam and find Vic in her office, typing away on her computer. I close the door and sit down, my knee jumping in anticipation. She looks up at me with concern.

"We have a lot to do today for you to be taking a break," she says.

"I want you to come with me on Monday."

"Where?"

"I'm getting a home inspection done on a condo I'm going to buy." I decide not to jinx it by using conditional words. I'm *going* to buy this place.

She lifts her hands from the keyboard and sets them flat on her desk. "Did you buy a place?"

"Not exactly." I explain what's going on.

"And you want me to come and not Lis."

"Lis has already seen this place. Sort of." I pause, taking a deep breath and lacing my fingers together in front of me, squeezing them tight. "I'm not doing this for her. I'm doing it for me. I think I've been scared to take any steps in my life. But this is the right one at the right time. It's a good place. Everything I'd put on my list because of her are things I want, too. I want to be able to have a pet. I want to be able to get a car. Did you know it only takes thirty minutes to drive to Grouse Mountain?"

Vic rolls her eyes. "You want a car so you can go hiking?"

I shake my head. "No. I want the option of having a car in the future because one day…" I hesitate, swallowing past the nerves. "One day, I want to have kids and I figure a car would be a good thing to have in that case. This place gives me that option. It's big enough I could start there and move to something bigger later if I need to."

"You've thought a lot about this and what you want."

I nod. "Out of all the places I've seen, the first one felt right. It felt like a place I could live and be happy. I just wanted a couple of little tweaks. This place has those exact tweaks."

She leans back in her chair, folding her arms over her chest.

"Okay. You've convinced me. So why me and not Lis?"

"Because, while I—" I stop myself from saying love. I've admitted what I want in the future out loud. An out loud declaration that I'm in love with Lis isn't something I'm exactly prepared for today. I clear my throat. "While I like Lis and hope to get her to change her mind about the relationship status, you are still my best friend."

She rolls her eyes again. "You sure know how to lay it on thick."

I grin. "I could add more. Maybe remind you about all the times I did things for you? Or get down on my knees and beg?"

"You idiot," she finally says, shaking her head and turning back to her computer. "The answer was always going to be yes. I just wanted to know why. Let me know what time."

The weekend passes by in a blur. We're so busy with all the events, I don't stop to think about the apartment until Monday morning. Vic and I go there before work and look around the place while the home inspector does his thing.

Vic agrees the place is perfect for me, and we return to work. It's a relatively easy day compared to the chaos of the weekend. Since it's the last Monday of the month, we all go to Derek's after to unwind. We're too exhausted to play a game so we just sit on his rooftop deck, Abyss lounging in her catio in the corner while we chat and drink.

It's Lis' first time up here and she sits next to me on the outdoor couch. It's small enough that her leg and shoulder brush against mine. I refrain from draping my arm around her and pulling her against me, but the thought

WHY NOT BOTH?

is there. When she looks up at me, I note her eyes have darkened to green.

I make the decision that, once this next week is over, I'm going to ask her out on a date again. After the bar and my office, she *has* to be ready for this. Right?

My phone buzzes with an email from the inspector. I open it and read through his report, finding nothing of note. I breathe a sigh of relief while, simultaneously, my heart rate kicks up as I send a reply to Sam telling her to put the offer in as we'd discussed.

"What are you doing?" Adalie asks.

"Nothing. Just had to check an email."

She taps her finger against her beer can. "Sounds work related, Spencer," she says in a sing-song voice.

I catch Vic's eye and lift my drink. "I guess I'll have to drink then."

She smiles. "Those are the rules."

I take my drink and the conversation moves on. Adalie tells us about how her sister Calista has quit her job, again. This time to try her hand at travel writing.

"Is she going to travel?" Derek asks.

"I don't know what her plan is," Adalie says. "I don't think she really has one."

We decide to call it a night early. Lis' head dipped to rest on my shoulder at some point and I find her eyes half closed.

"Come on, firecracker. Let's get you home."

I help her to her feet and we all troop downstairs to where an Uber is going to pick us up. We say good night and when I get home, I can't sleep. I'm too wired, waiting to know the fate of my offer. I can't sleep the next night either. Sam had said they probably wouldn't get back until Wednesday morning, so when my phone rings and it's her, I answer with shaking hands.

"Sam. Tell me good news," I answer, my heart pounding in my chest. Vic comes out of her bedroom at the sound of the phone. I put it on speakerphone. I don't want to hear this alone.

"Okay. Good news."

"Are you serious?"

"I am serious. They accepted your offer, Spencer. You can move in two weeks."

I sit down heavily on a dining chair.

"They accepted my offer."

"You gonna survive?" Vic asks.

I nod.

"Hi, Sam. I'm Vic. Spencer's best friend. He's just a little in shock right now."

Sam chuckles. "No worries. You want to come down to the office today and we can sort out all the last details?"

"Yeah. Uh. What time?"

"Whenever you're free. I'll be here until five."

I hang up and look at Vic.

"Are you going to tell everyone today?" she asks.

I shake my head. "It still feels so surreal." Then I nod. "I will. After I see Sam today. I'll tell everyone tomorrow."

"Or." She pauses, a thoughtful expression on her face. "Or you could keep it a secret and just invite them over when you move in."

A slow smile spreads over my face. "Closing is only two weeks away."

Vic frowns. "Two weeks. Isn't that…"

"I chose the day before."

"Are you sure—"

"It'll be fine." I take a breath. No one knows me better than Vic. She's been with me from the beginning. She was there when my mother died. So she knows how I get around the anniversary of her death. But this year is going to be fine. Because the day before is going to be the first day of my new future.

Chapter 29

Lis

Working two weeks straight is exhausting. There's another sold-out party tonight for the second night of the Celebration of Light. Including today, I have five more shifts then I plan to sleep all day. I arrive at Blue Vista and go straight to my office to get my notes for the evening when Adalie comes in.

"There's been a little change. One of your cooks called in sick. I have a replacement I can call if you think it's necessary."

"Who called in?"

"Terry."

"Don't worry about it," I say. "I can sort it out."

"You're sure?"

"Yes."

She sighs in relief. "Oh, good. Then I'm going home." She stretches. "I've been here for hours already and I don't have to be back until tomorrow night."

"I thought you weren't working tomorrow."

"I'm not. But there's an owners meeting. Last day of every quarter. They're usually only about an hour to an hour and a half. And Vic always supplies alcohol and dinner."

I blink, confused. "I thought Vic was the owner."

Adalie raises an eyebrow. "Didn't you read your contract? Under the Blue Vista Ownership section. It's all there. Since Vic fronted the money, she owns seventy per cent. Because we came up with Blue Vista together, Derek, Spencer, and I each own ten per cent."

I feel like I've just had ice water dropped over me and it makes its way into my veins.

"Right," I say, to cover the feeling of the whole world shifting under my feet.

"All right. Well. See you later." She waves as she leaves my office, so I must do a good enough job of hiding my spinning thoughts.

I open my contract on my computer and scan through it. Sure enough, there's a heading I'd read before, but then neglected to read anything underneath it. I hadn't thought how it might affect me or my job when I'd read it initially. I read it now.

Blue Vista Events is owned and operated by Victoria Sterling (majority shareholder), Spencer Cole, Derek Moritz, and Adalie Murphy.

It goes on to detail exactly what that means, but I can't read much beyond Spencer's name.

I stand in a daze and make my way to his office, closing the door once I'm inside.

He looks up at me with a smile that immediately slips when he sees my face.

"What's wrong?"

"You're not my co-worker."

"What do you mean?"

"You're my boss."

He stands and comes around his desk. "No, I'm not. I own ten per cent of Blue Vista. Vic insisted when we started it."

"Why? Why did she have to insist?"

"Because I don't want to own a business. My father's business ruined my childhood. His constant need to put the job before our family."

My mind races. I'm torn between feeling sympathy for what must have been a very lonely childhood and horror that I'd slept with my boss. Sure, I hadn't known it at the time. But this is way worse than having a relationship with a co-worker.

"Listen," Spencer says, taking my hand. "My stake in the company has nothing to do with whatever is between us. Once a quarter, we meet to discuss the business, what things we want to try and what things we want to stop doing."

"You could decide you don't want a head chef anymore. You could decide I'm not working out."

He considers this for a second. "We could. Together. Not me. But it's been working. We're not getting rid of our in-house cooking team. It was a smart business move."

He motions for us to sit. "Let me tell you the kinds of things we talk about."

I lower myself to the chair and he doesn't let go of my hand, as though he's afraid I'm going to run away. He sits in the chair next to me, turning it so we're facing each other directly, his knees on either side of me, caging me in. I can feel him watching me, but I'm staring down at where his legs frame mine.

"We decided back in university that we wanted to create a one-stop-shop for weddings. We wanted to have in-house catering, a relationship with a photographer and florist and baker. Contracts with the best out there, so people will want to come here just for that. We want to build more relationships, not remove ones we already have."

I look up. "If that's the case, shouldn't you have tried to hire someone for my position who already had a name for themselves?"

"We wanted to. But when we went through the resumes, yours stood out."

"Did you hire me?" I ask, my heart clenching painfully.

He shakes his head. "I saw all the resumes. The four of us got together and narrowed it down to the top five. Vic and Adalie did the rest. My job here has nothing to do with hiring or firing. To me, you were just a name on a piece of paper until you walked in the door."

"But you own part of the business. The business I work for. Isn't this a conflict of interest?" I motion between us.

"Not only would I never let it be one, Vic would never let it be one. Plus, remember, she owns seventy per cent. Even if Derek, Adalie, and I all agree on something, Vic's vote outweighs ours. She steers the ship."

"You're her best friend, Spencer. Of course she's going to side with you if things went wrong between us. That was always a problem. But now, you're part owner. Think of what this looks like from the outside. This is my first role as head-chef. If we get together, people will assume I got the job because of my relationship with you. I'll never be taken seriously."

"You'll prove them wrong. Based on what I've seen this summer, you deserve to be a head chef. Everyone else will see it too. I know Vic has some ideas on how to get your name out there more. Competitions and things. We were going to discuss them tomorrow night. Remember, we want our vendors, even the ones who work directly for us, to be part of what draws people to our business."

I look down to where his knees bracket mine, where he still holds my hand, my fingers warm where they're clasped in his.

WHY NOT BOTH?

"I just need some time to think about this." I gently pull my hand from his and stand, walking away as my fingers turn to ice.

Chapter 30
Spencer

The next few days are the busiest of the entire summer. That's the only reason I'm not going completely insane thinking about if Lis is ever going to speak to me again. If she does, it's at work and only about Blue Vista business. She has stopped letting me walk her home. She has stopped seeking me out for anything except things that are specifically my responsibilities. I have never hated my job until now.

The rest of Pride and the Celebration of Light go smoothly. Lis brings in Pride cookies she made for the parade. We all take the time to watch it as it passes by our building. Then we have to get back to work. We host three weddings that day.

With Pride and the fireworks happening on the same day, Vic wanted to let multiple people get married at our venue. We dropped the price for the one day, made a lower maximum guest limit, and had all three weddings happen together as one big party.

It was an interesting struggle to get three different couples together and sorting out wedding details, but it had been a fun and exciting exercise.

The three couples share their first dance as the fireworks start.

There's another wedding the next day since Monday is a holiday. Then finally, finally, we get to rest.

As we're about to leave, I ask Lis what her plans are for her days off and if she wants to go hiking. I'd intended to ask her out on a date, but now, I just feel like I need to get us back to our friend status.

Her smile is strained when she refuses.

"Oh. I can't. I have a hair appointment, then I'm going to get some wedding stuff done with Daze and Sophie."

They'd agreed to take the date I'd offered them in September, so the wedding is swiftly approaching.

"How's everything going with that?"

"They have their dresses. We went to this really cool consignment dress shop on West Hastings. Daze got this really cute, ethereal gown and Sophie got this simple, elegant one. They're going to look stunning together."

"That's great."

"Yeah. They only needed minor alterations, so those dresses are all taken care of. This week we're going to find my and the other maid of honour's dresses."

"That's awesome. I can't wait to see it all come together. Are you walking home? You want me to walk you?"

I hold my breath as I wait for her response.

"No. My feet are killing me. I'm going to take transit."

I want to go with her, but she said she needed time and I'm determined to give it to her.

A couple days later, I go through my morning routine of wake up, coffee, stare like a pathetic creep out my front window. When I move, I won't be able to do this. Maybe that's a good thing. Maybe I need to take a step back. Maybe Derek was right and I'm just going to have my heart broken.

After Lis runs past, I sit down at the dining table with my mug as Vic comes out of her bedroom, dressed and ready for the day, though I have no idea what she has planned.

I run my hands over the tabletop.

"I don't have any furniture," I say.

"No, you don't. Except in your bedroom."

"How did I get to be a thirty-year-old man with no furniture?"

She laughs. "A girlfriend asked you to move in with her and you freaked out and moved in with me instead."

"Well, if I'm going to move into a new place, I should probably get some things."

"Probably, yes," she says with a sage nod.

"And some dishes. I don't have any dishes."

"You have that mug." She points to it.

It came with a coffee gift set from some past girlfriend who thought we needed to exchange presents at Christmas. I can't even remember what I'd gotten her. We'd barely been dating a couple of months and she broke up with me shortly after Christmas.

The result being I have one mug. I don't particularly like it, but since it's mine, it's the one I habitually reach for.

"Let's go shopping," I say.

"Isn't this something you might want to do with someone else?" she asks.

"No," I say, standing. I know she means Lis. She also knows Lis isn't exactly speaking to me right now. "This is something I need to do for myself. And as my best friend, you are contractually obligated to assist me."

She raises one eyebrow. "Contractually?"

"Yes."

"I don't remember signing a contract."

"Okay. Maybe not a contract." Then I smile. "It's the law. The federally regulated best friend law."

"I'll need you to show that to me."

"No time," I say as I bring my single mug to the kitchen and load it into the dishwasher. "We have to get going if we're going furniture shopping."

I usher Vic out of the apartment and she agrees to drive us. She takes us to a few places. I look at couches, tables, and chairs for indoors and outdoors. But I don't buy anything.

"We've been at this for hours already, Spencer," Vic says as I drag her to another store. "We've been to five stores. Can't you just pick something?"

"I figure I'm going to have this stuff for a while. I don't want to choose the wrong thing. And I haven't found anything that really made me stop. There was that one sectional I liked. I might want to go back and order it."

She rolls her eyes. "You usually make snap decisions."

"I guess I've been second guessing things a bit lately," I say, opening the store door for her.

She touches my arm as she passes me, but doesn't say anything.

"This should be easier," I say as we walk into a kitchen supply store. "I don't think it's as big a deal to choose the exact right plate."

She examines the display of glasses in front of the store. "I guess that depends. I'm sure it would be more important to someone like Lis than to you or me."

"Hm. Maybe you're right."

"Oh no. Don't start this wishy-washy crap again. Choose something."

I find a simple set of dishes that's white with two blue lines around the edge. It comes with four each of dinner plates, dessert plates, bowls, and mugs.

"Look! More mugs," I say as I pick the box off the shelf and put it in a cart.

"Congratulations," Vic says. "What else are you going to get? Pots and pans? Coffee maker? Blender?"

"What do I need a blender for?"

"How should I know?"

"No blender. And I was thinking of waiting on the pots and pans and asking Lis' advice." We start toward the small appliances. "It makes sense to have a chef give advice. Right?"

"Yeah. I think so."

"She's going to talk to me again, isn't she?"

Vic casts a glance at me. "She talks to you now."

I shake my head. "It's not the same. Not since she found out about my stake in Blue Vista." We reach the coffee makers and I look through a few of them. "Except for the other day when she mentioned Daze and Sophie's wedding, she's only talked to me about business stuff. Nothing else. She won't walk home with me. And I haven't seen her smile."

"She smiles all the time."

I sigh as I turn one of the boxes on the shelf to read the features on the side.

"There's this smile she has. It's like we're sharing a secret. Like she's got a joke and I'm the only one in on it with her."

I turn the box around and check out the next one.

"Spencer. Are you..." she hesitates.

But I already know what she's going to ask. This time, I'm not afraid to say it out loud. I'd tell Lis tomorrow if she'd let me. "Yes. I'm in love with her."

"Since when?"

I laugh. "I don't know. The first night we met? Some time during the summer? You know how, in *Pride and Prejudice*, Darcy says something like *I was in the middle before I knew I had begun?*"

Vic looks at me with a raised eyebrow. "You've read *Pride and Prejudice*?"

"Of course not. I watched the movie. With Keira Knightley."

"Spencer. That line isn't in the movie."

"Maybe I read the book in high school? For English class?"

She crosses her arms over her chest. "I was in every one of your classes in high school. We never read *Pride and Prejudice*."

"Fine. I read it. I like Jane Austen. Happy now?" Vic laughs at me so I talk over her. "Anyway, it's like that. By the time I realized what was happening, it was too late to stop it." I lift a shoulder in a helpless shrug. "Pretty sure I wouldn't have stopped it even if I could."

We stand there without talking for a while, then I tap the box I'm looking at. "This is the one. What else do I need?"

"Cutlery."

"Right. Let's go find some."

I start to push the cart in the direction we need when Vic grabs my arm.

"You'll be okay, right?"

"I will. I've always got you."

She holds up her pinky finger. "No matter what."

I link mine with hers. "Even when I fuck up."

When I try to let go, she holds on. "And even when you don't."

Chapter 31

Lis

As the days pass, I try to bury myself in my work to keep from talking to Spencer. I take transit home or finish before he does and walk by myself. It's far lonelier than I expect it to be. I'm so used to having him with me that, now he's not, I feel his absence like a phantom limb.

Spencer doesn't push. Just like before, he gives me the space I'd asked for and now I'm getting tired of it. Nothing is resolved between us, but I miss my friend. I miss laughing with him and hiking and watching movies. I would even do the Grouse Grind with him again if it meant we could have back that easy relationship we had before.

Daze tells me, often, that I'm the only one getting in the way. By the next weekend, I'm finally starting to believe her. But on Friday, I notice a shift in Spencer's demeanour. He doesn't smile, and he doesn't talk to me at all. He spends as much of the day in his office as he can while still coordinating the rehearsal dinner that night.

Saturday is the same, but worse. On Sunday, I bake him some cookies.

I'm the one who put the space between us and now I'm not sure if I'm allowed to ask him what's wrong. So I just go into his office without a word. He looks up, his eyes haunted the way I've only seen them once before. I set the container of cookies on his desk and leave as silently as I came in.

I don't work on Monday or Tuesday. But when I go for my morning run, I stop by to see if he's working. On Monday, he is, and I give him a batch of cinnamon rolls I'd baked that morning. On Tuesday, he isn't there, but Vic is.

Oddly, however, the door to her office is closed. I stare at it in confusion for a long moment, glancing down at Cerberus as though he might be able to tell me why it's closed. The doors are almost never closed around here.

I knock softly.

"Come in," she says.

I open the door, entering with my backpack filled with baked goods and my dog trotting happily at my feet. He immediately goes to Vic and sits in front of her. "Sorry to disturb you. I brought something for Spencer. Is he here?"

She shakes her head, bending to scratch Cerberus behind his ears. I'm about to tell her we'll leave her alone when I catch a glimpse of her eyes. They're red rimmed.

"Is everything okay?"

Finally, she turns toward me. She doesn't say anything for a long time. When she finally does, it's quiet. "I broke up with my girlfriend, Emily. For real this time."

I close the door behind me and sit down on a chair.

"I blocked and deleted her number. Then I blocked her everywhere else I could think of."

Spencer had mentioned Emily a few times, usually after she'd spent the night at Vic's place. And after that single meeting with her, I definitely had my opinions.

"If you don't mind my saying, you deserve better than her, anyway."

She huffs a laugh. "That's number one."

I look at her in confusion and she pulls out a sheet of paper, handing it to me. At the top it says, "15 Reasons Not to Call Emily" except the 15 is crossed out and she's written 16 in its place.

I scan the list.

1. You deserve better.

2. She spends all your money.

3. She leaves you on read.

It goes on and on until I reach the last one Vic must have written in recently. *She wanted me to choose between her and Spencer.*

I slap the paper down on the desk when I finish reading. "That bitch! You guys have been friends since you were kids. How could she ask something like that?"

She lets out a breath and seems almost relieved. "Especially right now. She should have known I'd never abandon him. And not this week of all weeks."

I catch that statement, but she continues before I can ask about it.

"I've known for a long time she was all wrong for me, you know." She sighs and takes the list back, slipping it into the top drawer of her desk.

"So why do you keep going back to her?"

"It wasn't always this way. In the beginning, she was nice. She was sweet. I loved her." She tilts her head to the side. "It didn't hurt that my parents disapprove of me dating women in general and Emily in particular. They really didn't like how she never seemed to care what they thought of her."

"What changed?"

Cerberus lays his head on her knee. She smiles down at him and scratches him again. "I'm not sure which it was, exactly. A few things happened at the same time. It was almost exactly two years ago, and she asked me to go out with her. I told her I couldn't because Spencer needed me. Then she figured out who his father was and who my family was and suddenly things shifted. She wanted me to spend less time with Spencer. She was awful to him whenever we were together. Before we were together, she was cheated on and she accused me of being into Spencer. I told her she was wrong, but I'm not sure she's ever believed me. She also started making me pay for everything because I could afford it. I broke up with her."

She pauses, but I feel like she's not quite finished. I've noted the reference to Spencer and how he needed her almost exactly two years ago, but I wait to ask. Eventually, she picks up the story again.

"A month or so later, she called me, told me she was sorry for everything. I still loved her, so I took her back. It was familiar. I was lonely. She was sweet when we were alone. But whenever Spencer was around, which was obviously a lot since he lives with me, she would be obnoxious and awful. Over the last two years, we've broken up and gotten back together a bunch of times. It's always the same. One of us is lonely, we call the other, we're together for a while, but nothing is different."

"I understand those feelings. It's why I tried online dating."

"How did that go?"

I smile ruefully. "My last date asked me to donate my kidney to him."

She laughs and I laugh with her. Now that it's over, it is pretty funny.

When my laughter subsides, I say, "That was the night I met Spencer." Then it occurs to me why she might have felt relieved by my outburst. "Were you worried I'd ask him to choose between me and you?"

She returns her attention to where Cerberus is still resting his head on her knee. She hasn't stopped petting him. "I hadn't considered it might be a problem until last night when Emily asked me to choose."

"Spencer and I aren't even together."

She rolls her eyes, then looks at me like I shouldn't be so stupid.

"Regardless, I would never do that."

"Good." Her look turns hard. "Because I *would* fire you for that."

I lean forward. "I would want you to." We lapse into silence for a moment. "Do you want me to stab her? I'm pretty good with knives."

That startles a laugh from her and I smile.

"That seems a bit extreme, but I'll keep it in mind."

"I try to limit myself to assault. Don't want any murder charges."

"Of course. Very prudent. You make offers to stab people all the time?"

"My sister says you know I love someone if I do one of two things: bake for them or offer to stab someone."

"You should probably stick to baking."

"Probably less of a chance of me getting arrested. Though I suppose I could consider the idea of poison."

She laughs again and I'm glad to hear it. She usually portrays an image of an unbreakable block of stone.

Ready to do whatever it takes to ensure her business, and the people connected to it, succeed.

"You've done some baking for Spencer in the last few days," she says.

I try to keep my cheeks from heating. I am not at all successful. "I guess I have. Actually, I wondered if you could tell me more about this week."

She leans back in her seat. "He told you about his mom?"

I nod.

"The anniversary of her death is tomorrow. Every year, he goes to his dad's house and spends the day with him."

"I thought they didn't speak anymore."

"They don't. Except for his dad's birthday and this one day every year. The birthday isn't as hard, but this one is. I go with him, but I'm only marginally helpful. I would do anything I could to help him feel better. Losing his mom was really hard on him. She was the only real family he had. His parents had no siblings. His grandparents are gone. When she died, he and I were already best friends. He was the first person I told about being bi. I guess he needed a new family, and he decided I was going to be it."

We share a look. I understand why Emily might have been jealous of Vic and Spencer's relationship. I can see how Emily might have felt threatened by the love and protectiveness they feel for each other. But from where

I'm sitting, all I can feel is glad he has someone in his corner, someone who would be willing to go to bat for him, stand beside him in good times and bad. It makes me feel more like I'm part of something than excluded from it.

"You guys," I hesitate, unsure exactly what I'm trying to say. "You really look out for each other. I think that's amazing."

"I got your back, no matter what," Vic says under her breath. "That's all Spencer's doing, too. Right after we started university, Spencer had enough and cut pretty much all ties with his father. Then we met Derek and Adalie, and we all just sort of clicked. None of us have a particularly easy time with at least some of the family we were born into. Spencer decided we would be it for each other."

"I noticed."

"Actually." She stares at me for a long moment, contemplating. "I wondered if you would be able to do something for me?"

"What is it?"

"There's this photographer. I've been trying to get her to meet with me to have a sort of first dibs contract with her for next summer. I have a similar contract with our florist and the baker who does the cakes. Anyway. She said she was free to meet tomorrow, but then not again until later in September. I told her tomorrow is no good, obviously."

"Okay. What does this have to do with me?"

"What if, instead of me going with Spencer tomorrow, you go with him?"

"Oh. I don't know, Vic. We haven't really been…" I trail off.

"I know. And that's all on you. I'm not saying you have to get over it. As a woman in the business world, I get it. I date primarily women because most men I've met think they need to help me run my business. People—the public—like to see men in charge. Sleeping with the boss, even if you're madly in love with him," she shrugs. "It looks bad from the outside. Though he's not really your boss, I don't blame you for being cautious. What I am going to say is, if you decide it's not worth keeping you two apart, it's up to you to make the first move."

She's right. It's exactly the same thing Daze has been saying to me pretty much every day for the past two weeks. I pull the container of cookies I'd made that morning out of my backpack and set them on her desk next to her single decoration of a Pride flag in a bi mug.

"I baked these for him this morning."

She gives me a patient look. "Right. And you're not in love with him."

"I never said that."

WHY NOT BOTH?

I hadn't ever said I *was* in love with him, either. The more I think about it, the more I think it's probably true. And cookies and other baked goods are nice. But I want to help him more than just a few cookies.

"I'm supposed to work tomorrow."

She points to herself. "Boss. You can have the day off."

"Okay. I'll go with him. If you think it'll help."

"I do."

"You'll make sure he gets the cookies? There's a couple dozen in there, so you can have some, too. I'd like to make him something special tomorrow. Have any ideas for me?"

She shakes her head. "I don't think there's anything in particular he likes more than anything else. Why don't you make your favourite thing?"

"It's not sweet. My favourite thing to bake is a cheese bread."

"He'll love that. Who doesn't love cheese?"

I laugh as I stand. Cerberus looks up at Vic before he moves.

She scratches him behind the ears again. "Thanks to you, as well. It's amazing how just scratching a dog's ears can make everything feel a bit better."

"Come on, Cerberus. Let's let Vic get back to work."

He trots over to me and I clip his leash on. Just before I leave the office, Vic says, "Lis? Don't tell anyone about Emily, okay? I don't want to make a big deal of it."

"No problem. Maybe we can hang out some time and you can tell me all about it."

Vic smiles. "That sounds good. We could invite Adalie. Make it a girls' night. No boys allowed. Maybe even do some girly things."

"Victoria Sterling. I didn't know you liked to do girly things."

She lifts her hand, looking at her neatly trimmed nails. "I love a good mani-pedi. I know a spot. I'll book a time for the three of us."

"I can't wait." I hesitate for a second, then say, "I know it's not quite the same as Spencer, but I've got your back, too."

She smiles. "It is the same."

Chapter 32

Spencer

I wake up late in the morning. Actually, the afternoon. When I get up, my phone has a text from Vic and a voicemail from Sam.

Vic:
> Lis brought you some cookies. They're here if you want to get them before going to get the real estate stuff sorted.

Me:
> I just got up. I'm going to shower then I'll come down. Can I borrow the car today?

Vic:
> All yours. Keys on the hook by the door.

I shower before I listen to Sam's message, trying in vain to wash off the sadness and apprehension that's been covering me like a heavy cloak for the last few days. It doesn't work the way I want it to, but I get out, dress, and listen to the message. She tells me she has everything ready for me and I can come down to her office any time to sort out the final details.

So I grab the keys, stopping by the Blue Vista first.

"What's this?" I ask, lifting the container of cookies.

"She just stopped by and asked if I could make sure you got them. Seems she thinks you're in need of cheering up."

"She made me cookies and cinnamon rolls this week."

She spins her pen between her fingers as she leans back in her chair, assessing me. "Sounds like things are coming back around."

"I don't know. Until she says so, I won't make any assumptions."

"Derek and Adalie want to know if you want to go out tonight. Derek said drinks are on him if you want to get shitfaced."

I huff a laugh. "Maybe on Thursday."

"You going to your new place now?"

"Sam's office first. Then, yeah."

"When does your furniture show up?"

Over the last week, I'd gone back to the furniture stores and chosen what I wanted. Thankfully, the couch I wanted was the floor model, so I could have it whenever I was ready. The dining set had to be ordered and would take a few weeks.

"Couch comes on Thursday afternoon," I say. "Movers are coming to your place next Monday."

WHY NOT BOTH?

"When are you going to have people over? Reveal the big surprise?"

I shrug. "Ask me on Thursday."

She gives me a sympathetic smile. "Okay. Let me know if you need anything."

I meet Sam and spend more money in a single day than I've ever spent in my life. But everything goes smoothly, and she hands me the keys.

"That's it?" I ask.

"That's it," she says. Then she hands me a basket filled with a bunch of neat kitchen things, like a baking dish, an oven mitt, and some silicone spoons and something flat. "A little gift to say thank you for your business."

"What's this?" I ask, pointing.

"The spatula?"

"That's not a spatula. You'd never be able to flip anything with that."

She laughs. "It's not for flipping. It's for mixing, usually. Sometimes spreading things like icing. You really don't spend a lot of time in the kitchen, do you?"

I shake my head, trying not to think about Lis.

"Are you okay, Spencer? You don't seem as excited about your new place as I thought you would be."

I try to give her a smile. "I will be. It's just a bad day. Thank you for this. It's all stuff I need."

"I figured you might. Well, it was a pleasure. I'm glad to have helped you."

I leave her office and go to my new condo, carrying up my box of dishes and the gift from Sam. I unlock the front door and step inside.

Everything is quiet and empty. The sun streams in through the floor-to-ceiling windows, trying in vain to cheer me up. I should be happy. Maybe I shouldn't have tried to come here until the day after tomorrow. Or even the day after that.

I set my things on the kitchen counter, suddenly feeling very tired.

I return to the car and bring up more things. Vic and I had purchased a bunch of cleaning supplies. The previous owner had been required to clean before they handed over possession, but Vic said I might want to do it myself so I know what's been done.

I spend the day scrubbing everything. It's a good exercise to keep me from thinking too much. I order some pizza for dinner, having it delivered and ensuring I set up the buzzer so I know when they arrive.

After I eat—the only thing I've eaten today—I tidy up and sit on the floor with my back to the kitchen island, looking out the window with the view of the ocean. I watch that view for a long time, wishing my mom could be here, wondering what she would think of the place.

I'm still wondering when I fall asleep.

WHY NOT BOTH?

My phone wakes me, ringing loudly in the empty space. My neck and back hurt from how I've been sitting.

"Hello?" I answer.

"Where are you?" Vic asks.

"I'm at my place."

"You dumbass. You have no furniture."

"I know," I say, rubbing the back of my neck.

"Where did you sleep?"

"On the floor." I'm even more tired now than I had been before I fell asleep.

"Fuck, Spencer. Why do you have to be so…"

"Extraordinary?" I ask in a lame attempt at a joke.

"Extra," Vic says. "You coming home before your dad's?"

"Yeah," I say, groaning as I stand. I stretch, trying to work out the kinks from sleeping on the floor. "I'll be there in a few minutes."

"Good. I have something to show you."

"What?"

"Just come home, doofus." I hear her muttering something about idiots sleeping on floors before she hangs up.

I take another look around the condo, then just leave everything as I had the night before.

Chapter 33

Lis

My alarm goes off early in the morning, but all my favourite things to bake require kneading and rising times. I get out of bed and head to the kitchen. Cerberus watches me blearily then lays back down on my bed.

I gather what I need and start the dough. While I'm mixing the ingredients, Daze emerges from her bedroom.

"Are you baking at six in the morning?"

"Yes."

"May I remind you that you hate baking?" she asks, sitting on one of the dining chairs to watch me.

"You may."

"Okay. Lis. You hate baking. Why are you doing it? And at godawful o'clock, no less?"

"It's the anniversary of Spencer's mother's death."

"Shit."

I glance at her over my shoulder. "Take care of Cerberus today?"

"No problem. I'll tell Sophie."

"Thanks. I'll take him out while this is rising."

"Cheese bread?" she asks.

"Yeah. Vic said to make my favourite, so…"

The dough is sticky when I lift it from the mixer and drop it onto my already-floured counter. I knead and punch it into submission, then drop it back into the bowl, covering it with some cheesecloth. After I clean my mess, I go into my room to dress and convince my lazybones dog to get up. It only takes a bribe of one cookie and his ball to get him to follow me out the door. After an hour of exercise, we go back to the apartment. I grate cheese and roll out the dough, shaping it into the loaf I want before placing it in a pan and covering it again.

Sophie and Daze are awake now, drinking coffee at the dining table.

"What do I wear?" I ask.

"I'm certain Spencer isn't going to care at all," Daze says.

"We're going to his father's house."

They gape at me.

"It's some kind of tradition," I explain. "He's really upset about it. He doesn't have a good relationship with his father."

Sophie purses her lips, considering. "Well, do you want to look respectable or sexy?"

"Both. Respectable for the dad, sexy for Spencer."

Sophie and Daze grin at each other, then go into my room. I follow and watch as they open my closet and sort through, pulling out a flowy black skirt and my favourite red top. It has a scooped neckline and thick straps, the fabric soft and clingy.

Daze rummages through my top drawer and takes out my sheer, black, thigh-high stockings and a pair of lacy black underwear and the matching bra.

"No one is going to see the underwear," I say.

"Can't hurt," she responds. "And you said you wanted to be sexy today. Sexy starts with the underwear."

I roll my eyes but take them. After the bread is finally in the oven, I get into the shower, taking my time to wash my hair and shave. I tell myself I shave my legs mostly because the stockings will be itchy if I don't.

When I leave my bedroom again, dressed, with just some mascara and red lipstick on, I do a little spin to show them the full effect.

"Outstanding," Daze says. "Now. What are you doing with your hair?"

"I was just going to clip it up. Like I usually have it."

They stare at me, and I can see they think they're missing something.

"Spencer likes to steal the clip from my hair," I finally say, turning away to take the bread from the oven.

They break out into laughter and are still laughing when I turn back.

WHY NOT BOTH?

"Oh, Lis," Daze says, standing. She places her hands on my shoulders. "You need to admit to yourself that you are in love with this man."

"I—We're just—"

"Friends. I know. So are me and Sophie." She pats my cheek and I finish rushing around, gathering what I need.

Then, I'm out the door and walking the fifteen minutes to his apartment. When I arrive, I send Vic a text saying I'm here and she tells me to come up.

She opens the door for me after I knock.

"He's just getting dressed. I'm afraid he doesn't know you're coming."

"Why not?"

"I was going to tell him last night, but then he didn't come home," she says, exasperated.

A flash of jealousy and hurt sears through me. "He didn't? Where was he?"

Her eyes widen a bit like she's just said something she shouldn't. "I mean, he didn't come home before I fell asleep."

"Vic."

She closes her eyes and sighs. "It's nothing bad, I promise. It's just something he wants to tell people later. Not today."

"Okay."

She hands me some keys. "You can take my car." Then she hands me a piece of paper. "This is the address."

"Really?" I ask, noting the Mercedes symbol on the key.

"Yes. Thank you for agreeing to do this."

"Agreeing to do what?" Spencer asks, coming out of his room.

Vic turns toward him. "I asked Lis to go with you today. If you'd rather I come with you like usual, that's fine. I just thought she might help you more than I can."

He turns to me with bleak eyes. He looks so haunted. Like the Spencer I've come to know has left and all that remains is his shell. My heart breaks for him and in a second I'm wrapping my arms around his waist, pressing my body to his, trying to soak his pain into me.

He buries his face in the space between my neck and shoulder, crushing me against him as though he needs me to anchor him to this world. I hold him back just as tightly.

"Are you sure about this?" he whispers.

I know what he's really asking. Do I want to continue the friendship we'd been building before I'd found out he owned part of Blue Vista? And I do. I've missed him so much over the past couple of weeks. Even if he hadn't needed me today, I would have gone back to him.

"I'm sure. I've got your back no matter what. That's the Blue Vista motto, isn't it?"

He pulls back and gives me something resembling a smile.

"You look stunning, firecracker." He kisses my cheek.

"And you look like hell. Here." I let him go to get my backpack, reaching in for his hoodie and pulling it over his head. He bends down so I can manage, slipping his arms through the sleeves on his own. My heels today are only about an inch and a half, so he's still over six inches taller than me. Once it's on him, I find the container with the cheese bread. "I baked you this."

"You good?" Vic asks.

Spencer nods, holding the container. "I'll be fine. Thanks, Vic."

"I didn't do anything but ask her. I have a meeting to get to. You guys—" She falters. "I guess you won't have fun. But you know what I mean."

She leaves and I ask if Spencer is ready.

"No. Let's do it, anyway."

We go down to the underground, where Spencer leads me to a black Mercedes. It's not an older, used model like I'd hoped, but a shiny new one.

Great. Now I get to drive my boss' hundred thousand dollar car. Not intimidating at all. I should have just brought the One Car.

We get in and start the drive. Spencer programs the address into the car's GPS and I follow it to the Point Grey neighbourhood in Vancouver. When I pull up to a gated property, Spencer rattles off a code and I punch it into the keypad. The gates swing open and I drive up the driveway, my mouth dropping open as the house comes into view. I stop at the front doors and gape at the white mansion, all windows and columns with a marble staircase leading up to the front door.

After an awkward five minutes, I turn to Spencer, who hasn't moved at all.

"What are you waiting for?" I ask him.

"I just hate coming here." He looks over at me. "What are *you* waiting for?"

"The valet, obviously."

His smile is fragile, but real. I get out of the car and he comes with me. I take his hand as we climb the steps to the door. At this point, I wouldn't be surprised if he knocks, but he pushes it open and we step inside.

"Ah, Spencer," a man greets us immediately. "Welcome home, sir. Miss Victoria couldn't come with you today?"

"Hi Matthew. No. This is my—" He breaks off and looks at me. "This is Lis. Lis, this is Matthew. He runs the house."

"Runs the house," I repeat. "Like a housekeeper?"

Matthew chuckles. "Sort of. Right this way Spencer and Miss… Lis. Can I get you something to drink?"

"Water will be fine for me," I say. No way I'm having a single drop of alcohol if I'm driving that car home.

"Flat or sparkling?"

"Sparkling would be amazing."

WHY NOT BOTH?

Spencer doesn't ask for anything. Matthew leads us to a set of doors and the closer we get, the tighter Spencer grips my hand. When the doors open, I see a man between fifty and sixty years old sitting in a chair with a short glass in his hand, filled halfway with amber liquid. He's turned away from the door and doesn't look up until we enter. Then he does and I'm startled by how much Spencer looks like him. His hair is more silver than blond. But his eyes are the same clear blue and they have the same cheekbones and chin.

"Spence, my boy," he says with a smile, though I notice the sorrow in his eyes as well.

Spencer flinches at the sound of his name and I remember him telling me he didn't like being called Spence. In fact, in the almost four months I've known him, I haven't heard a single person call him that.

"Dad," he says, coming into the room and sitting on the couch across from his father. He pulls me with him and we sit together, thighs touching, his hand still gripping mine.

"You couldn't have worn something more appropriate?" the man asks. "You look like a homeless person. Where's Vicky?"

Vicky? What is with this man and his nicknames?

"She couldn't make it today. This is Lis. Lis, this is my father, Beckett Cole."

He turns toward me. "Lis? What's that short for?"

"Amaryllis."

"Hm. Well, wouldn't Mary be a better nickname for you then?"

I smile as sweetly as I can and say, "If you call me Mary, I might have to stab you, sir."

Spencer makes a funny noise halfway between a snort and a cough.

Matthew returns with my sparkling water and I take it with a grateful smile. He lets us know lunch is ready, so we follow him to the dining room. There's a huge table and we're spaced out so far that we'll have to shout to have any kind of conversation. I take one look and shake my head.

I pick up my plate and move it closer to where Beckett is sitting, then I pick up Spencer's, grab him by the arm and seat him next to me so I'm between him and his father. Beckett watches this with a scowl on his face.

"You didn't like the placements?"

"Not particularly," I say with another sweet smile. I have zero desire to ingratiate myself to this man. He can hate me all he wants. In fact, I hope he does.

"Well, then, Amaryllis, how did you meet my son?"

I sip the water, fixing my eyes on him. What is his insistence on calling people by names they don't want to be called?

"It's Lis. Only my mother and my sister call me Amaryllis, and only when they're angry." I briefly consider telling Beckett exactly how I met his son, but I'm not sure Spencer would like that. So I say, "We work together. I'm the head chef at Blue Vista."

"Oh. An office romance, then."

His tone is disapproving. I know he's thinking I'm sleeping with Spencer for my job, which is exactly what I feared. But sitting here, I don't care what this man thinks. He could think I'm the scourge of the earth and I wouldn't care.

Matthew returns and pauses, noticing the change in placements. He meets my gaze and gives me a brief smile before setting out the food, pouring Spencer some water and leaving us again.

"So, has Vicky seen any returns on that place yet?"

"Dad," Spencer protests.

"I'm just thinking about you, son. I want you to be well-established. Working there won't provide the life you need. You're thirty years old. You shouldn't be working for someone else. You should be working for yourself."

"Actually," I interject. "I think this is Blue Vista's most successful year yet. We've been incredibly busy."

I turn to Spencer for confirmation.

He nods. "We have twice the number of weddings this year over last year. We're already fully booked for next summer, and we've been discussing opening a second venue. Maybe something in Burnaby or Ladner."

"You only own ten per cent of the business," Beckett says. "You're hardly in a position to help make decisions."

My blood boils. The words coming out of this man's mouth make me want to stab him. Obviously just the hand or the leg. I clench my teeth, keeping my smile in place. Spencer is so stiff beside me that one wrong move and I'm afraid he's going to snap.

Spencer inhales a deep breath. "As I've explained before. I may only own ten per cent, but we make operational decisions together. We're a team."

Beckett rolls his eyes as though he doesn't believe what Spencer is telling him. "At least you've been investing your money well. Though I will never understand why your mother decided to leave it to you separately instead of including it in the trust I'm holding for you."

I'm about to make some smart ass comment—possibly something like, *You mean the trust fund you refuse to give him?*—when Spencer reaches for his glass of water. Instead of drinking some, he shifts the glass toward me.

I recognize the gesture immediately and turn toward his father. "Hey, Beck, have you ever hiked the Grouse Grind?"

"Excuse me?"

"The Grouse Grind. Spencer made me do it with him about two months ago. Honestly, it is absolute torture. I haven't forgiven him for making me trek up that thing.

Though he did follow through and go running with me after."

Under the table, I touch Spencer's arm, trailing my fingers along it until I can reach his hand. I lace our fingers together and he squeezes tightly.

"It's excellent exercise. The Grouse Grind, I mean. And the views from the top? Spectacular. Though I told Spencer, next time, he can hike it and I'm going to ride the gondola up. Did you know you can have breakfast with the bears? There's two of them up there." I launch into a full-on infomercial for the restaurant on Grouse Mountain where you can have breakfast during the two rescued grizzlies' feeding time. I don't stop talking long enough for Beckett to try to chime in or change the subject. When I finish talking about the grizzlies, I move on to talk about the zipline adventure they have, followed by information about the Christmas event they host in the winter.

I contain my sigh of relief when the phone rings and Beckett stands to answer it, moving across the room to talk. I've run low on Grouse Mountain tourism facts.

"Grouse Mountain?" Spencer says when his father is out of earshot.

I shrug. "I've been looking it up in case you try to drag me up there again."

He huffs a laugh.

"Are you doing okay?" I ask.

"What makes you think I'm not okay?"

"Well, you're squeezing my hand hard enough, my bones are creaking."

He looks down, startled, and immediately releases my fingers. "I'm sorry."

I grab his hand again, squeezing him just as hard. "Don't be. I'm right here."

He searches my eyes and I wonder if he's about to kiss me when Beckett returns.

"That was the office. I have to go in."

"Now?" Spencer says. "Today?"

"Emergencies don't wait for convenient times, Spence. You would know this if you ran your own company."

I want to stab him. Unfortunately, the knives within reach are just table knives. But if I stood, I could slap Beckett Cole across his uncaring face. Except Spencer still holds my hand, and I think he needs me next to him more than he needs me to slap his father.

Beckett leaves the room and Spencer slumps in his chair, completely deflated.

"Spencer? Are you okay?"

He's let go of my hand, staring down at his lap. I wait for him to look at me. He doesn't.

After a while, he sighs. "It's not the first time. It won't be the last. He wasn't even there the day she died. Why would the anniversary of her death be any different?"

He's a thirty-year-old man, but suddenly I can see the fourteen-year-old boy whose mother has just died and whose father isn't there. Whose father has chosen his job over his son. Again.

That's when it hits me. I've done exactly the same thing. I chose my job, one I hadn't even started yet, over him. Both job and relationship were barely a few hours old. And yet, when it came down to it, I chose the job and left him in the cold.

"Get up," I demand, standing as well.

His gaze snaps to mine, confusion tightening his brow. But he does what I tell him.

My hands fist into his hoodie, pulling him closer. "You need to understand something. I didn't choose the job over you because I didn't want to be with you. I *did* want to be with you. I *do* want to be with you."

"Then why aren't we together? Why me *or* the job? Why not both?" he asks.

"Because it's terrifying," I whisper. "What if we try and it doesn't work out? What if it all goes bad?"

"What if it doesn't? What if we live happily ever after, like Buttercup and Westley, or Rick and Evie, or Penelope and what's his name? James McAvoy."

A smile twitches my lips. "Johnny."

"Yeah. What if we have the greatest romance ever told?"

I roll my eyes, but he's still referenced some of my favourite movies, my favourite love stories. "The greatest? Don't you think you're being a little dramatic?"

He shakes his head slowly. And I know he doesn't. He believes every single word he's said. He believes I can have both him and the job. And why can't I? Why can't I have this amazing man who sees me, who is kind and funny?

I tug on his hoodie, drawing him closer. I don't think I could stop myself from kissing him, even if I wanted to.

Chapter 34

Spencer

Fire races through me the moment our lips touch, burning away the haze of grief and anger shrouding my mind. My hands find her hips, dragging her against me. Her hands release the front of my hoodie and snake up my chest, fingers threading into my hair, pulling my head closer to her. One of my hands makes a similar trip and I find the clip in her hair, opening it and letting it all loose, the way I like it best. Then I palm her ass, lifting her onto her toes.

"Spencer, I need you."

Blood rushes from my head to my dick at her whispered words, and I'm dizzy for a second. I want to push her against the wall and take her right here in my father's dining room. Sense prevails before I start tearing her clothes off.

"I would take you right here, firecracker, except I have no condoms."

She blinks her eyes open. They're the darkest green I've ever seen them, filled with desire. She catches her bottom lip between her teeth and I want to stop her so I can do that instead.

"I have an IUD," she finally says. "If you want…"

I search her eyes. "Are you sure?"

"Yes. I'm tired of fighting this, Spencer. It's been almost four months. I don't want to wait another twenty minutes to get all the way back to my place or yours. I want you right the fuck now. This place is a fucking palace. There has to be a bed or two kicking around we can use."

I chuckle and nod. "I know just the place. Come on."

I find one of her hands and lace our fingers together, tugging her with me as I leave the dining room and move to the back of the house. We pass a wall of windows and Lis comes to a stop, looking down.

"Is that what I think it is?" she asks, pressing her face to the glass.

"The pool? Yes. Lots of people have pools."

"It's inside! You have an indoor pool!"

"Not me. Come on." I lead her further, up the back stairs to the second level and down the hall, finally stopping at a door. The desire to get Lis into a bed where I can fuck her wars with the trepidation of seeing this room again, causing me to hesitate. "I haven't been in here in a while."

I take a breath and push the door open, letting Lis into my childhood bedroom. It hasn't changed since I left over ten years ago. She lets go of my hand to walk around the room. The same framed movie posters are scattered on one wall. *Army of Darkness*, *Alien*, *The Dark Crystal*, *The Exorcist*, *The NeverEnding Story*. The opposite wall has a gigantic window with the curtains drawn. Lis peaks behind them to see the view but leaves them shut. She trails her fingers along my dresser, looking at the items scattered over the top. A trophy from when I was in soccer, an old hockey puck, an empty frame. She holds it up and looks at me, the question in her eyes.

"The frame wasn't really my style. So I took the picture when I moved out. Left everything else."

Finally, she makes her way to the bed. It's huge and pretentious, just like everything in this house. But my old duvet cover is still on it, a galaxy of colours brightening an otherwise white room.

"Is it going to be dusty?" she asks, running her fingers over the blanket.

"Probably not. Matthew keeps the house clean."

"Is he still here?"

"Downstairs somewhere. He won't bother us."

She turns toward me with a smile that melts away all hesitation. "Get over here, then."

She holds out her arms and I don't need to be told twice. I take two steps and I'm there, lifting her and setting her gently on my bed where she lies back on my pillow. I kick off my shoes and climb onto the bed as well, hovering over her. My hand slides along her leg and I'm not sure if I love the feeling of the stocking she's wearing or if I want to rip it off her so I can feel her skin. I sit up so I can remove her shoes. They're not the red, fuck me heels I love so much. These are cute black shoes with a rounded toe and a much shorter heel. I take them off and drop them to the ground.

I kneel between her legs, one propped up on either side of me, and I skim my hands back along them, moving toward her this time.

"You have this whole business casual thing going on today," I say.

"I thought I should look somewhat appropriate to meet your father. If I knew what an asshat he was, I wouldn't have cared."

"Did you know the skirt molds to your ass and the shirt clings to your curves and a part of me has been undressing you in my mind since the moment I saw you today?"

She smiles slyly. "I also wanted to look hot for you."

"Mission accomplished, firecracker."

My hands reach her knees and start the slow slide down her thighs, catching the edge of her skirt and letting it fall to her hips, revealing the lace tops of her stockings, held up by black satin ribbons. She watches me as my hands move, her legs opening wider the closer I get to her core.

"You don't have to go slow," she says.

"Yes, I do. I intend to savour this."

When my hands reach where the skirt has bunched, I flip it up over her stomach, revealing black, lace panties.

"These are not business casual."

I trail a finger along the edge and her hips lift toward me, silently begging me closer.

"Spencer." Her voice is breathy, pleading. "Are you going to tease me all day, or are you going to fuck me?"

"I was thinking both."

She reaches for me, but I back away.

"Now, now. None of that. Do I have to tie you to the bedposts to make you behave?" I don't intend it seriously, but the way her eyes gleam makes me reconsider. "Maybe next time, firecracker."

She pouts then sucks in a breath as I run my finger up the slit of her pussy through the damp fabric of her panties. I reach the top hem and pull them off her, revealing soft, glistening lips begging for a kiss. I lean down, kissing the inside of one thigh, then the other. By the time I make it back to the centre, she's squirming underneath me. I wrap one arm around her leg, settling it over my shoulder and pressing my hand to her belly. My other hand presses the other leg out further, giving me all the access I require. Then, finally, slowly, I lick all the way up that swollen, pink pussy.

She moans as my tongue touches her. I find her clit and swirl my tongue around it, sucking on it, making her moan louder. I alternate between licking and sucking before I slide two fingers inside her and she sucks in a breath, her hips bucking. I hold her still with the hand on her belly, needing to lap up every drop of her. Her hands find their way into my hair, pressing my face closer to her. I taste slowly, teasingly.

"Spencer," she says, and I recognize the sound. It's been months since I heard it last. She doesn't need to tell me she's almost there. I can hear it in the way she says my name.

I keep my pace, sliding my fingers slowly in and out of her, licking and sucking at her clit as she starts to unravel.

"Fuck," she says, following it up with a moan as her climax squeezes my fingers tight. I stop moving them, but continue relentlessly licking at her clit, driving her higher until the moan turns to a scream. She slaps her hands over her mouth to muffle the sound. I lift up and remove her hands, replacing them with my mouth, and she kisses me desperately, licking the taste of herself off my lips.

I undo my pants and shove them down. My dick springs free, straining toward her wet heat. I hesitate for a second.

"You're sure about this?" I ask.

Her eyes find mine, the pupils blown out so there's only a thin ring of green around them.

"You've done the teasing. Now it's time for the fucking." She lifts her hips, her pussy brushing against the tip of my cock, inviting me in. "Fuck me, Spencer. Please."

I capture her lips again and drive into her in a swift, hard thrust, sheathing myself to the hilt. The knowledge that I'm inside her, with nothing separating us, almost makes me come right then. I hold still, gathering the reins of my control until I'm certain I can do this right. I sit up on my knees again, draping one of her legs over my shoulder, allowing me just that little bit more depth, before I start to move.

"Fuck, Lis. Your pussy is so fucking wet."

I slide out and back in, slowly, reminding myself of the feeling of her wrapped around me. Her hair is spread out on the pillow I slept on when I was a teenager, and the sight of her, open and ravishing, her clothes still on and in complete disarray, is so erotic that I move faster. She moans, her hands searching for something to hold onto as I drive into her again and again, finally ending up pressed against the headboard so she can meet my thrusts.

"You're so fucking gorgeous, Lis."

My thumb touches her clit, massaging gently, and she bites her lip, hard, turning the skin around those red lips pink. I know she's trying to keep from screaming. "Let it go," I tell her.

She shakes her head.

"Let it go, Lis. Let me hear what I'm doing to you."

Her eyes flutter closed, and another moan escapes her, but that's not what I want. I lean down, bracing myself above her, pressing her leg toward her chest, gaining another fraction of depth inside her.

"Let me hear you."

I thrust harder, massage her clit faster, and she shudders. She screams and I capture the sound, kissing her as her body convulses around me. Then I groan as my own release floods me. It's powerful enough I literally see stars.

I collapse, letting her leg slide to the side, and try to move beside her, but she wraps her arms around me and pulls me back.

"Uh-uh. Stay here," she says, her voice distant.

I smile. "I don't want to crush you."

"You won't. Stay here."

So I lay my weight down on her and she takes it, tucking her arms between us and holding my shirt in her hands, keeping me in place. I kiss her hair and her cheek and her jaw. She just lays there, eyes closed with a satisfied smile.

"How are you not uncomfortable?" I ask. "I'm not exactly light."

She shifts, tucking as much of her body underneath me as she can. "It's nice. You're like a weighted blanket."

I laugh. She shifts again, reminding me of the clothes still separating us. "I haven't had fully clothed sex in a long time."

She cracks her eyes open and they're shining with happiness and, if not love, something very close to it.

"It wasn't bad," she says.

I nip at her neck and she squeals and bats me away, laughing. I open my mouth to tell her I love her. Because she can hear it now and it won't freak her out, right? What comes out is, "You're going to stay this time. We're together now."

Our faces are so close together. I watch as the doubt floods into her features and my heart cracks.

"Don't say no," I say, not giving her a chance to speak. "If the answer is no, just don't say it."

She's silent for a long time, long enough that the answer *must* be no. Her expression remains troubled until she looks into my eyes and seems to come to a conclusion, the doubt fading away.

"Yes," she whispers. "We're together."

"Really?"

She nods.

"You're certain?" I shouldn't be giving her opportunities to change her mind, but I won't be able to survive if she goes back on it now.

She wiggles one hand out from between us to touch my face.

"I've missed you, Spencer. In the last couple of weeks, I've seen you almost every day and I've missed you. When I noticed you were sad and hurting, I just wanted to do everything I could to make you feel better. I love being with you. I want to be able to kiss you whenever I want, for you to hold me when I'm cold." Her eyes darken. "And I don't want any other women touching you like that bridesmaid tried to do a couple of months ago."

My lips tilt up. "Were you jealous?"

She sniffs and tilts her head up. "Of course not."

I laugh. "No. Of course not. So what are you telling me, firecracker? I need you to lay it out for me."

Her eyes find mine, the colour swirling between green and blue.

"Earlier, your dad mentioned a workplace romance, and I knew he assumed exactly what I'd feared all along. But it made me realize something. I don't give a shit what other people think. I want to be with you. I want the dream job and the dream man. I want everything. Does that make me greedy?"

I don't answer her. Instead, I crush her lips to mine and she holds me close, our tongues tangling. The hand that had been on my face slides around to the back of my head, her nails dragging across my scalp, sending tingles through my body.

Eventually, I break the kiss.

"Yes. You are very greedy. And I'm here for it. But if we don't stop now, I have a feeling we'll be staying a lot longer."

She wriggles beneath me. "Hm. Well. I kind of want to leave before your father gets back. So." She waggles her eyebrows, making me laugh. "Your place or mine?"

I grin. "Which is closer?"

I help Lis up and into the ensuite where I clean her up, straighten her clothes, then my own. I help her put her shoes back on, but I refuse to return the panties, which I stuff in the pocket of my hoodie. Then I take her hand and lead her back to the ground floor and the front door. Matthew is waiting there to say goodbye, and I grin at him.

"My girlfriend and I are leaving," I say. Fuck, it feels good to say those words out loud.

"Goodbye, sir," Matthew says as he opens the door for us. "It was nice to meet you, Miss Lis. And if I may say, I'm glad Spencer has found a girlfriend who makes him so obviously happy."

She squeezes my fingers and gives me that look. The same one I swear is telling me she loves me. Or am I just seeing what I want to find? Reading something that isn't there? I tug her close to me and kiss her, letting that word fill me up. Girlfriend. I want to scream it to the whole world. Lis is my girlfriend. Lis is mine. *Fucking finally*.

Matthew clears his throat and opens the door for us, bringing me back to the present. "It's nice to see you smiling again, sir."

"I smile a lot," I say.

"Not while you're here."

He's right. I only come here twice a year. I only see Matthew twice a year. And they're not very good days. He won't have seen me smile for a long time.

"You're going to want to wash the bedding in my old room," I tell him.

"Spencer!" Lis says.

I just pull her closer to me, wrapping my arm around her. Her face is bright pink. I kiss her temple.

Matthew just rolls his eyes and shoos us out the door, ever the professional. See nothing. Say nothing.

We get into the car, Lis driving again. Even though the brain fog of the morning has lifted and I probably could drive the car, she's had more practice at driving than I have. We decide to go back to my place since Sophie will be home and Vic won't be. Or not my place, I guess. Vic's place. I need to tell Lis I bought a condo and I'll be moving.

"I've been wondering something," Lis says as we drive through the traffic on Fourth Avenue, cutting into my thoughts. "And please just tell me to stay out of it if that's what you want."

She rolls her bottom lip into her mouth and bites down. The movement makes me shift uncomfortably in my seat, even though I know it's a gesture of concern and not seduction.

"Ask me whatever you want, Lis."

"Your dad is a dick," she blurts.

I laugh. "That's not really a question."

"You go over there every year. He's a dick. And the rest of the year you have no relationship with him at all."

"I don't want a relationship with him. He sends me messages every once in a while that I usually ignore. I see him twice a year on the anniversary of my mom's death and his birthday, and that's enough for me."

"But why? Why do you keep going when he treats you like that?"

I sigh. "I'm feeling generous today. And when I'm feeling generous, I can admit my father is not a bad man. He just… has bad priorities. He calls people by those stupid nicknames because he thinks it makes up for all the times he's not around. When I'm being even more generous, I can also admit that him pushing me to start a business or join his isn't really him trying to be controlling. It's because he cares about me. Well. Maybe a little bit him wanting to control me."

She snorts and I continue.

"Unfortunately, the end result is the same. He got worse after Mom died. He was always bad. She would have to constantly remind him we wanted him with us more than we wanted the money he brought in. Looking back, I think they really loved each other even though he never really understood how to show it. So when she was dying, I promised my mom I would always be there for him. In the end, I had to cut back for my own sanity. So now it's just the two days. His birthday isn't as difficult."

"Okay. Then I won't argue with you about it. And if you want me to come with you every year for the rest of our lives, I will do that. I do want to say one thing about it. Do you think, if your mom knew the kinds of things he says to you, she would hold you to that promise?"

My breathing stops. Does she know what she just said? Did she mean it? The rest of our lives? Surely now is the moment I can tell her I love her.

But I hold it back. "I know she wouldn't hold me to it," I say instead. "But it's the last thing I promised her, so I hold myself to it."

"All right. The rest of our lives then." Then she changes the subject before I can bring up the thoughts swirling around my brain. "Can you text Daze and Sophie? Let them know we're going back to your place and ask if they're okay to keep Cerberus."

"Are you going to unlock it?"

"While I'm driving a hundred thousand dollar car? Nope. Both hands on the wheel at all times."

I pick up the phone and type in the passcode she tells me. I select the app she mentions and find the group chat with her, Daze, and Sophie.

Me:
> Spencer and I are going back to his place.

"You realize you've just given me access to your phone," I say, checking through what else she has on there while I wait for the reply.

She snorts. "There's nothing interesting on it. A Pinterest profile loaded with recipes and hairstyles. The messaging app where I talk to my sister, her fiancée, my parents, and people from work. And a bunch of photos of mostly food and Cerberus. I deleted the dating app the night we met."

I turn toward her, frowning, but she's not looking. "I don't remember you doing that."

She glances at me before returning her attention to the road.

"It was before we met, actually. I didn't tell you this story?"

"No."

"I'd been on a date and he basically asked for my kidney. It was so awful I immediately left and deleted the app."

I laugh. "Are you serious?"

"Yes. Then Daze and Sophie browbeat me into going to the bar."

"I'll have to thank them for that. Might have to find the guy and thank him, too."

Her phone buzzes and I read the message.

> **Daze:**
> Are you going to be watching movies or did the outfit work?

> **Sophie:**
> Ten bucks says the outfit worked and they're not going to be watching movies.

I read the messages out loud. "What do you want to say?"

She sends me a quick smile that has my blood heating.

"What do *you* want to say? You've got the phone."

> **Me:**
> We are not going to be watching movies.

The reply is fast this time.

> **Sophie:**
> Finally!

> **Daze:**
> I didn't take that bet. And I told you so about the underwear. Did he steal your hairclip like you said he would?

I laugh.

> **Me:**
> That's not all I stole.

"What are they saying?"

"Sounds like they want us together as much as I want us together."

She huffs a laugh. The phone buzzes again.

Daze:
> ... is this Lis? Or Spencer?

I read back through what I typed. Oops. I said *I* instead of *he* in that last message. Too late now.

Me:
> Lis is driving.

Sophie:
> You better treat our girl right.

I glance at my girlfriend. Her hair is still down, clothes still slightly rumpled. She's tapping her fingers against the steering wheel as though she's impatient to get through the traffic. And she'd said the rest of our lives.

Me:
> I intend to.

Chapter 35

Lis

When I wake in the morning, it's to sun shining through the window, a dog sleeping on my feet—dropped off when we'd paused our marathon of sex for sustenance—and a man sleeping half on my body, our legs tangled together, arms wrapped around each other. I love the weight of him on me. Feeling his solidity, the fact that he's *there*. Right where he should be. I shift out from under him and his arm tightens around me, holding me in place.

"Where do you think you're going?" he mumbles into his pillow.

"The bathroom," I tell him with a laugh.

"Hm. Okay. But kiss first."

I chuckle, pressing a soft kiss to his lips, then pulling his hoodie on and slipping away to the bathroom. When I return, he's lying, stretched out on his back, arms folded behind his head, watching for me. Cerberus snores away at the foot of the bed like he'd been kept awake all night. To be fair, he kind of had been.

Spencer watches me, his eyes devouring as I make my way to the bed.

I crawl back under the covers, snuggling into his heat, and he holds me against him, stroking my back under his hoodie. It's still early and we don't have to be at work for a while. I would usually get up and go for a run, but today, I just want to wrap myself around him and stay there as long as I can.

He kisses me and my body heats. I want to fuck him right now. I want to climb over him and take him inside me until I can't tell where I end and he begins.

But he pulls away.

"Can I take you somewhere?"

"Where?"

"It's a surprise. But I want to take you somewhere this morning."

"We have time before work? I still need to take Cerberus home and get dressed."

"Bring Cerberus to Blue Vista. I can keep an eye on him while you're busy."

I roll my eyes. "And clothes?"

"You keep your work clothes in your office. Just grab one of my shirts and you'll be fine."

"You really like me wearing your clothes."

"I really do. It's like I have my name written all over you." He kisses me again. "Let's go."

We get up and gather what we need. Daze gave us dog food for Cerberus, so I bring that, and we leave. We start along the Seawall, but then turn and walk away from the water. We don't speak as we walk, but I glance at Spencer a few times, wondering what we're doing and where we're going. It only takes us ten minutes before we stop at a familiar building.

"What's this? Are we here for another showing?" It's the building with the first place we'd looked at together. Seems like so long ago.

"Not exactly."

He lets us in and we ride the elevator up to the tenth floor, where he unlocks a door and leads me and Cerberus inside.

It's empty except for a few boxes in the kitchen. He moves into it and points to the coffeemaker.

"I can make you a cup of coffee. It'll have to be black. I have no cream or sugar. But I do have mugs."

I look around the apartment. "Is this… yours?"

"Yeah. I got it a couple days ago."

"You bought a condo? And didn't tell anyone?"

"Vic knows. I didn't tell anyone else. I got a short closing, so it's only been a couple weeks."

I turn away from the windows that had drawn my attention and find him standing in the kitchen.

"This is amazing, Spencer. I'm so happy for you." I go to him, wrapping my arms around his waist. "This is where you were the other night. Vic said you didn't come home."

He nods. "I've ordered some furniture, but there are a few things I'd love your input on. Like pots and pans. Knives. That kind of thing. Maybe we can go shopping next week?"

My smile widens. "I'd love that."

He kisses me, drawing me tighter against him. My mind swirls. He bought a place. He'd told me his dream was to have a wife and kids. Buying a place is the first step in that dream. Suddenly, I'm more nervous about how long it's taken me to get here. I want to be the wife of that dream. I want to be the mother of those kids.

Daze was right. I have fallen in love with this man. I just needed to admit it to myself. Now that I have, I need to admit it to him.

"I love you, Spencer," I whisper, but I find I'm not nervous about saying it. I've never felt more sure of something in my life.

He closes his eyes and presses his forehead against mine. "You have no idea how many times I've almost said that to you."

"Really?"

He opens his eyes, searching mine.

"Did you know, the night we met, I saw you and I didn't see your sister? Have you ever wondered why that was? Because I have. For the past four months, I've been trying to figure it out. You're identical twins. If it was just looks, I should have been attracted to you both. But I only saw you, Lis. You're the only one I've seen since that night. You're the only one I want to see."

I pull his head down to me, fusing our lips together. My body presses tight against him. He breaks the kiss to begin a trail along my jaw to the spot beneath my ear.

I groan. "You have no idea how mad I am that there's no furniture in here."

He chuckles against my skin sending shivers through me. "There's a counter right there, firecracker."

"I can't have sex in the kitchen," I say, aghast.

His laugh is louder this time. He pulls back. "Don't tell me the chef has never had sex in a kitchen before."

"Of course not. I am a professional."

He gives me a sly grin. "That doesn't mean anything particularly relevant. We're going to have to christen this kitchen first, then. Though I warn you, I fully intend on fucking you in every room in this place." He tugs me against him again, pressing his hard cock into my belly so I know exactly how much he wants me. "As well as my office at Blue Vista. And your office. And your kitchen." He kisses my neck, making my head drop to the side to give him more access. His hands find the hem of the hoodie. "Do you know how long I've fantasized about stripping this from your body?"

"Since the first morning back in April?" I guess, my voice breathy. "I mean, that explains why you kept insisting I wear it."

"Got it in one, firecracker." Then he skims his fingers underneath the sweater, lifting it slowly up and over my head. "Like unwrapping the best gift ever," he says before his head drops and his lips fasten around one of my already hard nipples.

His arms press me to him, travelling down my bare back and pushing the skirt and underwear down my legs, letting them fall to the floor. Then his arms tighten around my ass, lifting me up.

I squeak and grab his shoulders, but he doesn't falter as he sets me on the counter. I make another squeaking sound as my skin touches the cold surface. He's laughing at me as his lips find mine. I bite his lip in retaliation, but I'm pretty sure it isn't the punishment I want it to be.

"Hang on a minute," I say. "Why am I undressed and you're still fully clothed?"

"Noticed that, did you?" he says with a grin.

He's wearing work clothes, so his shirt has buttons and I start at the top, undoing them, letting my fingers brush his skin as I work my way down.

"You're taking too long," he says, his voice husky.

"Do you want me to rip it open? Because that might be a little awkward when we get to work later."

He stops my hands and just yanks the shirt over his head, dropping it to join my clothes on the floor. He finishes the movement with his hands at his fly, pushing his pants down and letting his cock out to play. I reach between us, circling the velvety length with my fingers, stroking lightly from base to tip.

"As much as I love your hands on me, firecracker, I need to eat that pussy. This is the kitchen, after all."

My laughter changes to a gasp as he drops to his knees, spreads my legs wide, and drags his hot tongue along my slit.

My fingers thread through his hair as I try to pull him closer. The kitchen fades from my sight as my world narrows to his mouth and his tongue sucking and licking on my swollen flesh. I shift closer to the edge of the counter, giving him room to work as his tongue finds my clit and two fingers delve inside. I moan, my head dropping back.

"Spencer. I need more. Faster."

He doesn't respond with words, just takes the request and starts moving his fingers faster in and out of me, sucking my clit between his lips, making me jolt with the feeling. I'm trembling with need, rocking my body against his face, climbing higher and higher as his tongue laps against me. He finds the exact right spot, the exact right rhythm, and my fingers tighten in his hair.

"There. Don't stop. I'm so close."

I barely get the words out before the orgasm begins, tightening my body, shattering my soul. The shudders of my release haven't subsided when he removes his fingers from my pussy and stands, sliding me off the counter and onto his hard, eager cock. I sigh as he fills me, my muscles quivering around him.

"Lis," he groans in my ear. "You feel amazing. Your pussy is so hot and tight."

Plastered against him, my arms around his shoulders, my legs wrapped around his waist, I laugh. "Well, are you just going to stand there, or are we going to fuck?"

He presses me back against the counter, the edge of it biting into my ass, but then he thrusts into me again and I lose all ability to think of anything other than his dick stroking deep inside me. I cling to his shoulders, my fingers digging in as he drives into me.

"Tell me again, Lis," Spencer says, his thrusts hard and deep. "Tell me you love me."

"I love you, Spencer." The words come out on a sob as the pleasure builds and builds. "I love you. I need you."

My words devolve into moans and his mouth comes down on mine, devouring. I taste myself on his lips as my tongue meets his. The friction of our bodies touching has me on fire. Our mouths fused, my nipples crushed against his chest, my legs tight around his hips, which slam against mine. And at my core, his cock gliding in and out of my dripping pussy.

My body begins to tighten, pleasure ratcheting higher. Spencer pumps into me and my moans turn into a litany of his name over and over. I can't think of anything other than the feeling of him, his body and his heat. I explode, my orgasm shuddering through me on a wave of ecstasy. Spencer follows with a groan and my name.

We cling together as we come down from the high of the orgasms, our breathing heavy.

"Okay," I say, panting. "I can maybe get behind kitchen sex. But only if we sanitize after."

Spencer laughs.

I blink my eyes open, focusing on the window just beyond the kitchen.

"Can people see us?" I ask. The windows have blinds, but they're rolled up, letting anyone see in if they want to.

"Let them," Spencer says, his body still pressing me against the counter. "Let them see and be jealous."

"We should get ready and go to work."

He nods against my shoulder. "In a minute."

He lifts me so I can sit on the counter again, smoothing my hair back and finding a cloth in a drawer to clean me up before handing me my clothes back, including the hoodie which he slips over my head.

"I love you, Spencer," I say as he pulls my hair from the collar of the shirt.

He grins at me. "I know."

WHY NOT BOTH?

I smack him on his still naked shoulder. "You are not as cool as Han Solo."

He clutches a hand over his heart. "I am far cooler than Han Solo."

I tug him back toward me, holding him between my legs, wrapping my arms around him. "No one is as cool as Han Solo."

We kiss for a long time until my brain reminds me we should get to work. As I break the kiss and hop down to finish adjusting my clothes, Spencer grabs my hand.

"I love you, too, Lis. Possibly from the first moment I saw you."

It suddenly occurs to me I've probably loved him just as long. We could have had this all this time.

"How many favours do I have saved up?" I ask.

He shrugs as he steps into his pants. "I honestly lost count a while ago."

"Well, I want to cash them all in."

He sends me a sly grin before slipping his shirt back over his head. "And what favour can I do for you, firecracker?"

"Forgive me. For being such an idiot these last four months."

He pauses doing up his buttons to look at me.

"I made us waste so much time."

He takes my hands in his. "It wasn't wasted time. We got to know each other. We became friends. We set a solid foundation we can build from. There's nothing I would change about the last four months." He shifts his head side-to-side. "Well, maybe making sure you read your contract carefully that first day. But other than that."

"It's not going to be weird that we work together?"

"No. It's going to make everything better. Because now, I can kiss you whenever I want."

"And if any more bridesmaids come on to you, you can tell them your girlfriend is downstairs in the kitchen with access to lots of knives."

"I like the sound of that."

Chapter 36

Spencer

The morning of Daze and Sophie's wedding dawns bright and beautiful, except for one thing. Lis isn't sleeping next to me. It's in that moment I make a decision, though I can't do more than consider it before I'm up and getting ready for the day.

This wedding officially marks the end of wedding season. There are still a couple weddings in September, then a couple in October. But they're not every weekend after this one. There are no more fully booked weekends until next summer when we have even more than this year.

Lis stayed with her sister last night. We texted each other all night, but I miss her more than I rightfully should since we saw each other at the rehearsal dinner. Now that I'm fully moved in to my apartment, I can't even watch for her to run past along the Seawall anymore.

I shake myself from my maudlin thoughts. It's the most important wedding of the season and everything has to go perfectly. So I arrive early to make sure things are already operating smoothly. We'd done a lot of set-up the night before, including carting the big tents—that we all hope we don't need—to the rooftop terrace.

While it's not anyone who actually works for Blue Vista, it still feels like a Blue Vista family wedding. Tina is already hopping around the kitchen—hours earlier than she needs to be—ensuring everything is prepped for the dinner later tonight. Vic and Adalie are sorting out the staff. Derek is working with a small team to get the alcohol stocked behind the bar. Even our new on-contract-photographer is here with a couple of assistants taking some test shots.

Sophie arrives first, and I set her up in one of the rooms set aside for the bridal party along with her small entourage of her mother, her father, her maid of honour, and the hairdresser. I hand out flutes of champagne and get back to my job.

They'd only changed a few things from the original wedding, a few decorations and a few flower choices. They'd lowered the guest count from the original two hundred to a hundred and twenty. Even with the changes, they still saved a huge chunk of money over what a wedding here would normally cost.

I'm pouring myself a cup of coffee when the front door opens and there she is.

I should go directly to the bride. That's my job, after all. But first I have to kiss my girlfriend.

"I missed you," I say after I kiss her.

She laughs. "It's only been a few hours."

"Too long."

"And it's going to be even longer," Daze says, striding toward me. "We need to get ready."

"Miss bossy," Lis says. "She seems to think it's her day or something."

They slip their arms around each other, leaning together, and it's so beautiful to see how happy they are. Identical twins with identical smiles.

"Follow me to the rooms," I say, leading the two women and their parents to the other space for the bridal party. "Sophie is already here with your hairdresser. Would you like anything while you wait? Champagne, mimosas?"

"Mimosas would be lovely," Daze says as they settle into the room, hanging up dresses.

I nod. "I'll let Tina know."

Lis catches me before I can leave.

"We're going to do our makeup now, so this is your last chance to kiss me before the reception."

"That long?" I say, tugging her closer.

"I'm afraid so. Once the makeup is on, we can't mess it up until after pictures."

"Wouldn't want that." So I kiss her. Because what else can I do when she's looking up at me with those beautiful blue-green eyes filled with love? When we finally break apart, I tuck a strand of rainbow-coloured hair—newly brightened at her recent hair appointment—behind her ear. "I'll go get those mimosas. Four?"

"Yes, please," she says before returning to her sister, who is pulling out makeup and setting it on the counter.

When I return, I tell them to have fun today and if they need anything at all, to let me know. Then I get back to work. I check on Sophie, bringing her another round of champagne and letting her know everything is on schedule.

At the designated time, I'm waiting on the roof. Sophie is on one side behind a screen with her maid of honour. The guests are all seated and the photographers are ready.

Daze and Lis arrive and I position them behind a second screen.

The music starts and I watch Lis and Sophie's maid of honour, Kelly, walk down the aisle together in very different dresses that are the same dusty pink.

Daze and Sophie hadn't wanted to have one walk down the aisle to the other. So, once Lis and Kelly are in place, the music changes and the two brides step out from behind their screens, seeing each other for the first time.

Daze looks like a fairy princess in her romantic, ethereal gown with its delicate flower embroidery on the semi-sheer overlay. Sophie looks like a human princess in her sophisticated, fitted gown. At the bottom of her dress, a lace panel with flower embroidery flows into a short train the same length as Daze's. The matching trains and flower embroidery make it look as though they'd deliberately matched their dresses, though I know they hadn't. They blink away tears and link arms as they walk toward the start of their new life together, stopping under the pergola, decorated today with golden gauze and dusty pink roses.

I catch Lis' eye as the ceremony begins and wink at her. She rolls her eyes at me, but she's smiling, and I can't help but wonder what wedding dress she might choose to wear. Would it be something like Daze's or more like Sophie's? Or would she choose something completely different?

The sun holds throughout the ceremony. They take some pictures on the roof before walking across the street to get more on the beach.

The crew rushes around, making sure everything is in place for the wedding party to return. I check on the bar and notice Derek staring at the other end of the reception hall, his face pale. I glance in the direction he's staring, but I'm not sure exactly what he's looking at. Or who.

"Hey, you all right, man? You look like you just saw a ghost."

"Ava Calligan," he says hoarsely.

"Who?"

"The photographer's assistant. It's Ava Calligan."

"Oh, right. And who is Ava Calligan?"

"We dated. A bit more than eight years ago."

"Dated? You? You don't date."

"Mm-hm. And she's why."

I look again, noting the woman with the camera taking pictures of the cake Lis' friend made and the decorations around the room. She has long brown hair caught up in a messy bun with a headband to keep bits of escaped hair out of her face. She has a camera bag slung over her back and is completely focused on her task.

"Are you going to go talk to her?" I ask.

"I don't think so. We didn't exactly part on the best terms."

"What happened?"

His fist clenches at his side for a second before he visibly attempts to calm himself and relaxes.

"She told me to leave and so I left."

If ever there was a statement that didn't tell the whole story, it's that one.

"Right. Well, if you're not going to talk to her, are we done with everything else?" I ask, hoping to get him to stop openly staring at the woman.

"Yeah. Everything is ready."

He seems to snap out of his thoughts and heads back downstairs for something while I finish the last tasks before the brides return.

It's possibly the most flawless execution of a wedding I have ever coordinated. Daze and Sophie set a table aside for me, Derek, Adalie, and Vic. The photographers join us and I notice the tension between Derek and the one assistant, Ava, though they don't say a word to each other. They don't even look directly at each other for most of the meal.

After dinner is over, someone taps my shoulder and there's Lis, in her pretty pink bridesmaid dress with her rainbow hair tied up on her head in some elaborate style I can't begin to comprehend and am excited to take down.

"I know you usually don't like it when the bridesmaids hit on you, but I wondered if you'd make an exception tonight?"

I catch her hand and rub her fingers between mine. "I don't know. It's a pretty strict rule. I don't break it for just anyone."

"I understand. But maybe you'd like to dance?"

Sophie and Daze are out on the floor already, just finishing up their first dance as a married couple and other people are joining them.

"I can't say no to that."

She tugs me with her and I wrap her in my arms, holding her close.

"You never did tell me who taught you to dance," she says, smiling up at me.

"My mom. She told me women wouldn't be able to resist a man who could dance."

"What if you were gay?"

"I'm sure the same holds true for men."

She laughs and rests her head against my shoulder as we sway to the music. The rest of the night is a blur of laughter and conversation. Now that my job is pretty much over until the cleanup, I just enjoy my time meeting more of Lis' family, loving how she introduces me as her boyfriend. Loving the look in her eye when she says it even more.

When it comes time to throw the bouquets, Daze looks directly at Lis, points to her eyes, then points to her sister. Lis rolls her eyes in response but nods. Daze turns around and throws the bouquet over her head. It lands squarely in Lis' hands as though they've practiced this a hundred times. Everyone laughs and hugs Lis, who looks at me with a helpless little shrug and smile.

The decision I made when I woke up that morning solidifies in my chest. As I watch her among friends and family, I start to make a plan.

As the months pass, Lis and I spend all our extra time together. So much, in fact, that she moves in with me at the end of November. We spend Christmas with her family and I've never seen people more happy to just spend time together. It feels the way a family should feel.

WHY NOT BOTH?

New Year's Eve, Blue Vista hosts a party. My plan for the night is ready. I'd asked Vic if we could keep it low-key this year and just invite family and friends instead of selling tickets to the public. So instead of the maximum capacity of five hundred people, there's only about fifty.

Derek claps me on the shoulder while Vic and Adalie come up beside him.

"It's almost time," Derek says. "Are you ready?"

While I'd kept the purchase of my apartment secret from my friends except Vic, I'd told *this* plan to five people. Three of whom are here tonight, standing right beside me.

I take a deep breath, my gaze focused on Lis, laughing next to her sister on the other side of the room. "Yes."

"Are you nervous?" Adalie asks.

"Not even a little bit," I say with a shake of my head.

"You're that certain of her?" Derek asks.

"More."

Vic gestures in Lis' direction, crossing her arms over her chest. "Prove it then."

I check the time. Three minutes to midnight. I make my way over to where Lis is standing. In my peripheral, I notice a few other couples getting closer, getting ready for the countdown and the kiss as the year turns.

"Hey, firecracker," I say when I reach her. "Come here." I tug her against me and move us closer to the centre of the room.

"What are you doing?" she asks, giving me her I-know-you're-up-to-something-and-I-want-in-on-the-secret smile.

I check the time once more. One minute to midnight. I kiss her hand and drop to one knee. Lis gasps, her free hand covering her mouth. A few people had been watching me move and in about half a second, everyone has fallen silent.

"Lis. I love you. I know it's only been eight months since we met, but I'm as certain now as I've ever been of anything in my life. This has been the best year because it's the one I met you. But I want next year to be better. Will you marry me, Lis? Will you say yes so I don't have to spend a single second of next year not being engaged to you?"

Tears fill her eyes as I open the box. "Is that…?"

"Your grandmother's ring." The blue stone sparkles from its place in the box. "I asked your parents if I could use it to propose."

No one around us speaks as we all wait for Lis to answer. She just stands there and stares at me. My heart is pounding in my chest as she leaves me in agony, waiting.

Derek starts counting down from ten and, as people join in, it occurs to me what she's doing.

WHY NOT BOTH?

Eight.

"You're going to make me wait until the very last second, aren't you?"

Six.

"With a speech like that, how can I not?"

Five.

"You are terrible. And I love you."

Four.

"I love you, too."

Three. Two. One.

"Yes!" She launches herself toward me and I slip the ring on her finger, kissing her as everyone shouts, "Happy New Year!"

When we end the kiss, everyone comes over to hug and congratulate us. When Daze and Sophie come over to inspect the ring, Daze gives me a look.

"So you didn't buy my sister an engagement ring?"

"Daze," Lis says. "I love this ring. It's perfect."

"I know it is," she says. "I can still give him a hard time. He's going to be my brother-in-law, after all."

"Actually," I say, pulling the other small box from my inside pocket. "You're right. I didn't buy an engagement ring. I bought this instead."

Inside the longer box, I reveal a platinum chain with a clip on it.

"You forgot the charm on that necklace," Sophie points out.

I fasten it around Lis' neck and remove the ring I'd just put on her finger. "I know you won't wear rings while cooking. So I got you this, made specially, to keep it safe while you're in the kitchen." I clip the ring onto the necklace. "This way, you don't have to take the chain off to put the ring on it. And it'll stay safe, and right next to your heart."

"Okay, that's a little too sweet," Daze says.

Lis is speechless. She just lifts the ring from her chest to look at it, tears standing in her eyes.

"I see you, firecracker. It doesn't need to be one or the other. You can have both. You can have everything."

She kisses me, pulling me to her. She breaks the kiss and whispers, "Take me home."

Epilogue
Spencer - Three Months Later

I'm sitting in my office when someone barges in as though he owns the place. Surprisingly, it's my father.

"What's this I hear about you getting married?" he asks, waving the invitation around.

I stop what I'd been working on and steeple my fingers together. "I'm not sure what's confusing about this. The invitation has all the information on it. Shall I mark you down as coming or not?"

"I talked to my lawyer, and he said you haven't come to him for a prenup."

"Why would I go to your lawyer for anything?"

"So you went somewhere else for your prenup?"

Beckett doesn't sit down, so he's towering above me, an intimidation technique I hate. I lean back in my chair as though none of it matters. And really, it doesn't. I've gone long past letting this man hurt me.

"What do I need a prenuptial agreement for, Dad? The only thing I have of value is the condo I own. If something were to happen between me and Lis, I'd want her to have half. It's her home as much as it is mine, even though I'm the one who pays for it."

"You have a trust fund with millions of dollars in it."

"Actually, I don't have a trust fund. You refuse to give it to me. So, in fact, *you* have a trust fund."

I'm not sure what he's planning to say next because Lis breezes into the room with a smile, moving around my father like he's nothing, and leaning down to plant a sensual kiss on my lips.

"Hey," she whispers.

"Hey," I return.

Then she straightens and turns to my father. "Hi, Beck. So nice to see you. You know you don't need to RSVP to our wedding in person. A simple phone call would have been enough."

"What have you done to make my son refuse a prenup? You're nothing but a little gold digger and I'll see to it you don't get a single penny."

I want to stand and tell him to get out of my office for saying these things to Lis, but she presses down on my shoulder, ensuring I stay in my seat.

"I don't want a single penny from you or Spencer. I just want to marry him. Besides. He doesn't have anything in his name you need to worry about. Unless you want to give him access to his trust fund?"

"He knows the stipulations with regard to that."

"He does. So do I. I think it's just a way for you to try to control him. I have an idea, though. Something to make everyone happy. And a little bit unhappy. A perfect compromise."

My father lowers his eyelids, giving Lis his signature businessman look. "I'm listening."

"Give Spencer access to his trust fund and I'll sign whatever prenuptial agreement you put in front of me."

"Lis," I warn. I don't feel comfortable giving him that much control. She just squeezes my shoulder to keep me from commenting.

"*Any* prenuptial agreement?" my father asks.

"Any. I know Spencer just said he would want to split the condo with me if something happens and we get a divorce. But I'm also confident we're not going to get a divorce." She turns toward me with a smile. "Because I will never doubt again." She returns her attention to my father. "So include it if you want. Include everything. I don't need Spencer's money. I just need him."

I take her hand off my shoulder and tug her onto my lap, giving her a long, slow kiss. When she breaks the kiss, she turns back to my father.

"So what do you say, Beck? Do we have a deal?"

She holds her hand out across my desk. He's still standing there, just watching us. Finally, slowly, he extends his hand and shakes hers.

"I'll have the papers drawn up. I'll let you know when everything is ready."

He turns and leaves my office. Lis returns her attention to me.

"Are you sure about this?" I ask her. "I don't like the idea of you signing something that I don't get any say in. It's my money and if I want you to have it, then I should be able to let you have it."

"I think I remember you saying it's not real money, right?"

"The trust isn't. But the rest of it is."

She places her hands on my face, holding my gaze on hers, though she doesn't need to. "Spencer. I love *you*. I don't love your money. I'm going to sign whatever paperwork your father deems necessary. And it'll all be for nothing, because I love you and we are never getting a divorce. We're going to have the greatest love story ever told and we're going to live happily ever after."

She kisses me softly, then pulls back with a smile. "Besides. We're not just doing this for the money. We're doing this for a shitload of money."

"Mm. I love it when you quote *Spaceballs* to me."

Her smile widens, and she gives me a little shrug. "I just figured, why the money *or* the life you want? Why not both?"

The End

I hope you enjoyed reading *Why Not Both?* as much as I loved writing it. If you did, please consider leaving a review. Reviews help indie authors like me gain exposure which helps sell books. Which helps me create more books.

But wait! What was that at the end about Ava Calligan? Who is she and what is her relationship with Derek? You'll get to find out in the next book, *Why Not Now?* a second chance, holiday romance. It's available for preorder right now! It'll be out November 7, right in time for Christmas.

Preorder it Now!

Turn the page for a sneak peak at the first chapter.

Why Not Now?

Chapter 1 - Ava

"How are there so many hot people at this wedding?" my best friend and fellow photographer Bethany asks as we stand to one side of the room taking candid shots of the guests mingling while they wait for the grand entrance of the two brides.

Honestly, Bethany is better at candids than I am, but I've already taken all the stills we need until later.

"Aren't you married?" I ask.

"Yes," she says with a smirk. "But that doesn't mean I can't appreciate the view. I mean, look at those two over there. Mr. Tall, Dark, and Handsome, and Mr. Golden God."

I smile as I take another shot of the guests. Bethany and I shouldn't be taking pictures from the same location—our shots will all look the same—but she'd come over to tell me about all the beautiful people, so I figure I should actually look at the two men she's pointing out.

When I do, my breath lodges in my lungs and it feels like they've turned to stone.

WHY NOT BOTH?

"Fudge brownies!" I whisper.

"Whoa," Bethany says with a chuckle. "Watch the language. What's wrong?"

"I know that man," I say, turning us both so that we're not facing him. Though he hadn't been looking at me, I don't want him to see me if he hasn't already.

"Who?" Bethany looks around, but I make a hissing noise and she turns back to me.

"Mr. Tall and Dark," I answer. No way I can force the word *handsome* out of my mouth, even though he is that. Derek Moritz has always been my definition of the perfect man. At least, when it comes to looks. "Be cool."

She lifts her camera and scans through her recent images until she finds the one of the two men. I look down at the screen and there he is. Though I don't need to see the image to remember what he looks like. He was always the most gorgeous boy in school. We'd been friends for a long time before we got together. And when we did, I'd felt like the luckiest girl in the world. I would lose myself in the depths of those brown eyes, run my fingers through that curly, dark hair. And the memory of his strong hands and soft lips on my body—the first ones to ever touch me in those ways—has haunted many a dream.

"Who is he?" Bethany asks. "One of your conquests?" She gives me a sly grin and I roll my eyes.

Bethany likes to tease me about the men I've gone out with, casual hook ups only. She told me once that her teasing wasn't serious, but she wished I would learn to let people in. I'd told her I had no time for relationships between my multiple jobs and raising my sister.

"No. We dated. A long time ago."

She scoffs. "You never date."

"Nope. And he's why."

She looks at her camera again. "Don't tell me that's the infamous Derek."

"One and the same."

"You broke up with *him*?"

"Uh no. He broke up with me."

"Tell me again what happened?" she asks.

I sigh and take a shot of the flower arch over the head table, stunning pink wisteria and white roses with gold accents creating a romantic spot for the couple. "My parents died, and I got custody of Lacey. We'd been dating about two and a half years, friends for longer. I asked if he wanted to leave. He didn't sign up for the whole raising an eight-year-old sister thing, you know? Anyway, I asked, and he left." I shrug, trying to downplay the most painful time of my life.

"That's horrible."

"Yeah, well. It is what it is."

"Is he a guest, or does he work here?"

"God, I hope he's just a guest. I don't want to see him whenever we're here to shoot a wedding."

WHY NOT BOTH?

"Derek seems pretty chummy with Mr. Golden God. And I'm pretty sure *he's* the event coordinator," she says, taking some more pictures of the crowd. "And Mr. Golden is definitely with the maid of honour."

I don't bother to ask how she knows. She sees people in a way I don't. Bethany is better at capturing candid shots than anyone I know. Even better than Cindy, our boss, who tends to take all the posed shots.

"Which maid of honour?"

We'd just finished up helping Cindy with the wedding party shots before coming here to capture the grand entrance that should take place any moment now.

"Lis. The twin with the rainbow hair."

Before I can respond, the entrance starts, the emcee announcing the two maids of honour, Lis and Kelly, in their mismatched dusty pink dresses. They're exactly the same colour and length, but slightly different styles. The twin's dress is more flowy like her sister's wedding dress while the other bridesmaid has a more fitted one to match the other bride.

As I'm snapping pictures, I clearly see Lis turn toward the event coordinator, a coy smile on her lips. He's looking back at her with a matching grin. I'm just able to capture them both in frame before taking the picture.

"Good call," I say to Bethany, preparing for the brides to enter. "Maybe Derek is a friend or something?" Though if he was a guest, I'd probably have noticed him before now. "I mean, my luck can't be that bad, right? My one-and-only ex working at the same place where my boss just got a contract as the main wedding photographer?"

Bethany laughs. "You've done it now. You think Murphy's Law is bad, but the universe will wreak havoc with a statement like that. Hey, you still need a ride home tonight, right?"

"Yeah, if you don't mind." I hate asking for help, but with my car in the shop and all the camera equipment I had with me, Bethany had offered.

"Of course."

"Thanks. The new alternator goes in on Monday. Hopefully that solves the problems for a while."

The brides enter and we spend the next half an hour taking pictures until dinner. Since the brides had decided they didn't need pictures of people eating, I take a few stills of a perfectly plated meal and then head to the table Cindy said had been set aside for us with some other people who work at the venue. When I get to the table, Bethany is proved right, because there he is, sitting between the event coordinator and a black-haired woman with icy blue eyes.

I can't stop my hands from shaking as I sit down and his attention turns to me, our gazes colliding. For several heartbeats, he holds all my focus. Then he blinks, and the spell breaks. He turns back to his friend, a smile spreading at something the other man says.

Ah. We're pretending we don't know each other. Fine by me.

Cindy's voice pulls me back, and I realize she'd been speaking the whole time I'd been in the Derek induced haze. Thankfully, not directly to me.

"Adalie is the HR coordinator here," Cindy says, indicating a woman with riotous red hair seated next to me. "And then beside her is Vic, the big boss." Cindy and Vic share a laugh.

Bethany shakes Adalie's hand first, then Vic's. Cindy starts at the other side where she's going to sit and says, "You're Spencer, right?"

He smiles, holding out his hand to shake. "Yes. Event coordinator."

Then Cindy turns to *him*. "I don't think we've been introduced."

Derek gives her a smile and I wonder how she's not blinded. How is she not a puddle at his feet? Because I would be.

"Derek. Master of acquisitions." He stretches his hand across to her and they shake.

Bethany has gone around the table shaking everyone's hand as well, introducing herself. "Is that an official title?" she asks when she gets to him.

He shifts his head side-to-side. "No, but it's close enough."

And then everyone turns to me.

I don't want to shake anyone's hand because then I'll have to shake *his*. So I muster up a small smile and lift my hand in greeting. "I'm Ava," I say before quickly dropping my hands into my lap.

I'm seated between Bethany and Adalie, directly across from Derek and so, throughout dinner, while I'm trying to focus on a conversation with Bethany and Adalie about photography and painting, I keep getting distracted, listening to what he's saying, who's talking to him, why he's laughing.

And he laughs a lot.

It doesn't take long to realize, not only does he work here, but these four people who run Blue Vista Events are close friends.

Bethany gets up as soon as the speeches start and continues taking photos.

"Do you need to go as well?" Adalie asks.

I shake my head. "I'll take some more when the dancing starts. And I have a few more I want to get later. But I mostly take stills and portraits."

"You'll want to go up to the rooftop later, then," Derek says, and my heart stops.

It's the first time he's spoken directly to me all night. I turn to him and get lost for a moment in his brown eyes. They always reminded me of warm caramel.

"Get a few shots of the moon and stars over the bay."

"Yeah," Spencer chimes in. "It's a clear night, so it'll be good for that. Maybe we can take Daze and Sophie up later and get a few shots of them in the moonlight. Lis and Kelly, too."

Everyone nods and the conversation moves on. But Derek is still looking at me, like he can't look away any more than I can. Until the two bridesmaids arrive. Lis directs all her attention at Spencer.

The father-daughter dance is just ending, so I should head out there to take more pictures, but I linger to eavesdrop on the conversation.

"I know you usually don't like it when bridesmaids hit on you, but I wondered if you'd make an exception tonight?"

I watch as Spencer catches her hand, rubbing her fingers. "I don't know," he responds, keeping a serious look on his face. "It's a pretty strict rule. I don't break it for just anyone."

"I understand. But maybe you'd like to dance?"

"I can't say no to that," Spencer says as he stands.

Before they leave, Lis turns to Derek. "This is Kelly. She won't hit on you, but she is happy to dance."

He gives Kelly that grin, the one that would make me melt, though she doesn't. Then he stands. "I'm always happy to dance. You sure you don't want to hit on me?"

Kelly grins back at him. I hate how easy they are together. "You're not exactly my type, Romeo."

Spencer and Lis have already made it to the dance floor, wrapped in each other's arms, but Derek turns back to the table, his eyes meeting mine for just a second before he turns to Adalie and Vic. "You two want to join?"

Vic snorts. "You won't get me on that dance floor."

Adalie nudges her. "We will eventually. Have another drink."

I get up and return to my job. The wedding is a really beautiful one, different shades of pink mixed with creams and gold at each table, from the linens and floral centrepieces to the gold sashes tied around each chair. Tea lights flicker in glass holders on every surface. It's easy to find good shots. After a while, someone touches my elbow and I turn with a gasp, finding myself drowning in deep brown eyes.

"You want to go up and get those pictures?" Derek asks, breaking the spell, obviously not as jittery about running into me as I am about running into him.

"Sure."

"Spencer is going to bring the ladies up in about fifteen. Will that be enough time?"

WHY NOT BOTH?

I nod and follow him to a staircase and up to the rooftop terrace, stopping to grab my tripod and a different flash.

I'd been up here earlier during the ceremony, but the view with the moon and stars is breathtaking, even if the early fall night is a little crisp.

I've taken a bunch of shots before he speaks again.

"So you stuck with photography?"

Oh. We're *not* pretending we don't know each other. Cool. Excellent.

I turn back to him. He has his hands shoved in his pockets and his shoulders are a little hunched like he's almost as uncomfortable as I am.

"Uh. Yeah. Sort of. I've been in and out of it."

It strikes me as funny how that statement is true and yet tells such a small part of the story of the last eight and a half years of my life.

I take another couple of pictures, looking down at the screen before making some adjustments and taking the next ones.

And then I blurt out, "I thought you were going to be a doctor."

His face splits into a grin as he relaxes and laughs—actually laughs. The sound makes me melt, just like I always did. Sugarsnaps!

"No. Turns out, I hate chemistry. Stuck with it way longer than I should have. But Mom always said I could be a doctor." He rolls his eyes in obvious affection. "I went into business."

"That's… quite a change."

He shrugs. "Led me here. And I kind of like it here."

We lapse into silence and I take another couple of pictures.

"Have you worked here long?" I ask.

"Since the beginning. I'm a part owner."

Owner. So not only would I be seeing him any time I did a wedding with Cindy, he's my boss' boss. Great. Perfect. Thanks, Universe.

We lapse into an uncomfortable silence. I'm finished with the pictures until the wedding party arrives. So I just stand there, looking at Derek, holding my camera like a shield between us. After a moment that drags on, I say, "Well, this is awkward. Where are those brides?"

"Ava," he says. "It doesn't have to be."

"We're going to see each other at every wedding. You don't think that's going to be weird?"

"I'm not usually at the weddings. My job is almost always done before the vows and I mostly stay downstairs. Tonight is different because it's Sophie and Daze."

"What makes them so special?" I ask lightly, but I'm very curious.

"Sophie is Lis' sister."

"And Lis is dating Spencer."

"Yes. And she works here. She's our head chef." He lets out a breath and runs a hand through his hair, shoving his curls into disarray. "Look. What happened between us is ancient history, right? There's no reason it has to affect us or a working relationship between us now. Eight years is a really long time."

Eight years, seven months, and three days, but who's counting?

"You're right. We're both adults. There's no reason we can't work at the same place. We'll probably barely see each other. Right?"

"Right. It'll be fine."

The smile he gives me is a little bit off, not quite the teasing, joy-filled grin I remember. But then, Derek is a different person now. Just like I'm a different person. He's changed.

Maybe we'd been in love once upon a time. But now, we're little more than strangers.

Acknowledgements

As always, I have a lot of people I need to thank, without whom this book might never have seen the light of day.

First up this time is Jenn for telling me a story about a guy on a dating app asking for her kidney. No lie. I laughed and laughed and then begged to include it in a story. Thank you for sharing your online dating horrors, Jenn, so I could turn them into a four book series.

Next, A. Boss. Thank you for forcing me to be spicy when I wasn't comfortable with it. I think I've got it now. Also, thanks to A. Boss, Ellie Jennings, and Colleen, for being amazing critique partners. You guys are all amazing.

Thanks to my very talented editor, Mel, for helping me make this story really come alive.

My Team Hikes and Games peeps: Krys, Steph, Kim, Meagan, and Jenn (again) – you guys are the best cheerleaders.

Jamie – as always, one of my first readers. Thanks for being a fan.

To my writing communities, Author Ever After and Blood and Pulp (even though contemporary romance isn't your jam), thanks for hanging out with me and just being my writing friends. Especially Britta and Heather for making sure I give Vic the backstory she deserves.

If you're a regular reader and you've made it this far, I just want to point out how many people have helped me. If you're an aspiring writer, take this as your sign. It's so much easier to do this with the support of a community than trying to do it on your own. Find your people.

Finally, as always, thank you to Sean and Ryan for putting up with me when I spend too much time at my computer.

About the Author

Sarah is a lover of all things romantic. A storyteller since before she can remember, she loves to write stories—often about found families—with twisted tropes, swearing, and spice.

She writes fantasy under the pen name SP Neeson where you can find more of her favourite things, but with magic.

And yes, the u in "favourite" means she's Canadian.

Follow Sarah on Facebook and Instagram

Also by

By Sarah Neeson
The Blue Vista Crew Series
Why Not Both?
Why Not Now? – Coming November 2024
Why Not Us? – Coming Winter 2025
Why Not Forever? – Coming Spring 2025

By SP Neeson
Glamour Blind Trilogy (in four parts) – optimal reading order
Truth in the Smoke
Destiny in the Flames
Out of the Embers
Hope in the Inferno

Manufactured by Amazon.ca
Bolton, ON